Strangely Funny III

Edited by Sarah E. Glenn

Strangely Funny III
Copyright © 2016 Mystery and Horror, LLC
Published by Mystery and Horror, LLC
Tarpon Springs, FL

Sarah E. Glenn, Editor
Cover by Gary Piserchio

All stories in this anthology have been printed with the
permission of the authors.

ISBN-13: 978-0-9964209-6-9

Library of Congress Control Number: 2016905901

ACKNOWLEDGEMENTS
AND
THANK YOUS

We would like to thank Gary Piserchio for creating the cover, and writing a story to go with it.

We also want to thank Gwendolyn Kiste, who made her first appearance in Strangely Funny II, for her efforts to boost the series.

Thanks, Paul Wartenberg, for sharing your knowledge of the library with us: from Library of Congress Control Numbers for our books, to explaining the ins and outs of getting books onto library shelves.

Sarah and I appreciate all the writers who contribute to the continued Strangely Funny saga. You keep us laughing, and make publishing this series worthwhile.

TABLE OF CONTENTS

TABLE OF CONTENTS

THE MISLAID HEART
BY COLUMBKILL NOONAN

The Pharaoh Intef the Elder, ruler of all of Lower Egypt, son of Ra himself, husband to so many wives that he couldn't remember all of their names, and father to at least one ungrateful bastard, was dead, but he was not really terribly sad about that. Indeed, he was quite excited to begin his exalted afterlife in the land of the dead. Soon, Horus' sons Imsety, Duamutef, Hapi, and Qebehsenuet would come to escort him to Osiris, who would weigh his heart against a feather. If (nay, when, he thought) his heart proved lighter than the feather, he could begin his proper life.

Because the afterlife had no choice, really, but to be better than his *life* life. True, he had been Pharaoh, and had had many wives, and could do whatever he wanted. But Egypt wasn't what it used to be. The Kingdoms had fallen apart, so that there was always fighting between his own Kingdom of Lower Egypt and that of Upper Egypt farther south along the Nile. There was drought, which brought famine, which meant that everyone was starving and looked to him to save them. But of course, he couldn't just wave his hands, royal though they might be, and create food out of thin air, which seemed to be what everyone expected him to do. Yes, he was Pharaoh, but the Kingdom itself was quite poor, so that he wasn't able to live in the same glorious manner that his ancestors from long ago had taken for granted.

Indeed, there hadn't even been enough money for a proper pyramid. He had been forced to share a saff tomb with his father and grandfather and great-grandfather, who had all been poor Pharaohs like himself. Essentially just a long stone hallway with little cubby holes in which mummies were placed, the saff tomb was all that his beleaguered treasury could afford. As he lay there, ensconced in his coffin awaiting his resurrection, he hoped that his meager burial would prove enough to gain him an auspicious beginning to his afterlife.

He also hoped that he would be joined soon by the aforementioned ungrateful bastard. Intef the Younger was Intef the Elder's son by one of his many wives, and he had just designated him as his heir the week before. The little jerk had taken the first opportunity he could to murder his father, by luring him out onto a small reed boat for some "father-son time", then pushing Intef the Elder off of the boat and mushing his head beneath the thick Nile mud until he drowned on the stuff.

He wondered if the boy's mother, whose name he couldn't remember for the life of him (or was it for the death of him? he thought, chuckling at his own pun). Whatever, he thought, wondering if What's-Her-Face had put the boy up to this. Intef the Younger was welcome to the job. Intef the Younger could deal with the starving people with their hands always reaching out towards you, asking for food. Intef the Younger could deal with the treasurers, telling you that there was no money to build a new palace, nor even enough to keep up the ones that you had. Intef the Younger could deal with the wives, always asking for presents and attention. He could deal with the advisors, constantly warning of war, and trade deals gone awry, and political intrigues. And the little jerk could deal with ungrateful sons who mashed your face into slimy, smelly mud until you were dead. Yes, Intef the Younger could deal with all of those things, because Intef the Elder was happily moving on to the afterlife.

At last came the time of his resurrection. Like the sun rose from beneath the ground each morning, like the scarab beetles rose from their balls of dung each spring, so too did Intef the Elder rise from his coffin. He stood up, did a little dance to shake off his mummy strips, and looked around his tomb. Immediately, he felt like something wasn't quite right. His body felt odd and disconnected. His limbs were too loose, and his mind felt a little muddy. Oh well, he thought, maybe one just had to get used to the feeling of being dead. It was probably nothing to worry about.

But, just in case, he did a quick survey of his tomb to make sure that all was in order. Yes, there were the four canopic jars that contained Intef's organs, one for each of Horus' four sons. There was the human-headed Imsety, whose jar contained his liver. Next to him was the jackal-headed Duamutef, who guarded his stomach. Hapi, the baboon-faced son of Horus, was responsible for his lungs, and Qebehsenuet, the falcon, presided over his intestines.

He sat down to wait for the four sons of Horus to guide him and show him where to go, but they didn't come. At last he grew impatient, so he stood up and left his saff tomb, still feeling a bit woozy. He emerged from the stone tomb into an almost unbearably brightly lit landscape. Perfectly flat and floored with sand, there was no end in sight in any direction. Hundreds, if not thousands, of people milled about, looking as confused as Intef felt. It seemed a bit like being lost in the desert, thought Intef, with a great lot of other people.

At last he saw something that at least gave a semblance of order. A long line had formed off to one side, and it was moving slowly as it snaked its way over the horizon. An official looking person with a rat's head stood off to the side of it, holding a papyrus scroll upon which he scribbled furiously with a reed pen.

"Excuse me, Mr. Rat-Face?" asked Intef, with as much respect as was possible for a Pharaoh to muster for a rat-faced administrative clerk. "I am the Pharaoh Intef. Where shall I go?"

"Back of the line," said Mr. Rat-Face peremptorily,

without even looking up at the bewildered and affronted Pharaoh.

"But," protested Intef, drawing himself up and fixing Mr. Rat-Face with the most regally disdainful glare that he could manage, considering how discombobulated and strange he felt. "I am the Pharaoh Intef the Elder, and I do not wait in lines!"

Mr. Rat-Face sighed beleagueredly, then looked up with a sardonic expression and glanced from one side to the other dramatically. "Oh my goodness!" he exclaimed, bowing with a dramatic flourish of his hands. "I was in error. It seems that the line for overly demanding dead pharaohs hasn't formed yet. Why don't you go ahead and start it off?"

"Huh," said Intef, feeling extremely annoyed by Mr. Rat-Face's lack of respect but also feeling too physically strange to do much about it. "Where shall I start it?" he asked, hoping to get this unpleasant little interview over with quickly so that he could begin his afterlife, where the first thing he intended to do was to sit down and get himself together.

Mr. Rat-Face raised his little rat eyebrows and curled his little rat lip in a nasty little rat smirk. "Right there," he sneered, his little rat whiskers twitching with mirth. He gestured towards the end of the long line. "Right there", he repeated. "Just at the back of that line."

Then Mr. Rat-Face turned his beady eyes to look directly at Intef for the first time, to see the effects of his mean-spirited teasing. But when at last he really looked at Intef properly, (who, by the way, was staring back at Mr. Rat-Face with astonished affront), his eyes opened as wide as they could with alarm, and his whiskers quivered as though he had been presented with a terrible foul smell.

"Uhhh," he said, before regaining his composure. "You might want to..." he broke off, waving his paw in wide circles to indicate Intef's body. "You'll probably want to do something about that first." Then Mr. Rat-Face turned and scurried away, leaving Intef utterly confused, annoyed, and more than a little concerned about the state of his body.

He took a moment to assess himself. He really didn't feel very well. He felt woozy, and his limbs didn't seem to move properly. He felt like a puppet whose strings were loose and tangled, so that when he tried to move an arm, a leg would move with it, and vice versa. He ran his hands over himself.

His torso felt oddly lumpy, and he began to fear that things hadn't been put back together in quite the right way. Terribly anxious now, he checked his canopic jars, opening one by one. It was as he feared. Imsety, who should have his liver, instead had his intestines. Hapi, who should have his lungs, instead had his stomach. Duamutef, who was supposed to be the keeper of his stomach, guarded instead his liver, and Qebehsenuet, who should have his intestines, had his lungs.

"Oh Isis, mother of Horus!" he muttered angrily, once he realized the dreadful mistakes that had been made by his embalmer.

"Yes?" asked a beautiful lady in long blue robes, who, to his astonishment, suddenly began to materialize in front of him. Her tone, a bit peevish if truth be told, was that of someone who had heard their name called one too many times.

"Nothing, nothing," he said, sheepishly ducking his head with embarrassment as he realized that this must be Isis herself, and that his oath must have called her to him.

Isis rolled her eyes and sighed heavily. "Well, then don't call my name for no good reason, please! It is quite irritating," she said, then disappeared with a poof.

"Huh," said Intef, with some amazement. "That happened." Shaking his head, he went back to his assessment of his body. At last he reached the front of his chest, and found what it was that had so disgusted Mr. Rat-Face. The stitches that should have held his heart in the place where it had been put back in his body had come loose, leaving a gaping hole in his chest. His heart, of course, was no longer there, having fallen out at some point.

"Oh, this is dreadful!" he cried, and began to run around crazily in a circle (or, as close to a circle as he could, with his parts all in the wrong place and his limbs refusing to cooperate with each other). Intef needed his heart so that Osiris could weigh it against a feather, thus earning him his place in the afterlife. He had no idea what would happen if he came before Osiris without a heart.

"Use the Nubian embalmer, they said," he muttered. "Nubian embalmers are cheaper, they said. You can't afford a Greek embalmer, they said. Everybody's using the Nubian ones anyway, they said. Stupid Nubian embalmers." At last, he tired himself out with his running and his muttering, and he decided that there was nothing for it but to wait in line, and see what Osiris had to say about his predicament. Surely, his lack of a heart couldn't be held against him, since it wasn't his fault. So he stood in line, and waited, and waited, and waited, until at last he came to the front where Osiris waited with his four sons. Beside the god was a huge scale with two trays, one which was empty and another that held a feather. This was where Osiris placed one's heart, to make sure that it was lighter than the feather so that one might earn a place in the afterlife.

"Now we shall get things straight," thought Intef, as he stepped up to the god and his sons. He was so nervous that he was sure that his heart would have been racing (had he had one presently, that is).

Osiris smiled benevolently upon him. "Hello," he said, "and welcome to the afterlife. May I see your heart, please?"

"Well, see, here's the thing," stammered Intef. "It seems that, through no fault of my own, that my heart has been lost. I used a Nubian embalmer, you see, and, well…"

"Ah," said Osiris, "that is most unfortunate. I need to judge your heart against this feather, and I cannot do so, obviously, without your heart being present. Run along then and find it, and then you can come back to me."

"But," protested Intef, "I have no idea where to find it. Can't you, just, I don't know, make an exception for me?"

"No, no," said Osiris, growing impatient with the presumptuous pharaoh. He waved Intef away, and gestured to the next person in line to move forward.

"But it was the Nubian's fault!" cried Intef. Osiris ignored him, sending Intef into a terrible panic. He reached inside his linens, looking for the Isis knot that was supposed to be there, that would protect his body. He hoped that perhaps holding it might help him find his heart. But alas, the Nubian embalmer had not put the Isis knot in the cloths. Intef patted himself down frantically, searching for the knot, to no avail. The knot was simply not there.

"Oh Holy Isis!" Intef cried, forgetting himself in his consternation. At once, Isis appeared. "WHAT. NOW?!?!" snapped the lady, irritated with him in earnest now.

Panicked, he tried to cover his mistake. "No, no," he protested, turning beet red in embarrassment. "I said, 'Where's my holy Isis knot?' That's all."

"Ugh," sighed Isis, shaking her head in exasperation as she began to fade from view. "Sweet Baby Moses," she added, under her breath.

An old man with a long white beard, and long flowing white robes to match began to materialize. His eyes glowered beneath bushy white eyebrows. "You called me?" he asked. "Again?" Quickly Isis blinked out, followed immediately by the old man. Intef heard the echoes of their bickering for a moment, before the sound faded just as their corporal bodies had.

Osiris closed his eyes, and breathed in and out very slowly before opening them again. He gestured to his sons. "Help him find his heart, will you?" he said. "I just can't take it anymore with this scene that he's making right now." And so, to Intef's great relief, the four brothers stepped forward to help him.

However, the commotion that Intef had already caused was greatly increased when the brothers discovered the state of the canopic jars, and that each had an organ that another brother was supposed to belong to another brother. They bickered amongst each other, grabbing canopic jars from each other in confusion and yelling until at last Osiris had had enough.

"Shut up!" he yelled with a booming voice, so that everyone froze where they were. Sadly, this also caused the brothers to drop the canopic jars that they were squabbling so fiercely over. The jars broke, and Intef's organs fell to the ground where they disappeared with an anticlimactic "poof".

Intef began to run around in circles again, crying out, "Ahhh, my parts! My parts!" Everyone present began to talk at once, until the hubbub became almost unbearable. Osiris put his head in his hands in exasperated disbelief.

At last, though, Hapi came up with a solution to the problem. "Wait!" he shouted. "I know where the parts have gone!"

Everyone, including Intef, quieted down to hear what Hapi had to say. "I'm certain that Intef's parts have fallen down into the lower realm. Which means that must also be where his heart has gone! Let's all go have a look, shall we?"

And so Intef and the four sons of Horus went down into the lower realm to look for Intef's organs, followed by a dozen or so of the people who had been waiting in line (who had come because they had been so very entertained by Intef's antics and didn't want to miss out on any further entertainment).

They all tramped around in the dark and muck (for it seemed that the lower realm was much like a cluttered and dirty basement, where all lost things went to remain lost and that no one ever cleaned out). As everyone looked and poked around and remarked upon the strange and interesting things that they found, Intef found himself more and more distressed by his situation.

His emotions reached a crux when someone trod upon his liver where it lay, breaking a piece off in the process. The man picked up what was left, and exclaimed, "Oh dear me, so sorry. But no worries, I can put it back together!" So saying, the man picked up something that was most definitely not a part of his liver (indeed, it looked like nothing more than a piece of rotten melon that had been discarded), and began to jam it into place on Intef's liver. Soon everyone was doing the same: finding little pieces of Intef's organs (or, at least someone or something's organs) and fitting them together with whatever struck their fancy. A piece of a statue filled in his intestines; balls of dung, left by some industrious dung beetles, made up an entire side of his lungs, and a sheep's bladder filled the holes in his stomach. One woman even decorated his lungs with shards of cheap jewelry that she found in a broken casket (although, one must admit that the effect was quite pretty, after all).

As Intef saw all of his organs being broken apart and pieced together in such a hodgepodge sort of way, he became more and more upset. He reached for the Plummet amulet (a token that was for keeping one grounded and sane in the afterlife) that was supposed to be in his linens, for surely the embalmer could not have forgotten to put everything in there? But alas, the Plummet amulet was nowhere to be found.

"Where is my Plummet amulet?" he cried. "This is terrible! Oh, I feel dizzy!" he exclaimed, dramatically putting his hand to his forehead as he swooned. Oh Horus, Isis, Osiris!"

Everyone stopped and looked at him, cringing at his blasphemy and waiting for Isis to appear and give him what for. But, thankfully, the lady didn't show up. Perhaps she hadn't heard his curse over the raucous din that was being raised by the search party, or perhaps she was still arguing with Moses. Either way, everyone breathed a collective sigh of relief (even Intef, who quieted himself under the exasperated stares of so many people) and continued the search for the only piece of Intef that was still missing: his heart.

Alas, the heart was nowhere to be found. Try as they might, no one uncovered it, and the search party dwindled as people grew bored and, one by one, wandered off to go about their own business. At last, all that remained were Horus' four sons and a very dejected Intef, who sat sadly contemplating the prospect of an afterlife with no heart.

Suddenly, Qebehsenuet hefted his hand high above his head, and called out "Aha!" triumphantly. His brothers and Intef looked to him excitedly, thinking that he had found the prodigal heart. But all that was held in Qebehsenuet's closed fist was a small, golden, heart-shaped locket.

"Um," said Duamutef politely. "I think that might not be our fellow's heart you've got there. Maybe just a bit small and, um, gold. Maybe get something just like that, but, you know, made of skin and bones."

"There's neither skin nor bones in a real heart, you idiot," said Hapi happily, and a good deal less politely. "It's made of, you know, more hearty material," he said, and guffawed loudly at his own pun. The brothers fell to arguing over just what a heart was made of, and exactly whose fault it was that they couldn't find it, while Intef sat there shaking his head and staring at them, wondering just what it was that he had done to deserve such a ridiculous entourage in his afterlife.

But finally, Qebehsenuet remembered that he had had something important to say, before Hapi had so rudely interrupted him, and he yelled out loudly enough to quiet them all. "Remember," he said, once he had their attention, "that when Set chopped up Osiris and scattered him all about, Isis tried to piece him together but couldn't find quite everything. So she made his, well, you know, out of gold, and it worked! So if she can do it, we can do the same for this poor little fellow here."

Everyone nodded excitedly, and agreed that it was a smashing plan, and that there was no way it could go wrong. Even Intef, nervous wreck that he was by now, had to admit that the idea might work. Anyway, there was nothing else left to do but to try, so together they all rushed off to present Intef's shiny new heart to Osiris.

Of course, the line to see Osiris was just as long as it had been before, and Mr. Rat-Face was just as unhelpful as before, so they all had to wait for some time. They moved slowly forward with the line, shuffling their feet and rolling their eyes impatiently while they waited. And, of course, since Intef was dead, and missing the Isis knot that would protect his body from decomposition, there was an unpleasant smell that accompanied them, and made people start to scooch away from them, and even to let them pass ahead in line, so that Intef and his escort reached the head of the line quite a bit faster than it had taken him the first time around.

Qebehsenuet prodded Intef to move forward. "Put your new heart on the scale, and don't say anything," he said. "I bet he won't even notice."

So Intef did just that. As he stepped up to the scale, Osiris looked as though he'd rather see anyone but him. The god closed his eyes, opened them again, and sighed heavily when he saw that Intef was still there.

"You've found your heart, I presume?" asked Osiris tiredly.

"Um, yes," said Intef, looking back at the brothers, who all nodded encouragingly towards him. "It's right here." With that, he quickly dropped the golden heart on the scale, hoping that Osiris would not look too closely.

Osiris, of course, saw immediately that the heart was not a real heart at all, but instead a piece of jewelry. And it was not even real gold, but some sort of cheap, brassy metal. He closed his eyes again, and wondered why he had taken on this thankless job of ruling over the afterlife. It really could be quite ridiculous at times, and he just didn't have the energy for this nonsense today.

He looked at Intef, standing there in front of him, looking all around, trying not to look suspicious and so looking incredibly suspicious. He saw the state of deterioration that the poor pharaoh's body was in. His skin was droopy, and his limbs looked like they were on so loosely that they might fall off at any moment. But the worst part was the smell. The smell was getting progressively worse, so that Intef had become, truthfully, quite rank.

It was the smell that decided Osiris. "Very well!" he said, with a forced cheerfulness. "You pass! Your heart is lighter than this feather, so on to the afterlife with you!"

Imsety, Hapi, Duamutef, and Qebehsenuet gave a mighty cheer and danced about, thinking that they had fooled Osiris. Intef smiled happily, suspected something a bit closer to the truth but not really caring how or why he had passed; he was only glad that he was to resurrect after all. And it was none too soon. Hapi rushed over to clap Intef on the shoulder, and his arm gave a distressing lurch, as though it were determined to separate itself from the rest of his body. Everyone raised their eyebrows and looked around with some consternation, but at last Intef's spirit was resurrected, and soared free of its stinky cocoon.

The body disappeared with a poof (although, in truth, the smell lingered for quite some time after that, so that people who came to the top of the line remarked upon it. Weeks later, Osiris still felt as though he caught a whiff of Intef from time to time, causing him to huff heavily with annoyance and disgust each time). Intef himself flew away to begin his afterlife, and soon forgot all about the travails that he had had in getting there. The four brothers ran off in search of a new adventure, and Osiris settled back in to the long task of judging hearts, and all was well.

Columbkill Noonan has an MS in Biology, and teaches Anatomy and Physiology at a university in Maryland. An avid history buff, much of her writing, which could be best described as "supernatural historical horror", combines historical events with elements of paranormal fantasy. Her first novel, *Night Woods*, is available as an e-book on Amazon.com. She is currently working on her second novel, which was inspired by a trip to Scotland, particularly by the grim castles and spooky underground alleys of Edinburgh.

In her spare time, Columbkill enjoys hiking, scuba diving, and riding her horse, Mittens. To learn more about Columbkill, and to hear breaking news about her latest works, please visit: www.facebook.com/ColumbkillNoonan

SCOOTER'S CLOSET
BY DAVID BERNARD

The trouble started in October when Mama finally got the kitchen remodeled. I certainly don't begrudge Mama a new kitchen, after years of dealing with an ancient double sink that loved to back up and old cabinets that were usually swollen shut from all the layers of paint. When we moved to Critchley's Hollow some thirty years ago, the kitchen was already in rough shape, even by Tennessee standards. Even worse, the cabinets weren't original to the kitchen, so they didn't quite fit into the room right. And all it took was one collision with the corner of a counter to discover they were a little too low to be waist-high, if you catch my drift.

When the contractor pulled out the old cabinets, we found out how shoddy the construction really was – whoever installed the cabinets fifty years ago had just slapped the cabinets up against the old wall, not even stripping off the original wallpaper, which was as ugly as they day they covered it over, blue chickens, pinkish stripes and all.

To save a little on labor, my brother Scooter took some time off from his job at Gilman's Bowling Alley to help prep the walls for the new cabinets. Scooter was, to put it delicately, pretty useless with tools, so we set him to working over in the corner where the old stove used to be. It was about his technical skill level and all he had to do was pull off old plywood stuck on the wall. What's the worst that could happen?

That's where he found the closet. It was a shallow little

thing - barely a broom closet that someone had covered over with scrap plywood. It wasn't any use in the new kitchen, but Scooter got the idea to come in from the back side in the living room and make it into a built-in cabinet where Daddy could display his collection of Civil War junk. The closet was dry walled over with a new cabinet installed in front of it. Scooter said he'd cut through from the other side later on, when the kitchen was done. Personally, my money was on everyone forgetting it was there and nothing ever coming of it.

Everyone was happy. Mama had a new kitchen, and Daddy had a pile of scrap lumber to play with. I figured if I could get on the day shift at the paper mill, things would be perfect for all of us. I could go back to flirting with Britney-Jo at the Riverview Donut Emporium. On night shift, I didn't really stand a chance of hooking up with Britney-Jo. Of course, Britney-Jo hooked up with just about everyone sooner or later, but that's a different story.

One morning, I got back from the paper mill and Daddy was sitting in the new kitchen with a mug of instant decaf and a look that meant trouble. He just looked at me and said "Your brother is a pain in my ass."

I looked right back at him. "What did he break this time?"

Daddy sighed. "He hasn't broken anything – yet. He went through my lumber pile and dragged half of it in the living room to build that cabinet."

I knew Daddy would normally be thrilled with the thought of a new cabinet, but he didn't like anyone messing with his wood pile and to be honest, the thought of Scooter using power tools made us both more than a little nervous. We decided to make sure Doc Caldwell was on the speed dial, just in case.

I wandered into the living room and sure enough, there was Scooter, surrounded by enough tools and wood to build a two-car garage. He had a strange, faraway look in his eyes, like the one he got when he was watching Lucy Liu movies.

He was just staring at the wall, caressing the handle of the 20-pound sledgehammer Daddy bought to break up the old septic tank.

"So, you're going to build Daddy that cabinet after all?" I asked him, hoping I could convince him to try a different project, one simple enough to leave him with all ten fingers.

"I have to. The cabinet is calling to me," he answered, still staring at the wall.

I looked at the wall. I didn't see anything, and I sure as hell didn't hear anything. Scooter always was a little high-strung, which Mama blamed on breathing in all that disinfectant spray at the bowling alley. We didn't argue with her, because Mama was kind of high-strung herself. I decided Scooter just needed some time to think about how little he knew about carpentry. So I went to my room, figuring what was the worst that could happen? He'd break another finger and that would be the end of it.

I was pulling double shifts at the mill, just like every October. For some reason, the idiots in management keep forgetting that there's a rush on bleached kraft paper when the big printing plant up in Chattanooga starts printing up "trick or treat bags" and every year, we run out of inventory before Halloween and end up having to run extra shifts to catch up. And after two shifts in the refining room, all I wanted was a shower and a few hours of sleep, preferably without the sound of power tools or an ambulance driving most of Scooter to the hospital.

I got up that afternoon to find Scooter had already headed to the bowling alley. He had punched through the drywall and rough-framed in the little closet. It was surprising – both because I hadn't heard any hammering, and because Scooter did it without bleeding all over Momma's carpet. I used to do a little carpentry before I decided a steady paycheck at the mill was better than the ups and downs of the carpentry trade, and this was good work, better than I expected from someone who once broke two fingers and a Formica

17

countertop trying to use a hammer and a screwdriver to open a can of pistachios.

The next night's shifts were dull as usual. The only thing to talk about in the break room was the weird weather: fog at the wrong time of the year, and storm clouds with no rain.

Scooter was working in the little closet when I got home. I said hello, and he grunted in my general direction. Not quite as exciting as the talk at work, but close. I grabbed a shower and went to bed. That's when the nightmares started.

I was surrounded by fog, but there was something off about it. The color didn't seem right and it moved in ways I'd never seen fog move before. I couldn't see anything through the fog, but I knew I was up on Critchley's Mountain. I started running through the fog, but I didn't know if I was running after something or away from something. The fog started clearing, but it not like the sun was burning it off. It looked like dirty water, circling a drain. But instead of a bathtub, it was a hole in the ground. I went to look into the hole...

I woke up covered in sweat. I never could get back to sleep after waking up, so even with a lousy four hours of sleep, I got up and went downstairs. Scooter was stacking wood against the wall. He had started working inside the closet on the back wall. It was about half done. He was lining the walls with an elaborate pattern of tongue and groove planks that should have taken him weeks to complete. It almost looked like a spider web made of wood. It was an odd effect that made the closet look deeper than it was.

"Scooter," I asked, "Why you'd bother putting something that fancy in the back of the cabinet? You know Daddy's just going to hang his bootleg lithograph of the Battle of Kingsport back there and hide all that woodwork anyway."

Scooter looked at me and then at the closet. I suddenly realized he looked like hell warmed over. He had bags under his eyes, his skin was turning yellowish, and his goatee looked downright straggly. Scooter wasn't particularly vain, but he was the best looking clerk at the bowling alley (which still ain't saying much) and he was an eternal optimist. He felt you never knew when a busload of Titans cheerleaders would break down in front of the bowling alley. And since the girls would obviously head inside to call for help and stay for cheap beer and bad nachos while the bus was being repaired, you needed to look your best for your one shot. For Scooter to look this bad, especially during football season, meant he was either sick or spending too much time working on that closet.

He shrugged and looked at me again, but I doubt he saw me. "I need to get this cabinet done for Halloween. That's when the veil is thinnest." Then he walked out to his Kia and went to work. I went back upstairs to get ready for the next double shift, still wondering what the hell he was talking about.

A 16-hour shift on 4 hours of sleep was hellish. I managed not to fall into a vat of pulp, but I was hurting by the time I dragged my sorry butt home. After the nightmare, I was a little worried about getting any sleep. Fortunately, Halloween was so close that the printers had stopped ordering as much paper. Management decided to cancel the double shifts and offer vacation time instead of overtime. Normally, I'd take the money, but the way I felt, I took a week of vacation time. Tomorrow was my first day off in a dog's age and I needed it. It wasn't helping that the big news on the radio for the entire drive home was the weird reports of another heavy fog up in the mountains.

I was surrounded by fog, but it seemed darker in color in areas, giving it a look like a giant spider web made of smoke. I knew I was up on Critchley's Mountain, and this time I knew I wasn't just running, I was chasing something. I could hear things echoing through the fog – an evil laugh and a kid screaming in terror. The screaming was getting closer and I realized I was chasing some little girl. Suddenly, there was that hole in the ground again, with weird lightning coming out of it. Suddenly the screaming stopped. I looked and my hands were covered in blood. Only they weren't my hands; they were the hands of an old lady, wrinkled and spindly…

I woke up staring at my hands. They were still mine, from the bleach spots right down to the scar from when I was nine and tried to play with one of Daddy's Civil War bayonets. I looked at the clock. I had been asleep for ten hours but didn't feel like I'd slept at all. In fact, I still felt like death warmed over. Some vacation.

Momma and Daddy were out shopping and Scooter was at work. I grabbed a bowl of cereal and took a good look at the closet. Scooter's sudden skill in woodwork was almost as freaky as my nightmares. The panel was flawless and it was backlit in some weird bluish light. That made it even weirder; Scooter didn't know a circuit breaker from fire hose, let alone how to wire recessed lighting. I looked for a switch to shut it off and couldn't find it. He did a nice job through – between the light and the spider web lattice design, the closet looked twice as deep as it actually was.

I decided to head down to Jerry's Ye Olde Ale House. I was determined to get some sleep even if I had to pass out at a bar to get it. Just my luck, the place was crowded and I had to sit at the bar next to Cherokee Jim. I grabbed a copy of the Times-News and hoped I could avoid making eye contact.

Jim was putting down bourbon faster than normal, which was pretty damn fast. He was spooked and the only other time I'd ever seen that crazy old man spooked was one night while we were out on his jon boat night fishing in Brennan's Swamp and we startled a whippoorwill. Well, Jim went off on how Waguli was a spirit guide for the dead and we just sent him off to collect a soul. I don't recall anyone dying that night, although we did kill a six-pack or two.

Jim glanced over at the paper I was pretending to read. Oblivious to the fact I was ignoring him, he started talking. "You know," Jim said, "Critchley's Mountain is an evil place. My ancestors avoided it because the witches practiced black magic up there."

I switched to "Plan B," where I finish my beer and remember an appointment. Just as I was about to run screaming out into the parking lot, Jim said something about portals and fog. I sat back down.

Jim looked at the newspaper I had folded. The Times-News headline was about an 8-year old girl that went missing in the fog up on Critchley's Mountain. He looked at me, and I think he sensed I was really paying attention. "You people took over our land, but you never listened to our stories. This newspaper tells a white man version of a story that would have our shamans preparing for battle against great evil. That mountain was home to Utlunta the Spearfinger. She was an old Cherokee witch who could use black magic to call forth a fog that made her invisible."

I started getting a bad feeling about Jim's story, and I wasn't sure why. I bought him another round. He downed it in one shot and continued. "Utlunta was so evil that even food avoided her. So she could only eat the one thing that was pure and sheltered enough to have never heard of Utlunta – the liver of a Cherokee child. She got the name Spearfinger because she turned her finger into stone, sharp as an obsidian knife, which she then used to cut out the livers of the children."

"The grief of the parents grew with the number of children killed, and the elders, chiefs, and shamans gathered in the ancient council place on the Long Island in the Holstan River. It was decided that such evil could not go unchallenged any longer. The shamans gathered their strength and the many would act as one. But the elders remembered Utlunta's evil and knew even the combined might of the shamans would be no match for the witch's black arts. Instead, the elders advised that they must think like Ji-Stu the rabbit and trick her.

So under the cover of a moonless night, the shamans climbed Utlunta's mountain and dug a pit. Using their most powerful charms, they opened the pit into the land of death. Then they made a cry like a lost child. Utlanta, in her greedy hunger, did not see the pit and fell into it. The shamans then covered the hole with spider webs and enchanted the webs, sealing the portal to the land of the dead and trapping Utlanta."

I motioned for another round and this time, I finished mine off before Jim. I glanced at the headline again. "I don't suppose the trap was foolproof?"

Jim snorted. "Anytime you make something fool proof, they grow a bigger fool. Utlanta can escape the realm of the dead, but only if someone passes through the mystic spider web and takes her place. And the transfer can only take place when the veil between the worlds is at its thinnest."

I looked at Jim. "And Halloween is the day when the veil is thinnest?"

Jim nodded. "All Hallows' Eve, Samhain, Day of the Dead – take your pick. All the ancient cultures knew when the veil was thinnest and tried to make nice with any spirits that passed through. The Cherokee are no exception."

I got up. "Jim, I need to go see my brother. I think he's in trouble." Jim looked at me strangely and just nodded. I think he already knew what the trouble was.

I drove home to wait for Scooter. It looked like the closet was just about done. A little bit of molding and the doors were all that were missing. If I was right, Scooter had gotten himself mixed up with a bad situation. But I didn't know how to stop it without destroying the cabinet and looking like a nut.

I fired up the computer and went looking for Cherokee good luck charms, anti-evil talismans – anything that might cancel out the closet. Absolutely nothing was helpful except one site that said the hair of some sacred buffalo in Oklahoma was powerful. I didn't have time to drive to Oklahoma, find this buffalo and give him a haircut. I decided to wing it. I went digging in Momma's closet and found the old crucifix Aunt Nabby gave us a few years back. I think Aunt Nabby wanted us to hang it on the wall, but there was no way Momma would hang a crucifix in the house; "too Catholic for us God fearin' Methodists" was the quote, so the cross went into closet, only coming out when Aunt Nabby came to call. Aunt Nabby had a good sized nest egg, bad health, and a last will that changed beneficiaries frequently. Methodist or not, Momma wasn't taking a chance on her inheritance.

I took the crucifix and stood in Scooter's closet. The tongue and groove was just flexible enough that I could jam the cross down behind the woodwork; I heard it drop down on the floor where Scooter would never be able to find it. And if he did, he'd have to tear the lattice work apart to get at it.

Momma and Daddy got home and told me that Scooter had announced he was just about finished with the closet, all he had to do was hang the doors and it was officially a display cabinet. He announced he would finish it tomorrow night. Momma assumed it was to officially present it to Daddy as a Halloween present, but I kept remembering that part about the veil being thinnest on Halloween.

Scooter spent the night working on the molding for the doors. He was cradling each piece of wood like it was a baby. I was on the couch pretending to watch the TV, and the few times the sound dropped low, I'd swear he was talking to the closet. He stood up and grinned. By this time he'd lost so much weight he looked like a grinning skull with a bad goatee. "Tomorrow," he announced, "I hang the doors at sunset and it's ready."

He headed upstairs to bed. I looked at Daddy, who looked at me. I just shrugged. Daddy looked over at the stairway.

"You know," he started," I'm getting a little worried about that boy. He's acting like he's built something bigger and grander than a little display cabinet. Maybe your momma's right. It may be time to get him out of that bowling alley and away from all that disinfectant spray."

Daddy may have been a little worried, but I was downright nervous. Maybe Scooter was just proud of finally doing some quality woodworking. Maybe Cherokee Jim had just messed with my head. Maybe the nightmares were screwing with my thinking. All I knew for certain was that I had a lot of maybes and a really bad feeling about tomorrow's Halloween celebration.

I was standing near a hole up on Critchley's Mountain. The sky was full of lightning and every bolt showed the fog was getting thicker and thicker. I could hear the echo of a woman laughing and the screams of children. The lightning flashes showed the hill was covered with skulls. I knew they were the bones of children. I started to run, but I was trapped in spider webs that dragged me closer to the hole. Now I could see the hole was filled with blood.

I woke up gasping for air with my heart trying to pound out of my chest. It was Halloween morning. It was just after sunrise, and the sky was gray with streaks of red. It looked like it someone had smeared blood across the sky. I had definitely had better vacations. I decided to find Cherokee Jim. Maybe he had an idea of what the hell was going on around here. I didn't know where to look for Jim when the Ale House was closed, so I decided I might as well drive to the paper mill and pick up my check. I grabbed a cup of coffee at the donut shop, ignoring Britney-Jo, which would probably cost me in the long run. I started driving around aimlessly. I wasn't just killing time, I was trying to clear my head and shake the feeling something bad was happening.

I ended up by the logging road leading up Critchley's

Mountain. It was blocked off by police cars, state troopers and the county coroner wagon. I felt sick. I already knew what it meant. I saw Chuck Griffin, a deputy who was an old school buddy of mine.

I rolled down the window and pulled over by him. "Trouble on the mountain, Chuckster?"

Chuck looked at me grimly. "Yep. Real bad trouble. They found that little girl that disappeared. At least they found what was left of her."

My mouth went dry and I felt dizzy. "That's a real shame. You think it was a mountain lion that got her?" It was more of a last hope than a question.

Pete just shook his head. "No. She was cut up pretty badly, but the ME says it wasn't an animal. He says it was a knife or a straight razor – something really sharp. I can't tell you more than that."

I forced a smile. "Thanks Chuck, but I think I don't really want to know. You be careful out there." I turned around and slowly drove back toward the mill. I picked up my check and then stopped downtown for breakfast. I barely could taste it. Somehow, my nightmares were tied into that little girl's disappearance and it all started when Scooter found that closet. I just didn't know how to stop the nightmares or Scooter. I managed to kill enough time that the Ale House would be opening. I parked out front and went in. For the first time that I could remember, Cherokee Jim wasn't on his stool in the corner.

"Hey Jerry," I called to the owner, "Where's Jim?"

Jerry rolled his eyes. "He saw the morning TV news about that little girl getting killed on the mountain and just stood up and left. I was sweeping up next to him and heard him was mutter something about heading down to North Carolina to talk to some old guy and that was the last I saw of him."

Either Jim had gone to talk to a Cherokee elder, or he was hiding until whatever the hell this was blew over. Either way, it made Jim smarter than me. I went to the library instead and tried to find something that would help me get a handle on what was going on. Of course, all I could ask the librarian was how to find information on Cherokee folklore. I'm not sure they had a section on how to deal with your brother when you think he's under the spell of a Cherokee witch woman trying to escape Hell. I killed most of the day in there and came out with no new ideas. I went next store to the drugstore and picked up a couple of bags of candy and headed home to wait for Halloween night.

Momma took the bags of candy and looked out the window. "I reckon there'd be a few parents that would even let their kids out of the house with some maniac sex fiend out there cutting up children. Now this fog on top of it just makes it worse. I wonder why the mayor just doesn't cancel Trick or Treating and get it over with."

She poured the candy into a bowl just in case someone came by anyway. She looked out the window again and sighed. "At least this candy won't go to waste – your Daddy never met a bag of candy he didn't like."

Momma was right – both about Daddy and the weather. Fog was rolling in before sunset, and it was as thick as any I had ever seen. The storm clouds that had building all week were rumbling like a major thunderstorm about to let loose. We had about an hour before sunset. I went upstairs to get changed. Sitting in the middle of my bed was Aunt Nabby's cross, crushed into a little ball. I dressed in a hurry and backed out of the room, staring at the cross. I ran downstairs and looked in the closet. There was no sign of damage to the wood. There was no way to get that crucifix out from behind that wall without tearing out the woodwork, but someone – or something - sure as hell did.

Momma came into the room, handed me the bowl of candy and announced she and Daddy had decided to have dinner at Miss Reba's down the road and would be back later. I think they were a little spooked by Scooter and his crazy eyes. I wasn't thrilled about being there either, but something told me I'd better stick around.

Scooter's Kia rolled into the yard about 6:15. By my calculations, sunset would be about 6:30, so whatever was he was expecting to happen needed to happen in about 15 minutes. He staggered out of the car, with that wild look in his eyes. Frankly, I'd seen dead folks who looked better than he did. He was nothing but skin and bones, and the skin didn't look all that good. He came into the house and grinned.

"Scooter, how about we head down to the Ale House and have a couple of beers? My treat." I had never known Scooter to turn down a free beer, but he just walked past me like I was invisible.

Instead, he stood in the living room, watching the sun through the fog and storm clouds. I noticed he was looking right at the sun without blinking, almost like he was trying to stare the sun into going down faster. Once the sun was gone and the sky was filled with rolling black fog, he turned and attached the first door on the closet. The thunder got worse and sounded like it was right over the house. I decided that the second door shouldn't be attached, but I couldn't move. It was like I was glued to the floor. I watched Scooter slowly pick up the last door and attach the hinges. With a crazy look in his eyes, he gently closed the cabinet doors.

As soon as he did, the power went out and the thunderstorm broke like the gates of Hell themselves had burst open. Even in the dark with the power out, that damn closet still glowed blue. Somehow I knew it had to be that Cherokee witch. I discovered I could move again, so using the lightning to search the room, I ripped the doors off and just whaled on that spider web lattice work with Daddy's sledge hammer.

As soon as I knocked a chunk of the wood off the back wall, the blue light went out, the storm stopped and the power came back on. There was no sign of Scooter, but I knew where he was. I just didn't know how to get him back.

I fixed the doors on the cabinet and took down a big chunk of the spider web lattice. I hid the damage by hanging Daddy's lithograph on the wall, which covered most the back wall above the shelves, exactly as I predicted. I loaded up the cabinet with Daddy's bullets, buttons and rusted bits of swords and the other crap he had picked up in the woods with his metal detector and let him think Scooter had filled the cabinet for him.

I needed a plan to explain why Scooter suddenly disappeared. Before my parents got home, I drove Scooter's Kia down to the bowling alley and parked it with the keys in it. Hopefully, it would be stolen before too long by a member of the high class crowd that the bowling alley attracted.

What else could I do? Who'd believe me if I told them my baby brother got sucked into a display case for stray bullets from the Battle of Kingsport that was actually a portal to some sort of Cherokee hell?

I decided if I was going to lie, I was going to lie big. I told everyone that the reason Scooter looked so bad for the last few weeks was because he was under a lot of stress. Scooter, I lied, had admitted to me that he had knocked up a girl over in Biglerville. Now that the tests confirmed Scooter was the daddy, he decided to lay low before her daddy commenced to making plans for a shotgun wedding. Knowing Scooter and the girls in Biglerville, even Mama bought into that story.

That was two years ago. The child killings have continued and they've been spreading. Critchley's Hollow has armed citizens patrolling all night and Kingsport is on a sundown to sunrise curfew, for all the good it's done. The killings have spread beyond Sullivan County into Hamblen. Now the paper is reporting that there was another killing. This time it was in Jefferson County. This means the folks down in Knoxville are starting to get a little nervous. The State Police are getting crucified in the newspapers and there's talk about bringing the FBI in to help. They've tried everything from traps to psychics, but the mutilations have continued. The Cherokees figured it out first, since Spearfinger is one of theirs, but there aren't any elders or medicine men left with enough of the old knowledge to know what to do. Parents lock their kids up at night, but every month or two, I wake up from another screaming nightmare and somewhere another mangled little body shows up somewhere without a liver.

Cherokee Jim has sobered up enough to help try and find out how to reopen the portal. He's been going to every Cherokee reservation and casino he can find, looking for someone who might remember the old stories. I have him drop a blank postcard in the mail addressed to my Momma from every location he visits. She knows the blank card is from Scooter telling her he's okay without giving away any details to his location.

So I guess it's up to me. I quit my job at the paper mill and started doing carpentry work again. I figure that if our house had a portal, so does someone else and the easiest way to find it was to be the one who was cutting into the walls. And if I can find another door, maybe I can figure a way to open it so Scooter can escape. I figure I have all year to find one, since it only opens on Halloween.

It's not a great plan, but it's worth a try - what's the worst that can happen?

David Bernard is a native New Englander who now lives (albeit under protest) in South Florida, a paradoxical place where, when temperatures drops below 60°, locals break out parkas to wear over their plaid shorts and sandals. His previous works include short stories in anthologies such as *Snowbound with Zombies* and *Legacy of the Reanimator*. This is his third appearance in the Strangely Funny series.

SCREW KAFKA
BY GUSTAVO BONDONI

Goddammit, not this *again!*

I knocked on the door of number 23. I knocked again, and a third time before the door opened. An old woman sporting a prominent nasal wart stared up at me. "Ah, Greg, isn't it? I see you're turning into a large insect of some sort."

"Did you do this to me?" is what I tried to say, but I imagine it sounded more like "mim nu nu ti tume?" as it was bloody difficult to say anything with only half the human anatomy remaining.

Mrs. Woolfy had the nerve to look affronted and innocent. "Why would you ask me about that?"

I no longer had fingers to count on, but I still responded. "Well, there was the time I became a frog, multiple cases of boils, the locusts and sixteen treatments for evil eye."

"I had nothing to do with the locusts, but I guess I see how you could suspect me. But I will have to disappoint you this time. I wasn't to blame."

"Then who?"

"Ah, that is a conundrum. The last time you were a cockroach, I seem to recall that the pale warlock on the corner was to blame. But he's been eaten by a demon since then, so we'll have to look elsewhere. Would you like some tea?"

I attempted to explain that cockroaches almost never drank tea and stormed off. It is difficult to storm off when your legs are designed for stealth and scuttling, but I gave it my best shot. It made me feel better, but achieved nothing else, and I had the same problem as before at the end of it.

So I did the only thing I could think of. I went off in search of Gilda. She was always understanding about my problems, even if I suspected that she wasn't always completely faithful in other ways.

It was probably a mistake. The single word, "Ugh," and a slamming door were all I got for my troubles, and I finally gave up and headed where I didn't want to be.

"Man, you look like shit," Bernard said. A waft of pungent smoke drifted out of the room behind him. "You'd better come in. Are you like some sort of beetle?"

"Cockroach," I replied. The loss of my speech centers was progressing slower than I'd feared. Last time, I'd been completely mute an hour after the transformation started, with the entire fire brigade running after me with axes ten minutes after that. It had not been fun.

"Bummer. Beetles used to be worshipped by the ancient Egyptians, you know."

"Fascinating," I muttered.

"Want a joint?"

I wondered if he was trying to kill me, but decided he probably wasn't. He seemed to be off on some planet of his own where fumigation was either unheard of or considered a pleasant diversion.

I flopped onto a giant beanbag, being careful not to crack a piece of carapace. Exoskeletons looked tough, but I knew they were very brittle. "Can you get me some sugar?"

He looked at me, clearly disappointed, and shrugged. "Whatever floats your boat, man." He tried to hand me a large pottery jar, but looked at my limbs and laid it down on the floor instead. He looked at me again, shook his head in wonder, muttered "man, that was really good shit," and wandered off into the smoky gloom of the house.

"You really need to get that spell reversed," a voice from out of the fog told me.

"D'ya think?" I tried to say, but she clearly didn't hear

me.

"I'd hate to be stuck in that shell. It's only a question of time before someone manages to locate a really big can of Raid."

"Very funny," I said.

"I'm not trying to be funny. Those insect hexes can get you killed pretty easily. Kafkian ones are the worst. I wonder why it is that so many warlocks have that Metamorphosis obsession. I guess they think it makes them look dark and dangerous. I think it just makes them look like the losers they really are. I'm Gina, by the way."

I looked her over. She looked pale and overtly mammalian, and I knew that she would have looked a lot more appetizing to me if she'd been dead and decomposing for a couple of weeks.

Crap, the transformation was reaching the nerve centers. Screw Kafka, anyway.

"You'd never see a witch fooling around with roaches. After all, they're disgusting creatures when they're tiny, so what would you want with a giant one? Frogs, bats, that's good enough to punish someone with, without having to call an exterminator afterwards."

I grunted agreement. She was definitely preaching to the choir. I wondered idly how much longer I would get to keep my human thought processes. It wasn't making me particularly nervous, though.

"I'll help you."

That got through, all right. "Why?"

"Did you say 'why'? Easy, because I feel sorry for you. Bernard certainly isn't going to be of much use. He probably thinks you're just a piece of bad acid, or whatever it is he's on right now. But I can help."

"How?"

"I'm studying witchcraft. Nearly done with first year!"

Something in my mind, some instinctive self-preservation function, reacted, and I slammed into the door with a chitinous thud.

That was just about when I realized that most doors were designed for humans, not cockroaches. How did one go about rotating a knob with an insect leg, anyway?

"Oh, come on, all I need is a small snippet of leg hair. There we go." I felt a vibration which had no human equivalent, before I managed to locate a window and push my way out. Glass is not a problem when you have an exoskeleton.

Soon, I found myself in familiar surroundings: I was running down the street pursued by a screaming mob, at least one of which was a uniformed fireman wielding a large, serious-looking axe. Only the lack of pitchforks kept it from being a complete cliché.

Suddenly, I felt a wrench, an elongation of parts of my body and a contraction of others. The steady insectile scurry I'd been using so effectively to open the gap to my pursuers suddenly became disjointed. Something weird – well, weirder, at least – began to happen to my eyesight, and I nearly ran into a hydrant, mainly because I wasn't quite certain which of the many hydrants I was suddenly seeing I should avoid.

I gained some respite because the crowd suddenly stopped to stare, faltering for a moment. I was delighted to see that the guy with the axe went down when he stopped and the crowd behind was slow to react. I hope they trampled him to death.

But after that single hesitation, they came after me with renewed vigor, and I tried to high-tail it down the street.

It wasn't easy. I seemed to have more legs than before. A window I passed confirmed the feeling: the reflection showed one big-ass hairy spider. It was better than a cockroach, I guess.

Or maybe not. The cockroach could at least outrun humans on foot. This new shape simply couldn't. I tried turning to the left, into an alleyway, but misjudged the angle and hit the wall instead.

It was an enormous relief to find myself climbing upwards, for which I thanked the spider's reflexes as opposed to any quick thinking on my part. Sometimes, the human parts of the brain were a hindrance in these cases.

My pursuers milled about in front of the building I'd chosen for a few minutes before managing to gain entry. The fact that they were inside was cause for worry, but I had only a few moments to go to reach the roof.

The roof was a fairly typical example of its kind, with black tar and some kind of silver insulation covering a flat surface with a raised cabin into which a door was set. The drop off the side of the building seemed pretty long, but the spider in me was already plotting a trajectory for a line of silk to the next edifice over.

Sadly, that line had to be diverted, as one of my pursuers, puffing and red-faced, came through the door. He was soon wrapped in a white cocoon and rolled along the roof as he struggled to free himself.

But I was under no illusions. Pretty soon, the rest of my pursuers would arrive, and they'd probably be smart enough to use an elevator. I needed to move now.

It was a daunting drop. Even though my human thought processes were probably nearly gone, something deep inside, some primitive mammal, screamed from the subconscious layers of my being.

I had to stomp on that primal instinct and force myself to launch a strand. I had to shout down parts of me that said that the string would never support my weight, and that spiders only survived that sort of thing because they weighed sufficiently little that air resistance would keep them from hitting the ground as hard as I would when I fell.

But I managed, through an effort of will and discipline, to launch my thread and jump over the side. The thread held, and I swung majestically over the abyss between the towers.

It was a triumph of will over instinct, which makes it even more unfair that, as I traced my graceful arc, my body convulsed and changed shape again, causing me to lose my connection to the strand and fly straight through a window.

With what I felt to be almost superhuman patience, I digested that I no longer had an exoskeleton, just when the breaking glass would have made it useful right about then. I risked opening my eyes and crawled through what seemed like a hideously-decorated living room to a mirror. I got up slowly, and realized that, amazingly, Gina had actually hit the right species. I was human again, and the damage from the window seemed limited to a few minor abrasions.

Admittedly, I normally prefer to be much less feminine, and being shaped like I was, I would have preferred to have been clothed. Those mobs with pitchforks and torches are a persistent lot, and they would have marked precisely which window I'd flown into and would be making their way over. If they found me looking like this and dressed in nothing but a few scratches they wouldn't even bother trying to find the spider, they'd just get their entertainment elsewhere.

Time, therefore was of the essence, for that reason and also because I didn't want Gina trying to change me again. Human form was good enough to try to track down whoever had done this to me and get them to reverse it. I hurriedly ran to what seemed like a bedroom, jiggling in unaccustomed places. That is to say I was jiggling, not the bedroom.

I located a pair of too-big jeans which I held in place with a belt and rolled up, and a man's shirt which I knotted in place. Shoes were not in the cards – this was clearly a man's apartment, but at least I looked semi-decent. The door, fortunately, was on the latch, and I managed to duck down the stairs onto the floor below just before the mob coming up reached the one I'd vacated. I calmly called the elevator, waited while the mob disembarked on the floor above, listened while they started to knock down the door, and took the descending lift to the ground floor.

"Hi Gina," I said when I saw her waiting by the door. She took a second to understand what was going on, and then pumped a fist in the air.

"Yes!" she exulted. "I knew I'd gotten it right this time. You're human again!"

"I have much bigger boobs than I wanted," I told her.

"Who cares? Now you can investigate who did this to you originally. We're in the pink!"

"Yes, I have that, too."

"Stop it. Now, the first order of business is to make a list of anyone who might have wanted you out of the way."

"No, the first order of business is to get me a bra and some shoes. Then we'll talk."

"OK," Gina said, clearly wishing to get moving. "I think there are some shoes that will fit at my place, but my bras are not going to help with those."

In the end, we managed to use a combination of a t-shirt and a loose-fitting shirt from Gina's closet to solve the issue at least from a visual point of view. Her protestations that no bra would lead to sagging were met by my firm resolve to avoid keeping them any longer than necessary.

"OK, then who hates you this much?" she asked.

"Well, I hadn't had the faculties to think about it much so far today. There are a couple of guys at the office, I guess. Then there's my cleaning lady. She's always threatening to do terrible things to me if I don't learn to put my clothes in the hamper – but I don't think she has the talent. And then we also have..." I suddenly stopped and slapped my head. Gina looked at me as if I were mad, which I think is pretty unfair considering she hardly batted an eye when I was a huge cockroach. "Irene!"

"Who?"

"Irene. The last thing I remember last night was heading to the Olde Pub over on Krassnin Street and having three or four drinks. They had rum in them, as I recall. The problem is that that's the bar where I met Irene, and she still goes there. I remember seeing her and climbing on the table, and that's where it gets really fuzzy."

"Climbing on the table?"

"It seemed like the best course of action. I probably slept with her. I always hook up with Irene when I'm drunk."

"So, what's the problem, other than the fact that it sounds kinky when a girl says it?"

I rolled my eyes at her. "Irene is a little needy, in much the same way that Stalin was a bit of a sociopath. Every time we get together, she thinks it's for good, and we end up having a huge argument the following morning. Last time, I thought that was the last I'd see of her."

"But clearly it wasn't."

"Argh. I can picture it now. She probably asked me when I would marry her, and I probably said I'd rather be a cockroach, and voilà! People really shouldn't sell spells like that to crazy ex-girlfriends."

I paused for a second. "I probably didn't even need to tell her about the cockroach. She's totally into Kafka and dark stuff – she's always seemed like the type that would try to kill herself and fail, just for the attention."

I let out a frustrated sigh. "And now, I'll spend weeks tracking down the guy who made the spell, and then getting him to sell me the antidote."

"Well, there might be another way," Gina replied.

"What? What would you do in my position?"

"Honey, if I looked like you, I'd pop into the nearest modeling agency, find the prettiest pretty boy in there, and offer to give him an amazing time. Then I'd do it again with the next nearest, and so forth. I wouldn't stop till everything below my waist chafed like hell."

I shuddered. "Not even remotely interested."

"It's your loss, there's power in being irresistible."

"Even so."

"All right, then let's try this: how about you let me turn

you back? No, don't run, remember what happened last time. I'll just try anyway."

"OK, I'll listen. But letting first-year witches experiment on you is a good way of ending up dead."

"Now that you're not an insect anymore, it should be obvious even to you that we're almost there. I think I can have you back to your old self in about two more tries."

"Why two?"

"Well, first, I'm going to give you a form that will allow you to pay for all the help I've given you. I'm thinking of keeping your external beauty but making it more of a male beauty. And the big boobs... well, I'm sure I can find somewhere to put all that mass."

"Can't you just turn me back in one go? I mean, it's probably fun to be handsome and, er... huge, but what if something goes wrong. Or if you can't get me back on the second try? Or if you just say "to hell with it" once you get what you want? I might look better, but I want to be me! I like being me! And besides, isn't charging me that way a bit uncivilized."

"Don't be such a whiner. Even if you did manage to track down Irene's warlock. What do you think his price will be if you show up looking like that?"

It's always something, isn't it? "Crap. I guess I'll just have to trust you."

"Sure looks that way, doesn't it."

We walked in the general direction of Bernard's opium den. I wondered, somewhat despondently, whether that was a good idea.

"Have you ever had one of those days?"

"You mean when a crazy ex turns me into a giant insect to get their revenge?"

"Yeah."

"Nope. Can't recall any. I assume it isn't all that much fun."

I thought about it. "Beats going to work, I guess. Though

how I'm going to explain yet another day lost to a cockroach curse to my boss is something I just can't imagine."

"Better make that two days."

"Why?"

"You're pretty tired. I'm going to want you fresh and ready, so you're paying off my magic tomorrow. You may want to take a third day to rest afterwards, too."

"Oh, yeah. I guess that sounds logical."

I immediately resolved to mend my ways. No more crazy women, no more late drunken nights, and especially no more witches.

Just like last time.

Gustavo Bondoni was born in Argentina, which, he believes, makes him one of the few - if not the only - Argentinean fiction writers writing primarily in English. He moved to the US at the age of three because his father worked for a multinational company that bounced him around the world every three years. Miami, Zurich, Cincinnati. He only made it back to Buenos Aires at the age of twelve, by which time he was not quite an American kid, not quite a European kid, and definitely not Argentinean! His fiction spans the range from science fiction to mainstream stories, passing through sword & sorcery and magic realism along the way, and it has been published in fourteen countries and seven languages to date. Apart from over a hundred short stories, he has published two collections, a short novel, and a novella, with a third collection coming out in 2016. Follow his website at: gustavobondoni.com

SELFIE
BY GARY PISERCHIO

The ghosts are getting more aggressive. Which is weird, right? I mean, first of all they're ghosts. Vapors. Nothing corporeal about them. They can't grab me or stick me with a stick. And second —

Okay, let me back up. As you know, I've been going to cemeteries and taking pictures of ghosts. My Twitter handle is @_____. No, really, that's me. Most of you have heard of me. I mean, I'm pretty popular. Maybe not Kardashian popular, but, you know, not bad. Huge Twitter and Facebook numbers. I had that special on HGTV. I'm making a great — no, *fantastic* — chunk of change just off social media. And unlike the other ghost hunters out there, I actually see them. The ghosts, that is, not the ghost hunters. People say that makes me a medium to which I quip: No, baby, that makes me extra rare with fries on the side. They usually stare blankly at me after that.

Heh.

Anywho, back to the ghosts. That's why you're here. When I started taking selfies with them, they were all docile and confused. I'd point at a grave and say, "Rise!" and up they popped. Ghostly Pop Tarts. They'd peer around — sometimes they had eyes and sometimes just black holes in their face. I took a quick selfie, told them to go back to sleep, and I was off. Easy peasy.

Then it changed. I was out at the Mount Olivet cemetery on the outskirts of Denver. Me, I'm from the Bay Area. But I found early on that people dug the combo travelogue and ghost selfie. So I do little write ups about the cemetery for the blog, talk about the place on my videos — all with a nod to The Google. I picked the Mount Olivet cemetery because, you know what? Bozo the Clown was there. Okay, full disclosure (I quickly learned that phrase when followers online gave me shit over information I screwed up — claiming I was trying to trick them. Nope. Me just being an idiot). Google had information on this dead Bozo guy, but it didn't jibe with other Bozo the Clown information, so honestly, I don't know if he was really Bozo a long time ago in a galaxy far, far away or not. But his tombstone says it and I think that's pretty funny.

It was late October. The grass was greenish-yellow. But it wasn't very cold — maybe sixty degrees. I wore a light windbreaker. The air smelled of dried brittle leaves, which crunched under my feet. I trudged around the cemetery trying to find Bozo from the map I got online. It took me a little while, getting lost and all, but I found it. I had my GoPro attached to the top of my baseball cap. I started recording before I looked down at Bozo's grave. Pointing at it — honest, the pointing seems to help — I said, "Rise."

He sprang up from his grave. I was disappointed. "No makeup?" He was dressed like a business guy from the 50s — you know, gray suit and even the little fedora. He could have been anybody.

Then he lunged at me. Without thinking, I jerked backwards. "What the hell?" The ghost passed right through me. It wasn't cold or anything like they say, but it did seem like I felt a little breeze. Being startled like that, I got angry. I pointed at his tombstone and shouted, "Just stand over there!"

He complied. Whatever my abilities were — and I really had no fricking clue — ghosts seemed forced into obeying me. Sulking now, he floated over to his tombstone and hovered there, his back to me.

"Oh, geez, turn around!"

He turned and faced me. I shook my head. Maybe I'd summon someone else; this guy was being a jerk. But I went ahead with the pic. My phone was already attached to my selfie stick. I tapped on the Bluetooth to the stick and opened my camera app. I turned away from Bozo and automatically reached up and swiveled my GoPro around so that it was still shooting him. Then I held the selfie stick above me, so I could get the cemetery in the background; I had Bozo's head cut off. I stepped forward a few paces, got the framing I wanted, gave my trademarked (no, not literally) thumbs up and goofy smile, and took the pic.

Reeling in the camera, I was in focus as was Bozo. I didn't know how my smartphone camera could focus on both of us like that, but it always did. Then I frowned and squinted at the pic. There was someone standing in the background. Too small to make out on my camera's screen. I hadn't realized we weren't alone. I turned around and I'm sure I jumped a little. There were other ghosts behind us. Almost a dozen from the graves right around Bozo.

"What are you all doing out of bed?"

A group of ghosts like that—had I done that? Never happened before. But I wasn't about to pass it up. I took another pic with all of them in the background. That would get a sizable Retweet from my followers. They'd love it. Only one time, with twins, did I have more than one ghost in the shot. Not because I didn't think it'd be a great pic to have more than one ghost, but because I couldn't do it. If I commanded one ghost out of his casket, he happily slithered back into the ground when I commanded the next ghost up and at 'em. So my selfies always had one ghost in them, until that day.

With the group pic taken, I started the hike out of the cemetery. I was busy posting the pic to my social media sites and it wasn't until I was almost to my car that I glanced back and saw all of the ghosts following after me.

"Stop!"

They all stopped. I got a chill—a good one. A great one. I made them all stop. I was controlling more than one ghost. How awesome was that? I waved at them, a shooing motion. "Back to bed. Go." They all turned, it seemed rather reluctantly, and returned to their graves.

By the time I got back to the hotel, my Twitter feed had exploded per usual. I uploaded the video from my GoPro. It was shaky, of course, but that was part of the charm. The movie was actually pretty wicked cool. My GoPro was still pointed backwards when I walked to my car, so I had a shaky-cam movie of all those ghosts following me. I posted it to YouTube. People went nuts. It was awesome. I could see a huge spigot opened wide with cash pouring out of it and into my own private bank vault. Scrooge McDuck could go suck it.

But something nagged at me. I replayed the video from the beginning. Bozo pops up, looks around for just a sec, and then he lunges at me. I furrowed my brow and backed it up a few seconds. *Lunge.* He wasn't exactly coming at me. It seemed like he was lunging at my phone. But why—oh, shit.

Let me back up. Again. I'd forgotten about it, to be honest. You know, not really forgotten, but the memory was certainly misplaced until Bozo jiggered it free. It was, what, a month ago? I scrolled through my video files. Five weeks ago. That's when things began to change; I just didn't realize it at the time.

I double-clicked the video. There was the shaky cam. I narrated in the breathy voice I get when walking and thinking what to say and trying to be witty and trying not to biff into a tombstone. I was at the Mountain View cemetery in Reno, Nevada. I didn't get lost on that day and found the grave easily enough for Jessica M____. She was famous in Nevada for starting an equally famous saloon back in the late 1800s. I pointed and said, "Rise!"

The woman sprang from the grave. Nothing unusual there. But prior to that day and her in particular, the ghosts

44

didn't pay any attention to me or what I was doing. They seemed kind of bored. But now as I watched the video, I saw that she was watching me sharply. No, not me. She stared at my phone. Followed it with her head and eyes like a cat when you dance a toy on a string in front of it. She even cocked her head at one point. But otherwise, and the reason I didn't notice anything odd at the time, she floated passively by her tombstone. I did the usual: Turned away from ghost, swiveled GoPro, telescoped out selfie stick, took picture, reeled in phone, reviewed image. My back was still to her when I did that so the GoPro picked it up. She dove right at me. I didn't see it in real time—I only saw her dive later on when I watched the video. At the cemetery, I checked the image on my phone, it looked good, and when I turned she was gone. I shrugged—you could see the bobble on the GoPro—and then I turned off the camera.

When I watched that video five weeks earlier, it hadn't had any effect on me. Big whoop, right? I figured she'd gone back to sleep while I was checking the pic. Then a couple days, maybe a week after that, I was doing something with my phone. I think I might have been texting someone. Doesn't matter. What matters is that I was looking down at my phone when I see that woman's ghost, Jessica's ghost. It was just a flash, you know, but I definitely saw it. At the time it only made me pause for a moment. Yes, it was curious, but I immediately wrote it off as some weird smartphone time warp. Somehow there was a glitch in the Matrix and the picture I'd taken of her swam to the surface of my phone and flicked away just as quickly. That was all. Another shrug moment.

Until now. Now I wondered if there was some connection. Jessica was obviously interested in my phone, and then Bozo lunged for it almost immediately. And all those other ghosts chasing after me. I looked at my phone. Turned it over, held it sideways, shook it a little bit. What was it?

Well, one way to find out if it was actually the phone they were interested in.

I left my hotel, following Google Maps, and went to the Crown Hill cemetery. Still in Denver—well, a suburb of Denver. I drove into the cemetery slowly down a wide straight lane leading to a solemn white spire of a building that was, what, at least a hundred feet tall. Quite cool looking. Like a Gothic or Art Deco building out of an old, old movie. Before I reached the building, however, I turned into one of the narrow lanes that crisscrossed the cemetery. After a bit I stopped the rental car and got out. This was as good a place as any.

I put on my cap and turned on my GoPro, slipped my smartphone into the selfie stick, and tapped open the camera app. Ready. There were tombstones immediately on either side of the lane, but for whatever reason I tromped across fifty yards or so of graves before stopping. I looked around sheepishly for living people. No one was around. Funny I'd suddenly get shy. I grinned and held out both arms, hands spread wide. "Rise!"

Ghosts popped up like prairie dogs. And they immediately floated toward me. No hesitation. I was expecting the attention, but there were so many of them. They were a wave of fog rolling in. I quickly turned around and lifted my selfie stick and took several pics. I hadn't needed to turn. There were ghosts floating toward me from every direction. So many of them.

Now I tried to remain calm as they got closer, but honestly, I was getting a little creeped out. But I didn't run. They couldn't hurt me. That's what I kept telling myself. Then came the tugs on the hand holding the selfie stick. One after another. It was like holding a fishing rod with a pissed-off fish on the line. I had to grab the stick with both hands as the ghosts pawed at the phone. That's when I lost my shit. Just a little.

I ran. This wasn't just creepy, goosebumpy; this was WTF

overwhelming. I was afraid to touch my phone, so I held it away from me on the stick like it was something toxic. For all I knew, it was. There were so many ghosts. It was like running through the frothy cream of my Starbucks. I dodged between tombstones. The frothy cream was getting thicker and thicker. That didn't make it more difficult to run, just harder to see. I whapped my shin hard against a low tombstone and cried out. Man, that stung. Pain shot up my leg. But you bet I kept running.

And then I was on the asphalt of the main lane that led to the tall white spire. I kept running until I realized there weren't any more ghosts around me. My hand wasn't being tugged. I bent over, resting my hands on my knees, and tried not to pass out or throw up. Lungs burned. Legs were leaden. Head spun a bit.

After several moments I stood up and turned back toward the graves. The ghosts, those who hadn't disappeared into my phone, were floating there in a sort of rank formation. They couldn't come any closer. They were tethered to their bodies. They couldn't go more than about 50 yards.

They reached toward me. No, not me. Toward my phone. I could feel their yearning. They silently pleaded for me to bring the phone closer. I was still tense—it was a better word than scared—and snapped, "Go back to sleep." And they all disappeared.

Seriously, what was that about? Back at the hotel I sat at the little table by my bed for, like, an hour. In a daze. As it slowly wore off, I opened my laptop and hooked up my GoPro. I ran the video, but started to shake after only a couple of seconds and I turned it off. Ghostly PTSD? I'd deal with the video later.

Without thinking, I pressed the power button on my phone so I could Tweet the selfie.

Gaaahh! Dozens of ghostly faces stared at me from the screen. A tumult of faces percolating up like roiling water. It froze me. Enthralled me. It was like an acid-trip GIF file.

Then little tendrils, like vaporous snakes, writhed from the phone and wrapped around my hand. I couldn't feel it against my skin, but there was a little tug, not unlike when the ghosts had entered my phone. What were they doing?

The gray foggy tendrils grew and I finally recognized them as arms, the hands scrabbling at my own arm. I tried to drop the phone, but I couldn't. The tug got more intense. It wasn't just my hand; I felt it throughout my body. The ghostly arms grew larger and reached past my skin and yanked. Suddenly I was swimming. Floating. Surrounded by bright pinpoints of light. I knew, without knowing how I knew, that the lights were the other ghosts. *Other ghosts.* When I turned, I saw myself. If I was still in my body I would have gone nuts at the sight of seeing myself sitting in the hotel chair, arm outstretched to the phone. My eyes were open, but they stared blankly. I was dead.

But also I wasn't. I still felt like me, but I was—something else now. And then the voices hit me like a giant thunderous crash. A hundred voices clamoring. Begging.

"Shut up!"

Silence. I pointed, without an arm or a hand or a finger. "You."

And it spoke, though none of us talked like people do. It was some kinda weird communication, without saying the words. Not talking. Not hearing. Not telepathy or something like that. It was, I don't know, *understanding.* The ghost told me it—there was no he or she here—wanted to ride the waves of light.

Waves of light? As in the light to Heaven or something?

No.

In voices that weren't voices, they told me about the waves of pearlescent light they could see from their graves. It undulated above them. But they were bound to their bodies, only able to leave when I commanded. They saw that same light flooding into my phone. They were attracted to it without knowing why. Word spread among them—it was like a fricking social network of the dead—about my ability to raise them from their bodies. But now that they had escaped into my phone, they didn't know what to do. They couldn't see the waves anymore.

I told them I couldn't see the waves, either. Past the pinpoints of light that were the ghosts, there was void. But I thought I understood. Maybe. I told them I couldn't help them if I wasn't in my body. It was the body that controlled the phone. I couldn't do anything from in here.

So they tossed me out.

I immediately felt a pull. A sucking. Then I blinked—my eyes were dry and stingy—but they worked. I breathed deeply. My lungs filled. My heart thumped. At least I think—I held my hand to my chest for a moment, then sighed. Yep, it thumped.

"Oh, man," I muttered, shaking my head.

I looked at my phone. I gotta tell ya, I thought about chucking the goddamned thing. Instead, I pressed the power button. And there they were, except now I saw them in their true form—those beautiful twinkling lights. Being dead changed me somehow. I could now hear them—and you know that's not what I meant, I couldn't actually hear them. But I could now understand.

Taking a deep breath and crossing my fingers, I put the phone up to my ear and whispered one word.

"Rise."

The room lit up like Christmas and the Fourth of July were having funktastic '70s sex. The twinkling lights zipped about, swimming the currents and eddies of the cellular waves. It was brilliant and beautiful. I gawked at it, mesmerized. And then they were gone. After several stunned moments I might have wiped at my eyes.

So, yeah, my life changed after that. I felt honor-bound. I was on a crusade from cemetery to cemetery setting free the ghosts so that they could swim the shimmering waves. What they did after that, I sure as hell didn't know, but I chose to believe it was wonderful.

But full disclosure, I still took selfies and videos of the ghosts and put it all online. I might be noble as shit now, but I sure as hell wasn't above raking in the cash, baby.

Gary Piserchio lives in Denver and has a few short stories out in the wild. His weird western novella, *Night of the Monster*, about a US Marshal who also happens to be a vampire, is available on Amazon.

BREWED DARK
BY BRIAN HAMILTON

It all started with a cup of coffee.

Or a lack of one, actually. You see, there's this little coffee shop by the subway station that I take to get to Miskatonic University every morning. It's a bit of a ritual for me. Sure, the people running it are almost comically stereotyped hipsters, but I was happy to brave the stares from behind glasses and over obscure novels, and the comments of the scarf-wearing barista as he intentionally misspelled my name on the cup (last time it was Hoowyrd). The coffee was really that good.

This morning was a little different, however. There had been another massive snowstorm the night before, and while the college campus was closed, the library was open for its usual hours; mostly for the die-hards who needed to get into the off-limits section. Since nobody else seemed to want to leave their homes, I was the only one in the shop. I had ordered my coffee some twenty minutes ago, and was starting to get impatient. My expertly subdued coughs and "ahems," however, were going unheeded by the barista, whose thumbs were tapping against the screen of his phone. How long, exactly, did it take to brew a single cup of coffee? At this rate, I wasn't going to make it in to work on time.

I looked up from where I had been leaning against a pastel brown wall to stare out one of the windows. An Arkham winter framed the image of my face. Having been described, apologetically, as kind of "goatish" looking, I'm not exactly Prince Charming. But at least the full head of long black hair and the neatly trimmed beard helped. Somewhat. Turning away from my reflection, I saw that my coffee still wasn't ready.

"Hey," I said, walking up and putting my hands on the counter. The barista still didn't look up, keeping his eyes focused on whatever awful free-to-play mobile game was making the cutesy beeps and bloops that emitted from between his hands. He finally looked up, irritation sliding across his face, when I slapped the bell on the counter a few times. He probably hadn't expected anyone to use it.

"What do you want?" he asked, nose already climbing into the air. Part of that was probably because I was a good head taller, which threw the angle of his snark off by a few degrees.

"My coffee," I replied.

The barista rolled his eyes as he inclined his head to the door behind the counter. "I'm waiting on my co-worker," he told me. "I sent her down to the basement for more beans."

I looked at the door. "It takes twenty minutes to get a bag of beans up the stairs? How heavy are they?"

The guy's eyes went wide, and after a few taps at his phone he shook his head as he started walking away. "I swear, if she's down there smoking again, I'll-"

He didn't finish saying what he'd do, because as he approached the door swung open and a short, stubby woman appeared. I guessed that it was his coworker, and if she had been smoking, I was sort of scared to find out what. Her skin, a dark brown complexion, had managed to acquire a visible green tinge. Her black hair was stuck down to her head, as though she had been in a downpour or sweating heavily. There were puffy rings under her eyes, which stared into some distance that neither I nor her coworker could see. Either she was sick, or tripping hard.

Her coworker walked over and, putting his hands on her shoulders, asked "Hey, are you all right?" I thought the question was a waste of time; it was fairly obvious that she wasn't. The woman seemed to snap out of whatever funk she was in and looked at the guy. She opened her mouth to respond.

But instead of saying anything, her jaw continued downward, distending the skin around her mouth. Her coworker and I stood in shocked silence. I mean, I've seen some pretty weird stuff, but usually in dark alleyways or gloomy basements, not in the middle of my favorite coffee shop.

The woman started to vomit.

Now, I'm no stranger to the forced ejection of material from one's stomach, but usually there's some liquid involved. The woman seemed to have a torrent of small, brown objects pouring out of her mouth and onto the guy. They bounced off of him and clicked on the floor, and I realized with some revulsion that they were coffee beans. I thought that maybe she had been high enough to devour handfuls of the stuff. That possibility was shattered when the beans began to move, crawling their way across the floor and up the legs of the two baristas.

The entrance door was already swinging shut when the screaming began.

I stood outside, momentarily stunned. I thought I'd seen this enough times to get used to these kinds of occurrences when they popped up, but there's always some new aspect that manages to throw me. Chanting, ritual sacrifices, dumb jocks (or dumber geeks who should know better) in robes with virgins tied down to altars, that I could handle. But this?

I listened to the screams, muffled by the thick glass of the frost-covered door, and looked around. The few people walking past didn't seem to be paying any attention. The human mind can't process most of what happens when entities from the outer reaches and inner corners of space and time decide to intrude on our reality, so they're just ignored. Which calls into question why I was both able to see them happening, and why I kept deciding to get involved.

In this case, however, the answer to the latter question was pretty clear. They had messed with my coffee, damn it. So I pulled out my Menagerie.

The Menagerie is a large key ring with basically every religious and esoteric symbol I could find hanging on it. I inscribed it with glyphs and runes I'd taken out of a book in the lower levels of the Miskatonic Library, once it had stopped trying to attach itself to my face and shove a three-foot-long proboscis down my throat. It's a combination of eldritch radar and ethereal activity detector. Strange thing happening? Point the Menagerie at it, and hopefully it'll tell me what I'm dealing with.

This time, however, the only thing that was glowing was that little dried monkey head I had gotten from a tribe in South America. They had taken care of me after a portal in the depths of lightless Xal'Tch - the 3rd planet that orbited Pluto - deposited me somewhere in the middle of the Amazon. I wasn't happy to see the little guy light up, since I never really had any idea what it actually meant. Usually nothing good, though.

I pocketed the Menagerie and considered my options. I had a small collection of items of varying magical worth back at my apartment, but that was a good twenty minute walk back-and-forth. Who knew what might happen in that time? I pictured some sort of grey-goo scenario, only with humanity being devoured by waves of coffee beans. Nope, probably not a good idea to leave.

While I considered this, a college-age couple walked up to the door of the coffee shop and stopped, obviously put off by my presence. I have that effect on most people. Don't ask why. I stopped asking myself the same question years ago. I gestured somewhat lamely towards the door and said, "You probably don't want to go in there."

Deaf to the screams, the guy asked, "Why not?"

"It's… closed? For repairs," I replied, nodding. "Yeah."

The girl looked from me to the door. "The sign, like, says it's open." I followed her eyes to the door where, indeed, a small sign did proclaim that the coffee shop was open.

I shrugged and smiled in what I thought was a sheepish, apologetic manner. This apparently only further unsettled the couple, as the guy pulled his girlfriend through the door before I could say anything else. There was about a ten second pause after the door closed shut before the screaming intensified with two more voices. So I inadvertently learned how long I had before I was rushed if I went back inside.

I know it seems like I didn't try all that hard to stop them, but trust me, if I had, the couple would probably end up calling the cops. And they're the kind of people who'll stick their guns into places they don't belong. And for once, the movies get it right, with the screaming into radios and the wild shots fired everywhere and the monsters plowing through the police like sharks through conveniently-packaged chum.

Since the weather in Arkham had followed its normal pattern, I was wearing a decent pair of snow boots that I tucked my khakis into. These were heavy, clomping boots - the kind some GI back in WWII would have been happy to have stomping around in the Ardennes or on some Pacific island. Ass-kicking boots, really. Or bean-crunching.

So, picture this, if you will - a tall, lanky, pasty white guy in his late twenties dressed in a pea coat, khakis, and boots marching into a coffee shop and stomping on the ground like a New Zealand rugby player. There was probably some yelling on my part as well, but only because I had to drown out the screaming from the two baristas behind the counter and the couple on the floor in front of me. I considered myself fortunate, for once, for living on the fifteenth floor of an apartment building with three broken elevators as I brought my feet up and down, over and over again. Every time my foot hit the ground, there was a small, ear-piercing squealing noise, and dark fluid gushed out across the ceramic tiles, staining them from white to brown.

I thought I might have things in hand, until the four writhing lumps on the ground stopped screaming and all stood up as one. I jumped back as the two bean-things that had been the college couple lurched toward me. Four appendages that might have been arms extended towards me. I wasn't sure if the people were still in there, but I wasn't going to let them get too close. So I kicked the closer of the two in the chest. There was a squelching noise, more of those little squeals, and a spray of fluid splattered against the wall behind the bean-thing. My foot had gone right through its chest. I could feel the fluid from the crushed beans seeping into my pants. It was disturbingly warm.

I tried pulling my foot out. It reluctantly came free, but I ended up on my back, slipping in the dark liquid. The bean-thing still stumbled toward me. Convinced of its lack of a gooey human center, I frantically lashed out with my feet. One of my boots managed, with a single swing, to cleave through both of its legs. The thing dropped to the ground, and burst like an overripe fruit, a small wave of something that tasted like coffee strained through unwashed gym socks washing over me. Whatever was in these beans - or whatever these things were that just happened to look like beans - apparently couldn't take much of a beating. Which was fine by me.

I scrambled up as the two lumps that had been the baristas managed to navigate their way around the counter. Looking around, the only item I could really use as a weapon was one of the chairs that had been knocked over at some point. It was good, solid metal, although I didn't think the flower petal print on the seat was going to strike terror into the not-hearts of the bean-things.

As it turned out, the actual overall worth of the chair's ability to strike things in general worked out to be pretty good. After a few frenzied minutes of bashing, slipping, and more yelling I stopped, winded and soaked through with both sweat and that awful liquid that burst out of the bean-things every time I hit them. The coffee shop looked like a janitor's nightmare, with droplets of brown raining down from the ceiling and streaming down the walls in rivulets. Of the two baristas and the couple, nothing remained. Honestly, I thought I had done pretty well. Looking at the clock on the wall, I reasoned that I could make it home, change, and get to the library only a few minutes late.

Except for the matter of the basement door, where the woman had come up from and started this whole ordeal. Adjusting my grip on the chair, I walked over to and around the counter. The door was still open, the basement dark, and in the quiet absence of any screaming, grunting or squealing, I heard the faintest of noises. Straining to hear, I realized it was whispering. I couldn't understand the language, but to be honest I wasn't sure if that was a bad thing. If I could describe the tone of voice, it was almost as though the whispers gathered in your inner ear, and you'd happily jam something long and sharp into the side of your head just to get them to come pouring back out, rather than keep anything inside.

I pulled out my own cellphone - mercifully kept dry in one of the inside pockets of my coat - and hit the quick dial for the library. Because I was the one who usually answers the phone, I got the machine. "Bernice, it's Leng. I'm not feeling great today," which wasn't a lie, really, "so I'm calling in sick. Sorry." I hung up, acknowledging I'd probably have to go in early tomorrow. With a little less regret, comparatively, I went down the stairs.

You'd think for all the money they had apparently spent on making the place look pretty modern, they could spend a little money renovating what was down below. There wasn't even a light switch at the top of the stairs, which meant there was probably something at the bottom. And while my eyes can adjust to darkness quickly, what I was peering down into was a pitch black abyss. Each step on the stairs creaked loudly enough to raise the hair on my neck. I'm not really a stealthy guy, normally, but at this rate I might as well have worn a big neon sign that said "Eat me!" and gone down ringing a comically large dinner bell. I considered taking out my phone again, using any light was probably a worse idea.

It felt as though I had been creeping along for hours when I reached the bottom of the stairs, although truthfully it couldn't have been more than a few minutes. Oddly enough, the ethereal whispering had decreased as I ventured further deeper. I couldn't be sure, but I wasn't too hopeful that this was a good sign. It probably meant that I had done exactly what the voices wanted.

I panicked for a moment when something lightly brushed against my forehead, the chair swinging out almost of its own accord to strike at ink-colored nothingness. After my heart receded back from my throat to its normal position, I reached up and realized that it was the cord to an overhead light. Anticipating some horrible scene, especially after what had happened upstairs, I readied the chair again, and yanked down on the cord.

What the soft light revealed was a perfectly ordinary basement. Maybe in need of some drywall over the old bricks and some more cement to repair the cracks in the floor, but nothing more. Shelves were placed against the walls and filled with bags of beans and other supplies. A refrigerator hummed quietly in the corner. I wasn't entirely sure what I had expected. Probably something with more esoteric runes painted on the walls in animal blood, or a hole in the floor that ended at some terminal point which opened into a deep chasm, from which Things That Man Was Better Off Not Knowing About poured forth.

In fact, the only slightly suspicious item in the room was the empty coffee bean sack on the floor by the refrigerator. I walked over to it, chair held out in front of me, like a lion tamer approaching his deflated counterpart. The sack looked perfectly mundane. It didn't try to attack the chair when I tapped it, nor did it attempt to devour my foot when I gave it a small nudge. I squatted in front of the sack and gave it a couple desultory pokes with my pinky finger, the idea that if the sack had been biding its time, I could afford to lose the last finger on my left hand. It's pretty important to have these things thought out ahead of time.

Something was wrong here, and that wasn't including the bean-things. The whole scenario wasn't adding up. Not that it had to, especially when dealing with beings who laughed at logical procedurals like mathematics. But there had to be some catalyst, some spark that had set everything off.

Well, there was always the Menagerie. I pulled the ring back out of my pocket and instantly regretted doing so. My eyes had adjusted to the dimness of the basement, and the little monkey head was glowing so brightly it left an after-image in my vision in the moment before I was able to look away. The basement was bathed in a fluorescent blue-white light, with the shelves throwing dark shadows against the walls. Whatever was responsible for what had happened upstairs was down here, no doubt. Probably right on top of me.

Which meant I was only mildly surprised when the refrigerator violently shuddered, rocking back and forth in place, each impact bringing down dust from the basement's ceiling. The humming noise rose from its normal tone to a wailing, keening pitch. I fell backwards when the refrigerator jumped forward at me, moving nearly a foot in a single heavy leap. It jumped again, and again, each movement accompanied by the tortured squealing of metal on concrete.

The massive machine suddenly stopped, and so did the noise. For a few seconds, the refrigerator sat still, humming in place, completely normal if somewhat displaced from its original position. I sat there, stunned, the Menagerie glowing in my clenched fist. Sweat beaded on my forehead.

It almost felt as though I was staring down a large predator in the moment before it leaped.

"Well, what are you waiting for?" I asked.

As though responding to my question, the refrigerator's door swung open. There were no cartons of creamer in the fridge's interior - in fact, there wasn't anything resembling an interior. Instead, there was a riot of not-colors, oily collisions of expanding and contracting masses fighting in never ending chaos. Darkness shone through the portal, colliding with the bright light of the Menagerie. There was a noise that was a silent screech, a cacophonous whispering, both deafening and barely audible. It was the noise that flowed through the universe, the sound of beings that were so far beyond our concept of deities that they would laugh at the idea, if they could laugh at all.

Which was ironic, because I almost laughed when I saw what came crawling out of the rioting nothingness in the fridge. Had it been made of flesh - or some cosmic equivalent - I probably would have started weeping, or torn my eyes out.

Instead, it had been formed from coffee beans. Long brown pseudopods pulled its bulk from the yawning portal. White creamer flowed from orifices, spilling out onto the floor of the basement in waves. It mewled and gurgled from a hundred mouths, bean-teeth gnashing as brown liquid splashed and mixed with the seeping creamer. I couldn't see any eyes on the mass, but that didn't stop the dreadful feeling that this thing was staring at me regardless, hungry and malevolent.

I tried backing away, but couldn't get any traction on the floor - the creamer, greasy and vile, had spread quickly and all I could do was splash uselessly. The monstrosity pushed itself forward, sliding along the slick concrete. Behind it I could still see the portal to nowhere and every time, seemingly growing wider with each passing second.

The bean-monster shuffled towards me, each ponderous

shifting of its bulk causing ripples to spread out over the small white ocean that held me in place. Not wanting to end up in whatever its equivalent of a digestive tract was, I slipped and slid until I could reach out and grab one of the nearby shelves. Weighed down by coffee paraphernalia and supplies, it offered a decent anchor for me to pull against. Which didn't help when I felt something wrap around my ankle and begin to pull back.

I looked and saw that one of the brown limbs had stretched out and gotten a hold on me. Apparently the monstrosity had gotten tired of the somewhat limited chase and had just decided to reel me in. Another strong yank almost took my hand away from the shelves. If I was going to have any chance, I was going to need both hands.

So I threw the Menagerie at the bean-thing, hoping one of the mouths would choke on it. It seemed like poetic justice. The mystical symbol-ladened ring flew through the air, landing perfectly in one of the open mouths and quickly disappeared from view. I reached out and grabbed another pole on the shelf. If it wanted to eat me, I was going to make the otherworldly monster work for its meal.

That's when it exploded.

I didn't see the detonation, as I was fighting to hang on at the time, but there was a massive booming noise and I was tossed through the air, coming to land in a heap about halfway up the stairs leading up to the ground floor. Momentarily stunned, I couldn't do much else when gravity took over and I rolled back down the stairs, coming to a stop at the bottom on the cold concrete floor. Something metallic skittered across the floor and hit the wall next to where I lay in a heap. I stayed on the floor for a few moments. I could already feel the majority of my body turning into one giant bruise, so maybe being eaten and getting digested for the rest of eternity wouldn't be so unpleasant.

When I stopped feeling sorry for myself, I noticed that the background noise was no longer a chorus of insane wailing, but the normal humming that came from an old refrigerator. I turned, slowly, until I could see the rest of the basement.

It had gone back to normal. The refrigerator squatted in its original place, completely innocent of any unexplained movement. Its door was open, but I saw only the insides of a normal fridge, its bright white interior slightly marred by a tipped-over carton of creamer that had somehow opened up and was slowly leaking out.

As I pulled myself back up into a sitting position, my hands closed around an object that could only have been the Menagerie. I held it up for a closer inspection. It was no longer glowing with that eye-watering light. Gone too, I noticed, was the little shriveled head. I contemplated this and, deciding that this was one of those 'way over my head' sort of problems, I put the Menagerie back into my coat pocket. I stood up, slightly shaky, and made my way back upstairs.

When I opened the basement door – which apparently had closed at some point - I was greeted by silence. The room was still a mess, but all evidence of the bean-things and their caffeine-laden ichor were gone. Gone as well were the two baristas and the college couple. I put my hands in my pockets and kept my head low as I walked out of the coffee shop. My boots squelched across the too-clean floor.

The weather outside was normal, the cold just as bone-chilling and the wind just as biting as before. Checking my phone - mercifully dry and intact thanks to the stupidly large, waterproof case I had bought for it - I saw that the call I had sent to Bernice had still gone through. So I had the day off.

Sighing, I ran a hand through my hair, shaking it afterward to get the creamer off. I was pretty sure I had a kettle somewhere in my apartment's small kitchenette.

I really wanted a cup of tea.

Brian Hamilton is from Philadelphia, Pennsylvania. He's

an aspiring librarian, freelance writer, and a fan of horror literature - especially anything Lovecraftian. "Brewed Dark" is one of his first published short stories.

WHERE WERES CAN BE WERES
BY GIOVANNI VALENTINO

The full moon was just minutes away from rising into the night sky and I was more than screwed. My change was imminent and I was struck between work and home, on public transportation no less. I know I should have told my boss to go to hell when he insisted I had to stay late. He didn't want to hear about my doctor's note saying I had an irrational fear of the full moon. Since it was summer, anyways, he assured me I could make it home long before dark. Well, he didn't factor in the bus breaking down.

As my superior hearing kicked in, I could finally make out what the twitchy homeless guy in the back had been muttering to himself since I got on the bus. "I'm not a coward, mother. I can pull the trigger on the holy weapon. I'm just waiting for the right time." I hoped that weapon was homemade, since that bolstered my faith that he couldn't cause any trouble.

You may wonder why I didn't just get off the bus. I'd like to say I have a conscience and I could never live with myself if my wolf harmed another human. In truth, we were broken down in the worst neighborhood in the city. I was more afraid for my life than I was anyone else's. If you check the police blotters, someone gets shot or stabbed in this area every six hours. Well, I don't want that someone to be me. Sure, without silver, they can't actually kill me but it still stings. You think getting kicked in the balls hurts, try getting shot there. I had trouble taking a leak for months, in both forms.

With an equivalent of a kick in the face, my enhanced sense of smell turned on to the mixture of funk that hung in the air of this public transportation. Most of it was post work BO from riders whose deodorant wasn't strong enough for them, but a few people were special. The bus driver was a little too close to the line of legally intoxicated to be in that driver's seat. The faint scent of Calvin Klein's Obsession wafted over. This was a little weird for a public bus, but weirder when I noticed it was coming from the little Asian man in the front. To each his own.

I wish I still worked at the zoo upstate. That was great. Once a month, I'd make up an excuse to stay overnight. Some animal was always sick or needed observing. Then I'd hang out around near the "I'll huff and I'll puff" enclosure and wait for the moon to make its entrance. The pack at the zoo were a great bunch of mutts. We'd run around and play half the night, howling at anything that moved. They let me sleep in their pile with them.

The best part of the pack was Pandora. She was the only unmatched female in a pack of couples. Whenever I dropped by, she was the first to greet me with her tail wagging in the air. She'd watch intently when I'd play fight one of the other guys and always wanted to snuggle next to me in the sleeping pile. Nothing ever happened between us because even in my wolf form, I wasn't into the interspecies thing. And even if I were, it's impossible to put on a condom in wolf form and I wasn't going to be a deadbeat dad who only saw his kids once a month. Yeah, the zoo was a great gig, until someone learned to count.

They had just installed a new CCTV system without telling any of the employees. It seems somebody was taking home elephant tranquilizers for their own personal use. The bosses wanted to catch the perpetrator before the DEA caught wind of the missing stock. You just can't have powerful meds like that going missing in this day and age.

I snuck back into work freshly washed and shaved at the

local truck stop, wearing the new set of clothes I always keep in my car, and found the place in an uproar. Excuse the pun; they happen as the change gets closer. In reviewing the new footage, someone noticed that there were eight wolves in the enclosure last night and only seven this morning. So, of course, they jumped to the obvious conclusion that one of the wolves had escaped. It turned out that they had been missing a wolf for the last year, and no one noticed or reported it. I bet it was the elephant tranquilizer thief. They probably sold him on the dark net for a pretty penny to some exotic animal collector. So now, they're checking their inventory of eight vs seven in the cage and obviously one had escaped. They were not the sharpest tools in the shed.

All of a sudden my canine form was all over the local news with headlines like "Dangerous Escaped Wolf on the Hunt", "Alpha Dog mounts our fine city!" and "Killer Kanine Skares Kids". That last one really trended in cyberspace. God, I hate alliteration. I had to move away for my own safety.

If you're wondering why I didn't have a pack to live with, I'd been on my own since I was sixteen. I got into a stupid fight with my parents about me being able to watch 'South Park' and ran away. I didn't mean to leave forever, just until things calmed down. But while I was gone, two crazy hunters stormed our house. There were no survivors, family or hunters. All I have left of them was the lingering memory of their smell. A smell I've spent years trying to find.

As the moon peeked over the horizon, my muscles spasmed and I could see my fingers curling in. I was out of time with only one option. Run! I stood up quickly and rang the bell to get off the bus.

"Hey, pal, sit down!" The bus driver shouted. "Another bus will be by soon."

"I think I'm going to be sick," I made a retching sound to go along with the real twitching of my change. "Please open the door."

"Pal, this is not the greatest of neighborhoods. I'd be remiss in my duties if I let you out here," The driver said. "I've got a bucket up here if you need it."

Great, just what I need right now, a helpful soul. Maybe it was the wolf talking, but I really wanted to lift up my leg on him.

"No, seriously, I have to get off. I have Chorophobia," I loosened my collar and tie, hoping no one noticed the shag carpet growing out of my chest. "I tell you, I can't breathe."

"Chorophobia? That's a fear of dancing," the driver scoffed. "No one's dancing in here."

"I mean Clinophobia."

"That's a fear of going to bed!"

"No, I mean Coitophobia,"

"That's a fear of coitus." The driver laughed. "Don't worry, there isn't going to be any of that on my bus."

"What the hell is coitus?" I said, holding back a growl.

"That's sex, you idiot!" The driver said and the rest of the people on the bus broke into uproarious laughter. I couldn't hold it against them. I'd have laughed if it didn't make me think of Pandora.

"How the hell do you know all this?" I barked.

"I'm taking an Abnormal Psychology class online."

"Well, since you're the expert then, what's the one where you're afraid of enclosed spaces?" My right shoe slipped off, since my paws can't fill the size 13s I wear in my human form.

"Claustrophobia!" the driver spit out between fits of laughter.

"Fine, I have claustrophobia, the fear of enclosed spaces."

"No, you don't," The driver scowled at me. "You know what I have? I have a fear of jerkoffs like you that don't know how to sit down and shut up."

"Well, you know what else I don't have? A fear of kicking your ass!" I punctuated that statement with a low growl and a bark. That's definitely the wolf talking.

"Fine, asshole, have fun getting shot to death." The driver pulled the door lever and the side door swung open.

I barely made it out of the bus before the driver closed the door on me. If not for my lupine speed, he would have crushed me. I was so remembering his scent for later. Next month, I was going to dig up his entire lawn.

After the change was complete, I buried my wallet and keys for safekeeping. I felt bad leaving my favorite jeans and lucky underwear behind, but I missed laundry day yesterday and my super enhanced smell wouldn't let me go back for them.

You'd think I'd be all scary in my lupine form, and people would just leave me alone. Unfortunately, my wolf looked more like a larger than normal, ungroomed, Shih Tzu. I still have the enhanced strength and speed of a Were, just none of the intimidating presence.

I hustled through the streets looking for a good place to ride out the night. As further proof of the state of this neighborhood, the alleyways were fenced in and all the windows had bars on them. I found a homeless shelter about ten blocks away. This seemed like a good spot since it improved my chances of finding clothes and a shower in the morning. Their alleyway was open and filled with garbage bags, so I had food and shelter, the classic two for one. I was only there a few minutes before these guys jumped out of the shelter's back door.

"Hey, get out of here, you mutt," the first one said. From the smell of his clean clothes, I presumed he worked there.

"Hold on, Father Ryan," The second man slurred, his breath matching the bus driver's in its flammability factor. "Look at the size of that raccoon."

"We can make a few stews out of him," the third man said. He smelled like a music festival port-a-potty. What can I say? Enhanced smell can really suck.

With a loud yelp, I turned tail and ran out of there. A shot rang out behind me, and I felt a burning sting in my ass.

Limping away at the fastest speed I could muster, I eluded these possible diners but I heard one of them yelling, "Come back, big raccoon, come back. We just want to eat you."

I stopped at the nearest dark corner to lick my wounds, literally. It took several minutes of muscle flexing and leg shaking to force the slug out of my rump so my healing factor could kick in. I hate 22s. They sting like a bitch and dig themselves in deep. Looking around, I had no idea where I was now. Nothing but dilapidated houses and empty lots.

"Yo, Big Boss, take a look at this mutt," a man said.

Spinning around, I found a group of three fine young kids wearing matching jackets walking up on me.

"He be a bit mangy, but strong looking," Big Boss said. "What'cha think, Jazzy Jen?"

I had been wondering what they were doing out this late on a school night, but by their grammar, I could tell school wasn't a high priority to them. I hate to judge like that, but during the full moon I tend to turn into the grammar police.

From the smell, I knew Jazzy Jen was a woman. I let her approach me with her hand out. I couldn't tell if she was good looking or not because her face was covered in tattoos. All these kids had at least one, which I presumed was their gang tat, but she had eight by my count. She grabbed me by the scruff of the neck and pulled me closer. I licked her hand as she stroked my head. I always do better with the ladies in wolf form. This could work out. I'd play the sad lost dog and they'd take me home. I'd be safe until morning when I could steal some clothes and bail.

"He ain't got no collar, Big Boss. I guess nobody's gonna miss him." She smiled at me, and her breath hit like a slap to the face. I guess oral hygiene wasn't a recruitment requirement of the gang. "Can we take him home? We can call him Mangy Mutt."

"All right, doin' the night doggy style!" Shooten' Stan yelled, clapping his hands together.

"Shut it, Shooten' Stan," Big Boss lifted his arm and Stan instinctively cringed. "Ya, sure Jazzy Jen, we take him back to the lair. I doubt he be doin' well in de' ring. But he be great practice for King Killer Karl. Shooten' Stan, drop da rope 'round this mutt."

I wasn't sure which I was more annoyed by, being captured by dog fighting dirt bags or that I just joined the alliteration gang. I struggled and nipped at Jazzy Jen while Shooten' Stan threw a noose over my head. They wrapped part of the rope around my snout, cutting off my ability to bite or bark. As they pulled me along I tried to dig in against them, but they'd somehow wrapped the rope around so it could still choke me with a pull. I tried going limp, refusing to move, but they just dragged me, laughing.

This was not good. These types of bastards would put me in a cage when we got to their 'Lair' and I'd have a lot of explaining to do in the morning. Even if I came up with a good excuse for why I was there instead of the mangy mutt they picked up, they were more likely to kill me than let me go.

Along the way, a strangely familiar scent welled up in the air. I sniffed hard to draw it into my nose. I still couldn't place it, but it reminded me of home and the parents I'd lost. The scent got stronger when we got to this large old Victorian Style house. It had to be three stories tall, with the long porch covering the whole front of the house.

The gang stopped in their tracks when a young woman with a flashlight jumped in front of them, shining her light right into their faces. She wore a thin, silk robe, with nothing underneath it. This got the whole gangs attention, even Jazzy Jen's.

"What are you thugs doing out here? Do you know what time it is?" The woman shook her finger at them like an irate den mother. "Some of us need sleep. We have work in the morning."

"Baby, Baby, Baby! I have somethin' to help ya' catch

some Zs," Big boss said in the lewdest voice I'd ever heard, thrusting his pelvis forwards.

"Ya, Momma, I can help too," Shooten' Stan said, waving his tongue out of his mouth.

"Oh, eh, hello, ma'am. Nice night," Jazzy Jen's face flushed red and she turned her gaze downward.

"No, thanks, I only put out for people with at least ten tattoos on their faces," the woman said. My ears perked up. That familiar scent was all over the robed lady.

"Don't be so picky, honey. You should try a real man," Big Boss said.

"Or you can have me instead," Shooten' Stan chuckled and pointed at the woman.

"Do you hear da' things you say when you say 'um?" Big Boss rolled his eyes and slapped Stan in the back of the head. "You make us look dumb when you say dumb things like that."

"I … I… can get two more. You know, if you want me too," Jazzy Jen muttered, fighting to hold eye contact with the woman.

I saw the woman's nose flare a few times and she looked right at me. "Hey, that's my dog. Where did you get my dog?"

"That's not your dog, honey. It's our dog," Shooten' Stan pulled tighter on my rope, dragging me right next to his leg.

"Yeah, if this is your dog, what be his name?" Big Boss cackled.

She looked me right in the eyes, staring intently. Smiling, she said, "Bryant! Bryant Bentley Benson. That's his name."

Holy crap! That was my name. How the hell did she guess that? I guess now you can see why I hate alliteration. I let out a series of happy barks to signal that was indeed my name and pulled against the rope to get closer to her.

"That's nice, toots, but he ain't got no tags, so finders be keepers." Big Boss glared at her.

By the look on his face, I was afraid for the lady. I wasn't sure why she was coming to my rescue or even how she knew I needed it but I couldn't live with myself if she got hurt over this. When Shooten' Stan pulled out a big knife, which made me wonder how he got his nickname, I expected the nice lady to run to safety. I wouldn't have blamed her, but she didn't.

She stood up taller, throwing her shoulders back and said, "Maybe he's not mine, but we both know he's not yours, either. So why don't you leave him with me and I'll return him to whomever you have stolen him from?"

With a yelp of surprise and widened eyes, I looked up at her. That was grammatically correct. I think I'm in love.

"Just who's gonna make us, doll?" Big Boss spit at her.

"Yeah, you and which navy?" Shooten' San yelled, swirling his blade around to show off his skills. He only managed to cut himself twice.

Jazzy Jen only muttered out, "You're pretty, ma'am." And to my surprise, the lady looked over to her and smiled. How did she hear that? I could barely hear that.

"Just me and my puppies," the lady said, raising an eyebrow. She put both of her pinkies in her mouth and let out a loud, ear piercing whistle. Three large dogs leapt over the fenced in backyard and charged up to the sidewalk. They stopped just at the edge of the grass with their ears up and teeth bared. Two of them, a large mastiff and a Great Dane, barked wildly and ran back and forth. The last one, an enormous Swiss mountain dog, just stared at them, growling continuously. "So, which 'navy' do you guys have to back you up?"

Jazzy Jen yelped out, "Sorry, Ma'am." She turned and ran away, chanting "I'm so sorry," as she disappeared into the night.

Shooten' Stan's body tensed up and he stood frozen in place with his eyes open wider than they'd ever been before. A dark stain appeared in the crotch of his jeans and he collapsed to the concrete sidewalk.

Big Boss shook his head and rolled his eyes, "I'm surrounded by idiots."

The dogs on the lawn started jumping in the air, snapping and barking at the last gang member. Big Boss stepped into the street to avoid their attacks.

"I'd move on, fine sir, before I lose control of these dangerous animals." The lady knelt down and removed the rope from my neck.

"You better be wiping dat smile off your pretty face, girly girl. We be knowin' where you lives now. We can come on back at any times and 'take care of you' and your lil doggies," Big Boss stood in the middle of the street, shaking his fist in the air. "Just you wait for me, lil ..." The piercing sound of a car horn filled the air, punctuated by the thump of Big Boss bouncing off the hood of the oncoming car.

The Lady winced. "Let's go inside and call 911 for this poor man." They all ran up the path to the house and filed into the front door. She looked back and waved at me. "You too, Mr. Bryant Bentley Benson."

She didn't have to ask me twice, but if she kept calling me by my full name, I was going to fall out of love with her. I charged up the lawn and into the house. She closed and locked the door behind us, and then headed straight to the back door. I followed her.

Stopping in my tracks as I entered the back yard, I looked all the way up and whined in surprise. Their back yard was taking up the lot directly behind their house. The yard was completely enclosed by a ten foot high fence and covered with trees and brush, making it look like a tiny forest.

Over the fences, glass window panes like a greenhouse rose up as high as the roof. Each pane was tinted, letting light in but hiding us from any nosy neighbors. I could see the full moon shining down on us in all of its glory.

"Hi, I'm Katy Johnson and this is the Johnson pack," She waved her hand across the yard and wolves of different shapes and sizes walked out of the brush. I counted over twenty of them. "You're safe here for tonight and tomorrow. We'll help you figure out what to do next. You can interview to stay with us if you want."

If my wolf form could cry, I think I'd be bawling by now. I turned back to Katy and jumped up on her, licking her face and wagging my tail.

"Excuse me while I slip into something more comfortable." She stepped back for me and dropped her robe to the ground to reveal the most beautiful sight I'd ever seen. I turned my gaze to the side, not wanting to make a bad impression by staring at her rack just minutes after she'd saved my life. A cute, high pitched yap drew my attention back to her and in her place sat the cutest little yellow Labrador, wagging its tail at me. She jumped forward and licked my face. Other wolves crept up to us slowly and after a number of butt sniffs, I was tentatively accepted into the pack.

Just like at the zoo, we ran, we played, we dug up things and reburied them somewhere else and we howled at the moon without fear. Fun was had by all. Katy snuggled up to me when we all lay down at the end of the night. I felt the warmth of her body next to mine and thought: this could turn into something, something real.

In the morning, we all filed into the basement. They had a total setup for post-change needs like an open shower room with ten facet heads and a row of cubbies, each with fresh clothes. I got to use the stand-by robe for now, but Bruce, the Great Dane, said he'd lend me something once we got upstairs. As we ascended the staircase to the kitchen, the last of my night vision saw a sign over the door frame. It read, "Where We're Weres. All Along and Always." And for once, I got a warm, fuzzy feeling inside over alliteration.

And now I live with the Johnsons. I moved into one of their many spare bedrooms and they gave me a reasonable rent. They even hooked me up with a more 'Were' friendly job, a pet food factory that strangely closed every full moon and let its employees take home all the 'Wolf' Chow they wanted. To my joy, Katy was unattached and thankfully interested.

The best part about it was the safe place to change every month. It took me a few months and a thousand rides on public transportation, but I eventually found that bus driver's house. I brought friends with me during the next change. We dug up his whole garden, marked every tree and every piece of lawn furniture he owned, and left presents all over his front stoop. It Pays to Participate in a Pack.

Giovanni Francesco Valentino has struggled at the art of writing for four decades against many demons like self-doubt, chronic depression, OCD, and severe dyslexia. He has written a few memoir pieces about his struggles going undiagnosed for more than half his life, as well as almost a dozen humorous speculative fiction short stories. His long-term goal is to become such a famous science fiction and fantasy author that other people want to write fan fiction in his worlds. He is also the editor of the humorous speculative fiction anthology series, *Alternate Hilarities*.

THE TORTURED TEEN
BY NATHAN CROMWELL

Marla glared through the curtainless dining room window at a bright spring day that mocked her very existence, and at the two lame-o lovebirds laughing as they ran up the walkway, keys a-jingling in the man's hand. As she heard the locks jolted, she crossed the bare wood floor and stood in what passed, in this glorious excess of sunshine, for shadow. Not until the dork had carried the simp across the threshold and set her down and kissed her did the pair notice Marla: the man first, with a shriek, and then the woman, who turned to see what the fuss was about before adding a surprised "Oh, my lands". Larry pushed Mary behind him.

"This isn't a squat, kid—get out."

"Now Larry, the child only looks 'round fourteen. Maybe she's a runaway who needs somebody's help."

"Or she's a punk who reckons breaking into empty houses is—come here, girl."

Marla moved into the light so the couple could obscurely see the empty dining room through her black bathrobe and Emily the Strange pajamas. Larry shrieked. Mary crossed herself and uttered an even milder oath.

The couple sat in their car looking up the drive at the shimmering teen in their doorway. Larry leaned forward as though the change in position might make her vanish, and then, disappointed, back again. "Maybe she can't leave the house."

"Sugar, I don't think she means to harm us any. Maybe we should talk to her."

"The Realtor said this place was just built. She lied to us."

"I wonder why we didn't see the ghost at the open house, or our other visits. Poor girl, so young and trapped in that house."

"Should we sue? We can't afford a lawyer. We're near broke buying this place, so what do we do?"

She massaged the back of his neck. "We'll think of something. Let's talk to her. Maybe we can—"

Larry flipped the door open and strode up the drive. Startled, Mary fumbled her way out of the car and followed.

"Look here, young lady, we own this house and you're not welcome. I need you to haul yourself off to heaven lickety-split, get me?"

Mary caught up and touched her husband's shoulder. "Larry's just riled, sweetie. I'm sure—"

"Don't worry, lady, I know I'm not wanted. I never was."

"With that attitude, no wonder. Now skedaddle."

Mary sidestepped her husband and presented her sincerest face. "Oh, honey, I'm sure that's not true. Do you have somewhere you can go?"

Marla smiled grimly and held out her arms with thumbs and index fingers extended. "If there was, I would be there now and not with two double-L losers in suburb hell."

"You watch your mouth with my wife, missy."

"Or? You think you're the bosses of me? Anyway, I'm dead, so what can you do, huh? Now excuse me, I'm going to my room so I can reflect on all the good times from my brief life—all none of them."

The couple watched Marla sweep down the hall and slam through the closed door second on the right.

"That's not your room; it's my study, where I'm going to finally write my bestseller exposing Harriet Beecher Stowe and her Illuminati buddies as the brains behind Lincoln's assassination."

Eddy and Gwen honked as they pulled up with two apartments' belongings crushed into a medium-sized U-Haul. "Hey, lovebirds, sorry we took so long. We stopped to pick up ribs and beer. Say, why the long faces? Who's the ball of fun walking up behind you?"

Probably because they had not sunk deep into debt for the house, Eddy and Gwen had felt less obligated to help unload and return the U-Haul than to flee on foot. After emptying the van themselves, the couple dropped off the U-Haul and bought groceries. They passed the waning hours of the day unpacking boxes and listening to Marla judge their belongings. As they sat at the 'pathetic' candlelit card table eating off of 'white trash retro' dinnerware, Marla supplied idle conversation by recounting her theory that unhappiness was the only universal constant.

"Someday they will build an electron microscope so powerful they will discover that even atoms are depressed and miserable. And if they look real hard, they'll find even atoms are made up of bad vibes that—"

"Do you mind?" Larry snapped, sloshing wine from his plastic cup. "We're trying to enjoy our first dinner as homeowners and newlyweds."

"You got married and bought a house at the same time?"

"Damn straight. Signed the papers and got hitched in the courthouse this morning. We're spending our honeymoon in our very own brand new house."

"We'll throw a big ceremony down the road," Mary added. "And after we save up some money we'll go away somewhere for a real honeymoon, hopefully in a year or two. But moving into our own house on the very day we got married is so romantic."

"Forget romance," Marla sneered. "Start planning for what you're left with after it dies. Habit, probably."

"Go away."

Marla leaned close. "You wanna hear how I died?"

Mary cut into her ham. "Maybe later, dear, but just now—"

"Don't encourage her."

"But this poor soul…"

Larry waved his fork hand. "Go peddle your woe somewhere else, Eeyore. My wife and I deserve alone time, so starting now we're going to ignore you no matter what. How do you like them apples?"

Marla stomped silently out of the room.

"See? That's how you handle kids acting out for attention."

Later, in Mary's double bed and wrapped in semi-darkness, Larry began to demonstrate his more tender side, and Mary her more impatient one. Someone sighed.

"Just don't get pregnant and bring another loser into this pointlessness called existence."

"Holy crap! Get out."

"I thought you two were going to ignore me. How's that working? Well, goodnight."

The couple lay in the gloom, unsure whether Marla had actually left. Mary began to weep softly.

"It's no fair—we have to live with a sulky teen without the cute before and the mature after."

Larry was so angry as he comforted Mary, that she started comforting him back. He glanced in the general direction of his study. "I'll straighten this out tomorrow."

"Are you sure you don't have any liquor?" the Realtor asked again. The negative confirmed, she drew a huge breath, as if she could suck the various molecular constituents of alcohol out of the air, gather them in the back of her throat, and stir them with her uvula. She exhaled sadly. "Okay, if you put it back on the market this soon, we won't make a profit and you'll be out the fees you already paid, plus the new ones. And that's just if Miss Sunshine over there keeps out of sight."

"As if. What are the odds of anyone cool actually wanting to grace this neighborhood? They're all over in Cabbagetown or Five Points. And I might end up with even bigger losers. Besides, I can't leave. God knows I've tried."

"Just cram yourself where you hid from us before yesterday."

Marla shrugged. "I didn't hide. I grew up and died tragically in this house, but the first time I saw you lamebirds was yesterday."

"You'll definitely be selling at a loss," the Realtor said.

Mary shifted uncomfortably. "We had another question—"

"You got us into a bum deal. We think we deserve a full refund."

The Realtor blinked. "What? I did my—"

"How could a haint be in a house no one's lived in? Don't make sense."

"No, read the disclosure—this house is new! Before the city hosted the Olympics, it cleared the Techwood area to gentrify it. I can show you the records."

"But the haint says she died in this house."

"I assure—"

The doorbell rang. "Maybe it's another Jehovah's Witness," Marla smirked. "You want me to shove my head through the door and drive her off?"

"No, stop doing that," Larry growled. "We don't want word to get out that we're infested with a corpse from the world's worst sleepover."

Marla's eyes flared and her lips contracted, then she turned on her heel and stormed to her room.

"Well," Larry gloated, "We'll have to remember that next time we want some privacy. See that, darling? Just point out she's lamer than us."

"I'm not sure we should be so hard on her," Mary called

over her shoulder as she walked to the door. "She's only fourteen—leastways that's how she looks to me—and dead. Hello," she told the man wavering on their doorstep, "How can we help you today?"

"Good afternoon. Sorry to disturb you, but are you the Dunwoodys?"

"Yes, I'm Mary and that's my husband Larry over there by Tina, our Realtor."

"Charmed. I'm Father Charles McNabb from St. Mary's. You emailed us that you would be moving into our parish. If it's not inconvenient, I'd like to introduce myself."

"You're a priest?" Larry asked in a different tone of voice and volume than McNabb was expecting.

"Well, yes, if that's all right. I-I understood you were—"

"He's a priest, Mary, he's a priest!"

McNabb worried that his visit might be veering off course, but he tried again. "I—that is, we at St. Mary's—"

Larry shoved Tina aside and bounded to the stammering man. "C'mon, Father." McNabb was drawn down the hall to Larry's study. "This is our ghost. Can you get rid of her?"

Marla scowled with transparent contempt. "Get out of my room."

By all rights Father McNabb should not have been as surprised by proof of an afterlife as he was, but he rallied. "Er, hello?"

"So," Larry continued. "What do you need to perform an exorcism? We got candles and a Bible. We don't have holy water—is club soda near enough?"

"Oh, I'd have to review my notes," McNabb temporized. "Could I get back to you on that?"

"Sure, take a couple of hours and we'll see you back—"

"Oh, I won't be able today." He had planned to beg a week's time, but lost heart against their dismayed faces. "Tomorrow?"

"Oh, could you?" Mary cried, then looked embarrassed. "For the sake of this poor girl, of course."

"Nice save, lady. I never even noticed it."

"Yes, I suppose I could, that is, well, yes."

"Great!" Larry boomed. "We'll let you get to work. See you tomorrow, father. Well, Mary, we're set. You can always count on religion to save you."

McNabb showed up the next afternoon looking wan — he had been up until 2AM searching the web for instructions on exorcism and he still doubted he could pull it off. Mary, with fulsome grace, ushered him inside and forced sweet tea and donuts on him, which probably did his diabetes no good; Larry kept up a non-stop patter of confidence in the outcome; and the Realtor smiled encouragingly between nips from a flask she'd stashed in her purse. Marla, standing dourly in the corner, declared herself the most despised person in the house if not the world and announced that she was going to her room to prepare for an afterlife that would probably blow even bigger chunks.

McNabb coughed nervously and began waving a crucifix and a rosary. "In the name of Jesus, I declare: *Lorem crescunt in caelo puellis suavissimas modum.*" He laid the rosary on the 'super nerd-o' coffee table, pulled out his vial of holy water and began sprinkling it liberally as everyone else dodged. "In the name of the Church Triumphant and the Archangel Michael, I declare that this spirit is not wanted and must return to the land of the deceased." He looked around without much conviction. "Amen?"

"Is it over yet?" Marla yelled from down the hall.

Larry turned. "You must have done it wrong. Try again."

"Dear," Mary shouted, "Calm down. Father McNabb will sort it out. Won't you?"

"I have an idea, madam; yes . . . I know exactly what I must do. Please give me the evening to prepare and — and I'll pop by again — would tomorrow work?"

A desperate Father McNabb went home and spent the rest of the day surfing Catholic chatrooms for advice. Most of the replies were variations of "Tell them to move to the 21st Century" and "Have you tried blasting ABBA/Katrina & the Waves/Neil Diamond?" Finally, around 2 am, he received a glimmer of hope:

"I believe your problem is a SCIENTIFIC ONE, not spiritual. I am a PROFESSOR at the MISKATONIC INSTITUTE in Essex County, Massachusetts, only seventeen hours away, and would be DELIGHTED TO LEND MY EXPERTISE!!! Please contact me at hpl@mi.edu at your earliest convenience :)"

The morrow found the couple's mood much improved: over Larry's objections, Mary had bribed the ghost to stay out of the bedroom last night in exchange for switching the radio this morning from their usual country-western/easy listening preferences to the local college station. As a side benefit, their cultural horizons expanded, and they now hated the Pain Teens, Throbbing Gristle, and Skinny Puppy, bands they never would have known to dislike otherwise. As the two ate their breakfast Marla stood by the radio, nodding and eyes half-lidded, as if recharging her doom batteries.

"Did your parents let you listen to this crap?" Larry snapped.

"No, so I had to go my friends' houses. Oh, man, were my parents lame. Paul McCartney and geriatric Stones were as wild as those droops got."

"I'm sure they were nice people," Mary said doubtfully.

Marla snorted. "Hardly. A pair of frumpy, fat alcoholics who argued all the time. God, their noses were all bursty-veined and purple, and Dad had the world's most obvious comb over. Thank god I found Morrissey, or I'd have never stayed sane."

"Show some respect girly — they had you."

"Yes," Mary added. "They must have loved each other and you. Somewhat."

Marla shuddered despite the warmth. "Maybe. At some point. You know, they never talked about it, but they did let slip that something tragic happened before I was born that ruined life for both of them. Mind you, I was just cherry icing on the shit cake. Still, they could have tried a little harder not to suck."

"Now honeypie, that's not nice."

"And," she continued, warming, "They both had affairs they don't think the other knew about, but I did."

"Well, don't you end up like that," Larry instructed. He tapped his fingers on the table and looked awkward. "If they get up to that sort of nonsense in the next life, I meant."

Marla looked at the two and shook her head. "No matter what, no matter where, you get hurt. It's fate."

A strong and insistent knocking interrupted their thoughts. Thankfully. Mary answered the door.

"Are you Mrs. Larry Dunwoody?

"I'm Mary Dunwoody-Buckhead. Who are you?" She didn't like the look of the man on the stoop—bulky and clean-cut like a marine but with an air of having spent his entire deployment hiding in the latrine.

"I'm Chad Chadwell from the Journal-Constitution, checking up on the rumor you got a haint."

"Who told you that?"

"All over the Internet. Some collar named McNabb blabs it's a new, exorcism-resistant strain. May I assume he's right?"

Mary saw, over the man's shoulder, other cars arriving and more visitors accreting on her lawn. "Who are all those people?"

"Haven't been introduced to them, ma'am. Can I come in?"

"No, I don't think so. Let me get my husband."

He pushed forward. "Look, if I'm inside, you can close your door and no one else can come in. C'mon, give a local boy an edge over these out-of-towners. See those license plates?" He sneered. "New Englanders."

"Oh, my! Larry," she called without widening the door.

He walked over holding a slice of toast. "Who's that?" He glanced through the uncurtained dining room window at the crowd of young women gathering on the lawn and his toast landed with a buttery slap. "Who are they?"

A fist snaked around the reporter's torso and rapped on the door.

"Hello? May I speak to the Dunwoodys, please?"

"I got here first, pal. Take a number."

"But I'm here by the invitation of Father Charles McNabb to rid the house of its ghost."

The reporter grinned and pulled out his notepad. "So there is a ghost."

"Who's the choad?" Marla asked, thrusting her head through the door.

Chad shrieked and ran to his car, pulled a duffle bag from the trunk, changed his pants, and jogged back.

"Oh, dear," Mary fretted. "I'm so sorry."

Chad waved dismissively. "No worries; happens all the time in my line of work. Can I come in?"

Mary opened the door more out of guilt than sense. Both Chad and the striking man in the white lab coat entered.

"Wait!" Larry croaked. "Is that a journalist? Don't let him in!" Chad hustled towards Larry. "If he publishes anything about this house being haunted by the ghost of a miserable, whiney teen, we're sunk." Chad was almost nose-to-nose with Larry, writing furiously in shorthand. "We'll have to sell so low we'll be in debt for life. Or we'll be chained here, like that damned girl."

"Chad Chadwell, sir. Nice to meet you. How did this girl die so terribly that she walks still the Earth? You didn't kill her, did you? Is that bacon? Do you mind? I skipped breakfast to scoop the snoozers."

"Er, hello?" McNabb called out. "The door was open."

"Mary, shut that damned door!" Larry yelled while

86

glaring at McNabb, immobilizing both.

The stranger broke into a boyish grin. "McNabb! I'm Professor Ludson. You invited me to help you give up the ghost, ha-ha!"

"I said I was—I would call you. Why are you here?"

"To prove my theory correct. Ooh, PANCAKES! I've just driven all night. Can I? Thanks =P"

McNabb floundered for a second. "But-but you said it would take seventeen—"

"Got a Fuzzbuster, so I made pretty good time. The laws of physics are pretty ironclad, but speed limits are more, how shall we say—we won't! Ha-ha. Mmm. The chocolate chips are a nice touch."

"Excuse me," Larry snapped. "Who are you?"

"Oh, are you the unfortunate homeowner? Nice to meet you. I'm Professor Ludson, a crypto-physicist over at Miskatonic, and I'm here to help."

"You're a what?" asked the Realtor.

"We examine the unproven branches of science. You've heard about cryptozoologists, right?"

"No."

"They search for creatures that have been reported but not confirmed."

"Wait," Chad said, pushing into Ludson's face, "I hear about them sometimes at the paper. They hunt crazy crap like bigfoots and melonheads, right?"

"Well, yes, but they've also investigated things such as the Devil Bird of Sri Lanka, which turned out to be bubo nipalensis, a new species of owl; and the so-called African unicorn, a thing described as a mix of a zebra and a donkey with a long neck, and that turned out to be an okapi, the giraffe's only living relative; and did you know that the kangaroo and platypus were once considered HOAXES when first reported? True fact: even when the Aussies sent a stuffed platypus, the Brits thought they were being pranked."

"And how are you a crypto—"

"Physicist. I'm here on a hunch connected to STRING THEORY, something that by its very nature is UNPROVABLE. :(Still, it seems to be holding up in explaining a lot of contradictory phenomena, so until someone brings everything together with a better UNIFICATION THEORY, we'll go with it. Say, could we let my audience in?"

Larry's lips worked in ways that did not quite match the sounds coming out. "Audience? Wha?"

"Just a small group to witness either my TRIUMPH or temporary setback. I texted them something GRAND might occur here today." He opened the door. "Come in, everybody!" He turned to the room. "We can't disappoint them after they drove so far. And fast."

"I say, excuse me, professor," McNabb murmured. "What exactly are you planning to do?"

Ludson clapped his hands together and rubbed. "Listen: according to string theory, ALL the universe, even down to the last ATOM, is made up of tiny strings vibrating at different frequencies. The frequencies combine variously to form all we know and can observe."

"No," McNabb said, "I'm afraid God does that."

"If God exists, then he—or she ;p—is also composed of strings."

"Oh, I really must differ, if you don't mind. I do not believe the omnipotent one would be party to these silly strings of yours."

"Then what? Is God carbon-based? Silicon-composed? What?"

McNabb considered the matter. Doubtless he would be up past 2 am fretting. "I suppose we mortals cannot know. Since He predates the creation of the universe, some unknown, er . . . proto-substance?"

"Oh, spare me your crypto-theology. Now, to hand: string theory posits that there are COUNTLESS regions of space that form POCKETS which have in themselves uniform environments with their own constant natural laws, little universes within the grander one, if you will. Now, normally time scuds over these multiple universes as smoothly as a board over ball bearings, but sometimes a pocket gets jostled and, until it settles back, an anomaly results."

"You lost me when you started explaining," Larry said.

Chad was nodding as if he understood. "What causes these anomalies?"

"An excess of DARK ENERGY," Ludson replied, noticing Marla for the first time. "That force which is slowly pulling our universe apart. Say, is she our little blip?"

"You suck as hard as everyone else who's insulted me today. I have a name, you know."

"Now," Ludson continued, "in what I call a TIME BUBBLE, the regular flow of THE or A universe is interrupted, and someone can get trapped in it and cease to move forward. I believe this young lady was ripped from her normal time stream as she died and was pulled into a riptide of disruption and is now stuck like a big ol' bug in amber, and thus she remains, unchanging as the world moves past her."

Tina took another draw on her flask, which seemed to be helping her understand the professor. "That must be really rare."

Ludson shrugged. "Not as much as you'd expect. Small, temporary rents exist all the time, I believe: an old cuss who just won't die, say, or animals that are supposed to be extinct suddenly discovered in a later era. In fact, I came up with this theory while waiting in line with my niece at Disneyland, where I believe a RATHER SIGNIFICANT time anomaly occurred."

Larry snatched for the last pancake, but not as quickly as Chad. As he watched the larger man chew, he considered. "Say, if we're in an anomaly, are we frozen, too?"

"No, for the anomaly cropped up elsewhere, and she is

centered there. We are merely seeing its manifestation."

Larry sighed. "I almost had it until you kept talking."

"I must say," McNabb added, "That I am deeply disturbed by your reducing the spiritual to mere science. It seems, if you don't object, blasphemous."

"Duly noted," Ludson replied. "Okay, I need a couple of strapping volunteers to help bring in my equipment."

"Oh, Larry, he's got equipment," Mary squealed. "That sounds so confidence-giving."

"You watch, it'll fail," Marla prophesied as four of the women followed the scientist outside.

Another of the professor's ardent fans, a young woman whose Milky Way print t-shirt was demonstrating exactly how curved space could get, stepped forward. "Oh, it'll work. Herbert's a genius. You can rely on science. And Herbert."

Tina tipped back her head and violently shook her flask, and then put it back in her purse. "So why haven't we heard about him?"

Another woman bounced forward. "A cabal of conservative scientists that operates behind the scenes has been keeping him and his RADICAL IDEAS down."

"I can believe that!" Larry exclaimed. "In fact, back in April of 1895 the Illuminati, led by — "

"Oh, my God, spare us," Marla cried. "I am so tired of hearing half-baked conspiracy theories about Harriet effing Stowe."

Larry's outraged retort was silenced by the entrance of a figure in a hooded grey robe who was directing four young undergraduates as they lugged a fused collection of tubes, duct tape and wires.

"Just put my GROUND-BREAKING equipment over there, by that shabby card table."

"What's with the cool getup?" Marla asked.

"Protective clothing, of course. Very dangerous, messing with time and the universe."

Mary regarded the machine. "Do we get robes?"

"No, it's REPEATED exposure you have to watch out for! Do you wear lead shielding when you get an x-ray? No! JUST the technician. Well, here goes," he said flipping the switch, catching everyone mid-flee. Marla vanished. "SUCCESS!! Now they'll be forced to reinstate me =D"

Larry looked around, open-mouthed. "She is gone! Oh, professor, you did it!"

Mary began to cry. "We're so grateful. Bless you. Would you like more pancakes?"

"Yes, please, I'm quite hungry," Ludson called from the tight scrum of his fans' congratulatory hugs.

She began to crack eggs into the bowl. "One thing I still don't understand," she mused aloud.

"What?" asked McNabb, hoping to supply an answer after being so irrefutably upstaged by science.

"The girl said she was raised in this house, not the low-income one that got torn down. How is that possible?"

McNabb regretted speaking up, being equally stymied.

"Must have been from the future," Ludson called out. "She was in an anomaly where time was DISTORTED. No reason she could not someday be born and die in this house."

"How far in the future?" Mary asked, clutching her abdomen in sinking dread.

"No telling. But you needn't worry. If you have a girl, just name her something different and it'll kick the problem to SOMEONE IN THE FUTURE." He sighed contentedly. "Just like the deficit and global warming."

"Larry, do you remember what-what her name was?"

"She didn't say."

They both looked at the professor.

"Well, at least you know her approximate age and HOW she died, so you can forestall the events—"

"Did she tell you?" Mary whispered, but she could already read the answer on Larry's face. "If you had only let me talk to her like I ask—"

"If you hadn't kept interrupting me all the time…"

Ludson walked over and nudged the box of pancake mix closer to Mary. "I guess you should have asked her more questions."

"We can't let her end up like that awfu—that troubled girl," Mary sobbed. "We'll raise her so she feels loved and has plenty of freedom."

"Like hell," Larry replied. "Punk like that had too much freedom. We need to be strict so she knows what's what."

"No, she'll rebel."

Larry rounded the counter and pulled out the bottle of wine they'd hidden from the Realtor. "Let's just think this out. We're only in trouble if it's a girl. How many weeks before the ultrasound shows gender?"

"You monsters had better not even be considering early termination!" roared McNabb.

"He's right, we can't," Mary moaned. "For better or worse, we're struck. We'll just have to love her all the more."

Tina lurched up from the couch. "Okay, I just worked it out—this can't be my fault, so I'm not getting sued!"

"Wait!" Larry said. "Now the ghost's gone, we could still sell the house for a small loss, right?"

Tina considered. "Who's going to buy a house if they know they're gonna end up with a child who dies young and unhappy?" She began staggering towards the door.

"But how would anyone even find that out?" Larry called after her.

"Let me help you, ma'am," Chad said, grabbing Tina's elbow. "I'm heading out anyway—got a story to file."

The rest watched through the living room window as Chad poured Tina into her car, got into his own, and began to follow the potential news item as she wove down the streets.

"I can't stay long, either," the professor added. "Got to start typing up my paper. This house, this proving ground of man's great leap forward in knowledge, will become FAMOUS, I tell you."

"Oh, Larry, what will we do?" Mary moaned as she wrestled the bottle from her husband.

Ludson laughed.

"What's so funny?" Larry growled.

"Oh, sometimes I just think funny thoughts."

"Such as?"

"You know how 'those who forget the past are condemned to repeat it'? Well, in your case it should be: 'those who ignore the future are condemned to live it'. Really, if a ghost showed up in MY house I'd be a little more curious about it. HEY! I don't see any pancakes getting made X-("

The professor's jibe had caught Larry at a rather inopportune time, a point in his already jangled life when his last nerve was already so taut you could break a camel's back with it. Consequently, Larry's brain searched for a handy valve with which to relieve the pressure, and the professor's pretty-boy nose suggested itself. As it so happened, the time anomaly had fallen back into place but, like a dropped stone raising a plash before sinking, it threw out a small droplet that enveloped the area currently occupied by Larry's fist. Thus, as everyone watched, Larry's punch rocketed halfway to the professor's nose, then sped half the remaining distance, then half that.

"Looks like an AFTEREFFECT of the anomaly," the professor chuckled. "Lucky for me. Now students, watch this—his blow WILL NOT LAND, for it must always travel half the remaining distance, and caught by time and outside our usual governing laws—"

Then the globule popped, and the universe proceeded again in its orderly and predictable manner, and all was right with the world.

Nathan Cromwell is a living, breathing, swearing

teleprompter for the human race, and he does some of his best work on public transport. A military brat, he is from no one place. He did hover in Indiana long enough to earn a BA in English which he has never used for any job ever unless you count this. He has worked in the retail, security, and fitness industries and has acquired all the concomitant bitterness they offer. That hard-won fruit he passes on to you in his stories.

Many of his stories are online, and you can find links to them at: nathancromwell.wordpress.com

HAPPY BIRTHDAY AARP BOY
BY DAN FOLEY

Jacob was in the hot tub with the chick from 2B. They were both naked, and things were just getting interesting when a gravelly male voice tore him from the best dream he'd had in weeks.

"Wake up, AARP Boy, it's your birthday."

"Go away," Jacob muttered, and then sat bolt upright when he realized someone was in his bedroom. Not good, since he lived alone.

"Who ...," he blurted out, and then he saw the Danny DeVito look-alike perched on the end of his bed. A scruffy, balding, fat, bearded, cigar smoking, Danny DeVito look-alike to be sure, but there he was, except he was smaller than DeVito, a lot smaller.

"So AARP boy, it's your birthday, what have you got planned?" the DeVito look-alike asked through a thick cloud of exhaled cigar smoke. Before Jacob could answer, the intruder said, "Jesus, the ventilation in here sucks," and broke up the cloud with a pair of ratty wings that sprouted from the middle of his back.

Whoa, still dreaming, Jacob thought, and actually pinched himself to see if he could banish the apparition and get back to the chick in 2B.

"You're not dreaming, AARP Boy, I'm as real as you are, so get used to it," the DeVito thing said.

"Who are you ... what are you?" Jacob managed to mutter, still having a hard time believing this was happening.

"I'm Sam, your birthday fairy, AARP Boy," it told him.

"What the hell is a birthday fairy, and why do you keep calling me AARP Boy? I don't belong to AARP," Jacob asked, still half asleep but waking up fast.

"I'm a birthday fairy, you idiot. I just told you that. And it's not AARP like in the American Association of Retired People, it's AARP like in Another Aging Roly-Poly," Sam told him.

"Roly-poly? I'm not a roly-poly," Jacob argued.

"Really? Look in the mirror, AARP Boy. Or, better yet, look at me," the fairy told him.

"What do you mean, look at you?" Jacob said.

"Me, look at me. I'm a fucking fairy pariah, and it's all your fault."

"My fault, what's my fault?" Jacob asked.

"Me, this, the whole package. Fairies are supposed to be beautiful — thin, fair-haired, happy creatures. Not short, balding, pot-bellied caricatures you might find in a Maurice Sendak story."

"Fine, great, it's my fault, but, again, what the hell is a birthday fairy?" Jacob demanded.

"A birthday fairy: every human gets one," Sam said. "We all start out soft and cuddly with beautiful wings, and then we grow, right along with our human. And, every year, on our human's birthday, we give them a special present."

"What the hell did you ever give me? I don't remember any special presents," Jacob told him.

"You want me to go over them?" Sam asked.

"Sure, go ahead," Jacob said.

"Okay, you won't remember this, but when you were one, I taught you how to walk. Everyone was so impressed that you walked so early. I have to admit, it was a bit selfish of me since I got to spread my wings and fly as soon as you were walking, but hey, I was young too. And these," Sam said, flapping the ratty wings behind his back, "were beautiful."

"You did that, you taught me how to walk," Jacob said.

"Yup, that was me," Sam said before shifting to his left, lifting his leg, and cutting a massive fart."

"What the fuck?" Jacob said, gagging on the noxious cloud that filled the bedroom.

"Your fault," Sam said, flapping his wings to clear the air. "This happens every time you drink beer and eat hot wings."

"That's disgusting," Jacob said, and then felt a crippling stomach cramp.

"Hang on Champ, here it comes," Sam said, and a few seconds later, Jacob also cut a wet sounding fart.

"Whoa, good one, better check your shorts for skidders after that baby," Sam told him through another cloud of cigar smoke.

Jacob waved the vile, blue cloud away from his face and broke into a deep, hacking cough.

"Smoker's cough," Sam said, and motioned to the pack of Camels on the bedside stand. "Go ahead, light up, it ain't gonna' to bother me," he said, and took another long drag on his cigar.

Jacob leaned over and snagged a Camel. He lit it with practiced efficiency and then coughed up a loogie that he spit into a tissue from a box on the bedside table.

"Now that's disgusting," Sam told him.

Jacob was coughing too hard to reply, so he just flipped the fairy the bird.

Sam ignored the gesture and asked, "You want another one, one you should remember? You were eight. You climbed that tree in the back yard."

"I fell out of that tree and broke my arm. Some present," Jacob said.

"If I wasn't there you'd have broken more than your arm. You'd have broken your damn neck. I saw you; I knew what was going to happen. I was just a little shit then. I wasn't strong enough to completely stop your fall, but I slowed it

97

down and all you did was break your arm. I strained my wings so bad I couldn't fly for a month. But, I did get a Medal of Valor for that one, so it wasn't all bad," Sam said, and then grabbed his stomach. "You gotta' stop with the hot wings, you're killing me," he said through gritted teeth.

"And how about that bike when you were ten? Without me, you never would have gotten that bike. You were ten dollars short on the price, and ten dollars was a lot of money back then. Who do you think dropped that bag of quarters on the street right in front of you? Me, that's who. You know where I got those quarters? I swiped them from the tooth fairy, and she was pissed, made me work it off collecting teeth. That was a job I didn't enjoy."

"The tooth fairy? You expect me to believe the tooth fairy is real?" Jacob said.

"Hey, I'm real; you're talking to me, aren't you? Of course the tooth fairy is real," Sam said.

"Right, and Santa Claus, and the Easter Bunny and leprechauns," Jacob said.

"Don't be ridiculous; Santa Claus and the Easter Bunny are fictional characters. Leprechauns, on the other hand, are another story; you don't want to mess with those buggers," Sam said, and started to lift his leg again.

"Hey, get the hell out of here if you're going to fart," Jacob said.

The fairy ignored him and let go with a long, loud, ripper. "Sorry about that, Bud," he laughed, and used his wings to push the latest blast in Jacob's direction.

"Okay, the next one's my favorite," Sam said. "You remember that smokin' red-head you scored on your twenty-first? I arranged that."

"You did not, that was all me," Jacob told him.

"Come on, you were a nerd; she was at least a nine, maybe even a ten. This is how it went down. You went out drinking, alone. You were feeling sorry for yourself and you got a pretty good buzz on. What you didn't know, and never found out because you never saw her again, was that it was her birthday, too. So, you're getting a little drunk, she's getting a little drunk. That means I was getting a buzz too, and so was her fairy, who, by the way, was as hot as she was.

"Now, you may have been a nerd back then, but I was a one hot dude. I had gossamer wings, a full head of hair, and six-pack abs. You got it on with the red-head; I got it on with her fairy. That was it, the best birthday ever, for you and for me. It's been all downhill from there."

"Downhill? What do you mean, downhill?" Jacob demanded.

"Well, for one thing, you started smoking those damn cigarettes that year. That got me started on these fucking things," Sam said, waving his cigar in front of Jacob's face.

"Hey, I tried to quit," Jacob said.

"Bullshit, you can tell that to yourself, you can tell that to your friends, but you can't tell that to me. I hate these fucking dog turds, but if you don't quit, I can't quit," Sam told him, shaking his cigar in Jacob's face.

"You remember your thirtieth? I nudged you into getting a membership at the gym—epic fail. I really wanted that one, for the both of us. There were some really hot fairies there. It lasted for what … two months, then you stopped going and we got this," Sam said, patting his pot belly.

"Hey," Jacob said, "Are you the reason I won that trip to Puerto Rico on my fiftieth?"

"Of course it was me! The Big Five-O. Every birthday Fairy is allowed one big splash like that, and believe me, there was a lot of competition for that trip. I had to make a Power Point presentation to the Fairy Board, and believe me, they are not an easy sell. I had to convince them that winning that trip would turn your life—and mine—around. At that point I looked so bad, what with the smoke-stained teeth, the pot belly, and the thinning hair, that it was more of a mercy gift for me than an opportunity for redemption for

99

you," Sam said.

"Well, you done good on that one," Jacob said. "That was one great trip."

"A great trip? What world are you living on, AARP Boy? That trip was a disaster," Sam shouted back, so agitated he almost fell off his perch at the foot of the bed.

"What do you mean, disaster? That was seven days of sun and fun in the middle of winter, and I got to bring a friend," Jacob shot back.

"Oh, big deal, a friend. You brought your brother, for Christ's sake. You were supposed to bring a chick … a chick, you idiot, not your bar crawling, porcelain-bowl-hugging, asshole of a brother."

"Hey, we had a good time … no, make that a great time," Jacob told him.

"If you call getting drunk every night, sleeping till noon every day, and waking up hung over every morning a great time, then it was a real blast," Sam said. "Me, that's not my idea of fun."

"Looking at you, I'd say that's exactly your idea of fun," Jacob said.

Sam got quiet, took a long slow drag on his cigar, blew the smoke, out in a stinking blue stream and said, "That trip, that's when I started hating you."

"Hating me … why?" Jacob asked.

"Because of these," Sam said, and shoved his torn and battered wings in Jacobs face. "A fairy's wings are their pride and joy. I had gorgeous wings. They would actually shimmer in the sunshine. You remember the day you woke up on the beach with a wicked sunburn? Nah, you were probably too drunk. Well, I remember. I woke up on the same beach, and my wings were burned to a crisp. When you started peeling, pieces of my wings started flaking off. I'm lucky I've got these left."

"Hey, I'm sorry, all right? I had no idea you even existed. How was I supposed to know the damn sun would burn your precious wings?" Jacob said.

"Yeah, well, that doesn't mean I can't hate you for it, AARP Boy," Sam told him.

"Could you stop calling me that ... please?" Jacob asked.

"Nope," Sam replied. "You're AARP Boy to me. Live with it."

Jacob started to reply, and then stopped. A puzzled look came over his face and he said, "Why are you here? How come you were never here before?"

"Because we're not allowed to show ourselves to our humans. Humans aren't supposed to know we exist." Sam said.

"Then why ...?"

"Because this is a special case," Sam said. "I'm retiring. This is my last birthday with you, AARP Boy. I went back to the Fairy Board, with another Power Point, and presented my case. I waited for a day that you had been drinking beer and eating hot wings. Then I went in, treated them to a little gastric distress, showed them this pot belly of mine, and filled the room with cigar smoke. I think it was the wings that did it, though. When I unfolded them, two of the board members actually got sick, upchucked right there in the board room. That's when they gave me permission for this year's gift."

At this point, Jacob shifted uncomfortably on the bed before asking, "What gift?"

"This one," Sam said and pointed at Jacob.

At first nothing happened, but then Jacob felt a tightening in his chest.

"I'm really going to enjoy my retirement. I've got a membership at Club Fairy along with a personal trainer. I'm going to kick these things," Sam said waving the cigar in front of Jacob, "and when I'm healthy enough, I'm going to get a wing transplant. They're doing wonders with growing wings these days."

"What's happening?" Sam gasped as shooting pains ran

down his left arm and a fist seemed to close around his heart.

Sam smiled, cut one last, ripping fart, and said, "It's your birthday present, AARP Boy: the board approved your heart attack."

Dan Foley currently lives in Connecticut. He grew up in New Jersey and then spent over seven years in the U.S. Navy. Much of that time was spent on nuclear submarines. He credits both of these factors for his slightly disturbed sense of humor and writing style. He is the author of the novel *Death's Companion*, *The Whispers of Crows*, a collection of short stories, and the novella *Intruder*. He has also published in various anthologies and magazines in the U.S. Canada, England and Australia. His next novel, *Abandoned*, is scheduled for release in June 2016. Find him at: www.deathscompanion.com

QUASI-THERAPY
BY RUSCHELLE DILLON

"So, let's go back and discuss how you feel about your mother? It sounds to me like she might have something to do with your...*issues*." Emanuel inquired, hoping that this would finally get to the root of the problem.

The doorknob on the closet door shook wildly. Emanuel had struck a nerve.

"I see you aren't ready to talk about your mom right now and that's all right. But eventually, when you are more willing, we do need to come back and visit that topic. Okay?"

The doorknob stopped its feverish dance.

Emanuel tried a less clinical approach.

"How about I take off my shrink hat and you and I just talk like *de hombre a hombre*... Do you think we could try that?" He rolled his r's like his mother taught him when learning to speak Spanish all those years ago.

The closet door cracked open.

"That's a good start. Thank you." Emanuel sat on the only piece of furniture that was left in his old bedroom; his mattress. He ran a hand through his receding hairline and sighed.

"Look, Coco, you and I have been through a lot together."

A low growl rumbled from the closet.

Emanuel tapped his leg nervously. "You scared la mierda out of me when I was little."

The growl turned into a guttural laugh.

Emanuel reclined to the far side of the mattress which

was pressed up against the wall facing the closet.

"Yeah, you laugh. I was afraid to get out of bed to pee for years because I thought you'd 'get' me. I had to pee so bad that I wet myself. Mom put rubber sheets on my bed."

The amusement from the closet grew louder.

"And not that that wasn't embarrassing enough. I developed bladder infections because of you." Emanuel stammered as he recalled his boyhood trauma.

The laughter was joined by the pounding of a large fist against the back of the not so large closet.

"I'm glad you think this is funny."

A smile smeared across Emanuel's face. Although it was uncomfortable to hear Coco laugh, he knew it meant there could be some hope for a promising outcome.

"Okay, maybe it sounds funny now..." Emanuel steered the conversation into less comfortable territory.

"It wasn't until I was eleven years old that I realized you were all bluster. You wanted to get me, but you couldn't."

The hearty laughter stopped.

"Once I realized that you could potentially get me at any time during the night and you didn't, you couldn't..."

A deep reverberating rumble juddered the room.

Emanuel continued, "...well, that's when we called a truce."

Opening his briefcase, Emanuel pulled out a stack of large cards.

"Would you humor me, Coco? I'm going to show you some pictures or ink blots. Take a look at each one and tell me the first thing that you see."

The rumbling lingered followed by a single gravelly word.

"No."

Unrelenting, Emanuel kicked the closet door open a little more. It was dark inside. The closet was not deep, but it was not shallow either. If something wanted to hide in its shadows, one would have to know exactly how to shift and contort oneself inside the closet to become one with the shadows. It also helped if the something was as inky and black as a shadow itself.

"Come on. I think you'll enjoy this."

Plucking the top ink blot off the stack, Emanuel glanced at it and showed it to Coco.

"What do you see?"

Reluctantly, Coco answered him.

"*Conejillo de indias.*" He replied in his low and gritty timbre.

Emanuel spoke out loud as he jotted his answer down in a note pad.

"Guinea pig. Okay."

He held up another ink blot.

"How about this one?"

The picture looked sort of snake-like but Coco's answer was anything but.

"Me."

Emanuel looked quizzically at the picture and shook his head.

"Okay...sure. It's your interpretation. Next one."

The succeeding ink blot resembled a squat totem pole with six arms. Emanuel barely had it off of the pile when Coco blurted out his answer.

"Me eating Manny's Guinea pig when he escaped from cage and ran into the closet. What was his name? Bembe?"

Emanuel's mouth dropped open in disbelief.

"You ate mi mascota. My pet guinea pig?" he stammered.

The closet exploded with immodest hilarity.

"You told me it escaped out the window. You fiendish bastard, I loved that Guinea pig! How could you eat him?"

Coco thought about it for a moment before he answered.

"How could I eat him? With ketchup packet from clown restaurant. That's how I ate him. Guinea pig very tasty."

He snorted at his own wit and added, "Could not help it. It bit me. I bite back."

Emanuel strained to keep his composure. It disturbed him that Coco ate his pet. It disturbed him more that Coco still called him Manny. No one called him Manny anymore. So he bit back.

"So is that what you would have done to me if I bit you? Eat me with ketchup?"

"No." he replied with a chortle. "Ranch dressing."

Coco enjoyed the delicious scent of tension oozing from Emanuel. The closet was once again alive with robust laughter.

Agitated, Emanuel continued.

"This really isn't funny." he snapped but Coco carried on unfazed.

"Ate your cat too. It peed in my closet."

Emanuel bristled, "Dammit Coco!"

He persisted on poking Emanuel with his revelations and the use of his nickname.

"Manny?"

"I need a minute to myself, Coco. I need to process all this."

Coco barely let five seconds pass before he spoke again.

"Manny?"

Reminding himself of his purpose as to why he came back to the house, Emanuel sucked in a deep breath, filling his lungs and slowly released it. He couldn't let the tender feelings of his youth interrupt the objective of the here and now. He faked half a smile.

"Yes, Coco what is it?"

Coco could barely contain himself, his laughter was so raucous.

"Ate Mom, too."

The closet door kicked open a bit wider as Coco carried on hysterically.

Emanuel slammed the closet door shut.

"You did not! I was at her funeral. Now you're just making stuff up to piss me off."

Annoyed at Coco, yet relieved at the comic relief he offered up, Emanuel stuffed the remaining ink blots back into his briefcase. He used this as an opportunity to discuss the future of the family homestead.

"So...I guess you know Mama passed away a few months ago?"

Emanuel's words compelled Coco to restrain himself. He was quiet for a few minutes before he answered.

"I miss Mama. She sang pretty songs when she came in room. She was nice. Smelled nice too- like cookies."

Emanuel's mom had passed away suddenly a few months past. He never knew anything about his father other than the name they both shared. His mother told him that his father had brought her over the border from Mexico to start a new life but once he found out she was pregnant he left. That's all his mother would ever tell him and that answer sufficed because his mother worked hard and raised him well. She encouraged him to be a good boy and go to school and make something of himself. And Emanuel did just that. After receiving his degree in child and adolescent psychiatry he moved two states away and launched a successful practice. With his mom gone and no other family there, would be no need for the homestead.

He chose his next words carefully.

"As of noon tomorrow, this house will no longer belong to me. This room will no longer be mine. Do you understand what that means, Coco?"

Underneath a throaty sigh, Coco whispered, "Yes."

"You can't stay in here."

Emanuel opened the closet door and gently rocked it back and forth. Hoping his words would be as gentle.

"You can't stay...here. You need to be honest with yourself and accept yourself. Unfortunately, because of who you are you may find that you're not liked. You may even be hated, but the rewards outweigh the backlash. Coco, you need to come out of the clo..."

Emanuel was cut off midsentence by the closet door swinging completely open. Inside it was so dark Emanuel thought it had been swallowed up by a black hole. Coco's green eyes were the only thing that gave credence to the void followed by his thick voice.

"Manny?"

"What is it?" he answered.

Coco slowly closed his eyes and murmured, "Not..."

A weighty pause enveloped the room.

And as slowly as he closed his eyes he forcefully popped them open and growled, "... gay."

Coco's declaration only strengthened Emanuel's resolve.

"I'm a therapist. I'm a therapist because of you, Coco. I want to thank you for that. And because of what you did for me- I want to return the favor and help you." Emanuel returned to the old mattress and sat like he did when he was a kid; 'cross-cross-applesauce.' His child-like posture came out of nowhere. It immediately made him feel uneasy...just like he felt when he was a kid.

He continued, "I deal with adolescents who can't come out of the closet. You don't have to feel persecuted like you may have eons ago. It's 2016. There's nothing wrong with being gay. Some of my best friends are gay...and black."

Calmly Coco whispered, "Manny?"

Emanuel looked intently at the dark space in front of him and cocked his head.

The monster snarled, "Gonna eat you now, Manny."

It was Emanuel's turn to laugh, "You can't eat me. Besides, you couldn't eat me years ago and you can't eat me now. You're not that kind of monster."

Emanuel could hear Coco shift inside the closet. But could see nothing but the darkness except the occasional flicker of Coco's green eyes.

"What kind of monster am I, Manny?"

There was a hitch in Coco's voice he remembered from his youth. It heralded the monster's intimidating temper tantrum. Which would mean toys and clothes tossed from the closet with the force of a miniature tornado. Wire coat hangers whipped like speedballs, sometimes imbedding in the drywall, and in extreme cases the closet hinges ripped from the wall.

Although the closet was emptied years ago, he hoped his learned techniques in anger management would keep the monster's wrath at bay. De-escalating the situation and stroking the monster's ego would be his best chance.

"I meant no disrespect. You are-and always have been- a formidable beast. I still remember the lullaby my mother would sing to me in Spanish if she thought I was being naughty.

Emanuel cleared his throat and softly sang, "Sleep child, sleep now...here comes the Coco and he will eat you."

As he reminisced a smile broke across Emanuel's face. He missed his mother.

"Foreboding little song--like many nursery rhymes and lullabies and fairy tales. They were meant to scare children. Adults made them worse than they were. No parent would want to tell a child they would be eaten if it they knew it were to indeed be true. They embellished to make a bigger impression on an already impressionable child. You're no child eater. You're a *fear* eater."

With no opposition to his theory, he continued.

"The horrid little song did what it was meant to do--it kept me in check. My fear kept you full. Until I realized you weren't going to 'get' me. But what I couldn't, and apparently still can't figure out, is why you refuse to come out of the closet."

As if he was hit by a stroke of clinical genius, Emanuel snapped his finger and pointed at the closet.

But in his excitement he blurted out in Spanish, "*Usted es impotente!*"

"What?" the monster roared.

Emanuel repeated it in English "You're impotent!"

Coco growled, disgusted, "I know the meaning. Getting angry. That is not good...for you."

The error of his words hit him. Attempting to rectify the situation he created he stuttered, "J-J-Just l-l-let me explain."

As if Coco hadn't heard Emanuel's last plea he snarled "*Mi pene es grande!* I am like a monster bull. *La Coca amaban mi pene.* Love it."

Emanuel rubbed his eyes. Although he could not actually see Coco's grande bull penis, the mental image his mind created was disturbing. And rubbing his eyes was all he could do to try and scrub it from his brain.

He struggled to amend his last statement.

"I'm sure your manhood or...monsterhood is quite impressive to the females..."

The monster cut him off.

"I was a sexual god. I fathered hordes of bastard creatures. Some still write..."

It was Emanuel's turn to interject.

"I'm not talking about that...any of that. I'm saying you can't come out of the closet because you have performance anxiety..."

Coco went on the defensive.

"I once had sex with a harem of polyvaginal females in the ball court of Chichen Itza. Mayan Warriors cheered me while I satisfied each one."

"But..." Emanuel began.

Once again he was silenced by Coco's braggadocio.

"I satisfied them all multiple times!"

Unexpectedly, Coco's voice veered off.

"Although... there was one very superb female that turned out to be a eunuch. But it was honest mistake. That does not make me gay?"

Coco's paused and quickly added, "Does it?" sounding almost desperate.

Before he could confess another sexual escapade, Emanuel launched into his explanation.

"I meant performance anxiety where you are afraid to leave the closet because of what might happen if you do. It's like having stage fright."

Somewhat satisfied with the explanation, Coco purred, "Stage fright?"

"Yes, stage fright. Apparently at one time you were out of the closet. So what happened between then and now?"

Taking a verbal swing, Emanuel asked as calmly as his voice would let him, "Was it the eunuch?"

Coco pounded on the back of the closet.

"He said his name was Conchita!"

"It's okay, Coco." Emanuel said attempting to comfort him.

"You said you didn't know. You can't blame yourself…"

The monster let out a gut punching wail, "He had four beautiful teats, resplendent with thick ebony hair, a thatched tongue, and mites that ate from his sacred hole …just like my mother!"

The walls in his old bedroom began to shake as the monster shrieked. The tremor emanating from his throat could rival a passing freight train. The neighborhood had to feel its echo.

At that moment Emanuel knew that there really was a monster lurking inside that closet. Now if he could just lure him out. He had to lure him out. At noon the following day the house would be filled with the sounds of a new family. A family with three young children who didn't need to fear falling asleep in their beds at night. They did not need to sleep with fear. Emanuel needed to make certain they would have a happier childhood than he had. Even if that meant dragging Coco out of the closet.

An ancient monster suffering from an Oedipal complex would take more than a few hours to 'fix.' Emanuel would have to draw Coco from the closet another way.

A Catholic, Emanuel crossed himself and whispered, "*En el nombre del Santo Padre, y mama y* Sigmund Freud… forgive me."

As he kissed his fingers and sent it to the heavens he took a deep breath and jeered, "Is your name *el Coco* or is it *el Cono*? Because I'm really having a tough time making the distinction."

Calling a monster a 'pussy' was a long shot at best. Coco might not physically hurt him, but the monster might get a full course meal because battling the unknown can be petrifying, and petrifying is delicious.

The closet door slammed shut, splintering the wood at the lock.

Emanuel raised the stakes a little higher.

"Really, you're just going to slam the door, *el Cono*?" he mocked.

"I don't see how anyone could be afraid of you. You are weak. You don't even deserve to be called *papa-negro* or boogeyman." Emanuel hissed as he pounded on the closet door. "In fact, when I was a boy I smashed the neighbor's mailbox with a baseball bat. I got away with it. No one ever knew. Not even you."

The closet door pulled shut even tighter, splitting the wood down the center.

Adding insult to injury, Emanuel continued.

"And it wasn't always the cat that peed in your closet!"

With that, the closet door flew open, knocking Emanuel backwards. He fell onto the mattress, his head hitting the opposite wall.

His head echoed, not only from the crack to his skull, but with Coco's thunderous roar.

Blood seeped out of the gash in his head and down his neck. Emanuel felt his head to make certain his brains were all there, because his next action would make him question that.

"That's it. Come on out and face me. Or are you embarrassed because you wanted to have sex with your mother but had to settle for a pansy-ass eunuch instead?"

The closet door began to disappear in terrifying blackness as the monster began to pour out. His arms spanned across the entire bedroom as he dug his thick fingerless claws into the plaster, slowly yanking himself free. As his head and torso slowly began to emerge, Emanuel instinctively pressed himself against the wall to give the monster room to make his grand entrance. It was like watching a flayed elephant emerge from a mouse hole. Emanuel's eyes bulged at the beast.

Without thinking, he sputtered: "How the fuck did you fit in there?"

With his phosphorescent green eyes fixed on Emanuel, Coco cocked his massive head and snorted in response. The exhalation thrust Emanuel further into the wall and coated him with a spray of opaque snot. The outline of the closet was swallowed up by Coco's grotesque sinewy frame. As he shook and jerked to free each leg from their vice, a viscous ooze dripped from his bulk, evaporating all color from the room. When the monster finally stood, he was immense.

Emanuel was face to face with the monster from his childhood closet. His boyhood nemesis, *El Coco*. Neither the storybooks nor his rich imagination could manifest a beast so dark and so hideous. Emanuel attempted to burrow himself deeper into the plaster of the wall--further away from *El Coco*'s putrid breath dripping all over him--but could not. He wanted to run but there was nowhere to run-- nowhere to go. The room was enveloped in the darkness that was *El Coco*.

Realizing he had just succeeded in persuading the monster out of the closet, his next thought was dire: "Now what?" Unfortunately, his thought was interrupted by a wood-cracking thud that caused him to clamp his eyes shut and flinch. He wasn't prepared for what was splayed out in front of him. Almost as large as the closet monster himself, was the monster's alarming penis.

This was not the monster his mother had told him about!

His mother warned him to be good or *El Coco* would snatch him from his bed and eat him for supper. None of the stories ever discussed, included, or alluded to the monster's schlong.

With that, *El Coco* leaned forward. A fine inky mist of snot parted Emanuel's hair.

Pointing a sharped finger at his manhood he sneered, "Do I look like pussy to you?

Emanuel needed to think quickly. Fear was taking over. Emanuel could feel his legs turning to pudding. Under his breath he absentmindedly muttered, "Oh shit, oh shit, oh shit."

Coco grinned a shiny black grin. "Petulant child. I *am* the boogeyman."

Emanuel's legs buckled as the words trickled from his lips. His knees sunk into the old mattress. He knew Coco would be feasting on the terror radiating from his pores, but he swallowed hard, attempting to stave the quiver in his voice, and cried, "You did it, Coco! *We* did it. You are free from the closet. You can finally leave this house and explore the world again."

He forced a smile and through clenched teeth, he fished for an answer, "This is a proud moment for you. You were ready to come out of the closet. I just gave you the push you needed. Isn't this exciting?"

Attempting to stand erect, Coco bashed his head into the ceiling. Plaster and dust showered Emanuel, but dissolved into Coco's murky hide. His eyes darted from one side of the room to the other.

"Yes. I am out of the closet. I am free," the monster paused for a moment. Filling his lungs with air that wasn't stale or musty or rife with mothballs. As he exhaled, Emanuel was blown back on his behind and again pressed against the wall. He had not been out of that tiny hole of a closet for almost 100 years, and the freedom felt good to the creature.

Gently, almost sweetly Coco cooed, "Thank you for that, Manny."

Relieved that the monster's mood had shifted--and luring him out of the closet was a success--Emanuel slowly stood and wiped the sweat from his forehead.

A genuine smile tore open his lips.

"I'm sorry I had to resort to childish name calling. That wasn't how I wanted to bring you out of there. I'm a psychiatrist sworn to help people. Again, I'm sorry if I hurt your feelings. But I am thrilled to see you out of that closet." Emanuel relaxed his posture.

"I know I have no right to ask you for anything but...*por favor* put your--um... *grande pene de distancia*? It's a bit disconcerting."

Not wanting to antagonize Coco again, he was quick to add a compliment.

"But it is very impressive. I can see where you would be a hit with the ladies." Lightening the situation, he quipped, "Just how large are these poly-vaginal females..."

But his stab at levity was quickly dismissed.

"I, too, am sorry, Manny."

Emanuel was comforted hearing the monster's apology. He was even more comforted knowing that the family moving in would be Coco-free. He had done what he had set out to do. Now he needed to send Coco in the proper direction--which was anywhere but this house.

"It's okay, big guy. We both made some mistakes today. But now that you're finally free, you can go anywhere you..."

Once again Coco disrupted him.

"No Manny. I'm sorry."

It was Emanuel's turn to interrupt him.

"I heard you, Coco, and it's okay. We'll move past this..."

Suddenly, Coco bent down until his face was inches from Emanuel's.

"Manny. I'm sorry I have to eat you now."

Emanuel let out a nervous laugh.

"You really had me going, Coco. Just like when I was a kid. But honestly, could you please put that thing away. You really shouldn't leave the house with not-so-little Coco hanging out."

Raising his raspy voice in protest, the black beast shouted:

"You have been bad, Manny. I am *El Coco*, the monster in your closet! And I eat bad children." An obscure claw twisted out from the shadow and wrapped seductively around Emanuel's face and mouth.

"And you were correct about my...persuasion, Emanuel. I am gay," he whispered as he grabbed his colossal penis and gave it a squeeze.

Emanuel felt lightheaded. He thought it could be from the loss of blood from his head, but he couldn't be certain it wasn't from the rush of fear that drained him of all confidence.

Stumbling over his words he stuttered, "Y-Y-You're n-not-not not that k-k-ind of monster."

The monster tilted his head and smiled. And continued to smile. As his mouth and jaw grew larger and wider, it enveloped the entire room, digesting everything in its wake--including Emanuel. *El Coco* would savor every last scream.

With a full belly of 'petulant child' *El Coco* slipped back into the closet. Emanuel was wrong. He wasn't ready to come out of the closet. *El Coco* was that kind of monster.

Ruschelle Dillon is a freelance writer whose efforts focus on the dark humor and the horror genres. Ms. Dillon's brand of humor has been incorporated in a wide variety of projects, including the irreverent "Caustic Cookbook" and novelette *Bone-sai*, published through Black Bed Sheet Books as well as the live-action video shorts "Don't Punch the Corpse" and "Mothman".

Her short stories have appeared in various anthologies

and online zines such as Strangely Funny III, Story Shack, and *Weird Ales*, due out in 2016.

Ruschelle lives in Johnstown with her husband Ed and the numerous critters they share their home with. When she isn't writing, she can be found teaching guitar and performing vocals and guitar in the band Ribbon Grass Acoustic Group.

Stalk her on-

https://ruschelledillon.blogspot.com/
https://www.facebook.com/ruschelle.dillon

PATIENCE MY UNSPEAKABLE NIGHTMARE
BY SYLVIA SON

Nothing weird, Nora was promised.

"You need to upgrade your home security," Deb nagged for the tenth time. After the fourth break-in in her apartment unit, Deb told her she had no choice. "If you're not careful, you'll be next."

"By getting a dog? They're just as expensive as getting a new alarm system, and I don't like dogs."

"That's okay. I know this place that sells something close to what you might need. It's better than a dog."

What was better than a dog, Nora thought? Tigers? Bears? Flying sharks? None of it sounded reassuring.

"How different? It's not illegal or anything?"

"No," she hesitated to elaborate. "Not illegal. Different. It's downtown next to this vintage record store. It specializes in exotic life forms that are compatible to your needs. Trust me. It's totally legit."

"All right." What choice did she have? "As long as it's not weird or anything."

She imagined a back end place with dangerous looking sign and dangerous-looking people hanging out in the front with who knows what in wooden crates.

Her suspicion was half rewarded as they stood in front of the store.

The place to be truthful was a dump. Situated in the more rundown part of the city. There was even graffiti on the side. Someone had spray painted a series of loops and geometric shapes all over the stained brick store. On the door there was a sign that said Everything Pets, but the front windows were painted over.

"Are you sure about this?" For the fifth time.

"Just get in." and she shoved her through the door.

At the front counter, a man was polishing the metal studs on a dog collar. He stopped polishing as soon as the door opened.

"Hello, I'm Vic," the seller said. "Are you looking for something?"

Deb cut in. "Yes. You see," she ignored Nora's constant poking at her shoulder, "My friend here needs one of your special breeds for home security."

"I understand." He stepped out from behind the counter and led them to the back. They walked past bags of dog food and the further away they were from the front, the more nervous Nora became, believing she was going set up into a trap.

They ended up standing in front of a playpen in the corner and there were mutterings from inside. The clerk stood by the pen.

"That's it?" Nora said. She kept a certain distance away.

"Yup. You can pick any one you like."

Nora took a step forward and leaped back when she heard a low "rah rah" and almost collided into Deb.

"Whoa! Nora, would you relax? I don't think they bite."

"Oh they bite," the seller said enthusiastically.

Now Nora wasn't so reassured about doing this anymore, but she would feel like an idiot if she backed out now.

She carefully inched herself back to the pen and peered over the edge and hoped to God it wasn't perverse.

Actually, it was not what she expected.

All over the floor of the pen were several pulsating basketballs covered in shaggy brown, dark brown or black hair.

"They're not what I expected," she said out loud.

The seller took that as a personal offence. "What were you expecting?"

Nora didn't know. Tentacles? Claws? "I don't know-- whoa!" She pointed back in the pen.

As if on cue, one of those basketballs rolled on its own and two bird feet pushed out from its body from one end and two feathered antennae uncurled from the other end. Bright red eyes popped open and a mouth that was as wide as it body opened and exposed huge set of teeth. It looked up and down its surroundings, then stopped to stare at Nora and barked at her. Rolling itself onto its feet, it ran around in circles, bumping into other sleeping basketballs, which startled them quite violently. Now there was a playpen full of bouncing balls, yapping as if the floor were electrified.

"What did you do?" Deb accused.

"Nothing," Nora shot back and backed away.

"You must have startled them."

"I didn't," she pointed at the first one to freak out. "He. She. It did that."

Vic waved the concern off with a shrug. "Don't sweat it. They get excitable a lot."

Completely unfazed by the little monsters losing their little minds, he picked up a medium-sized plastic bag of candy. He scooped up a handful of gummy bears and scattered it all over them. The hairballs stopped what they were doing, stared at the gummy candies, and immediately scooped them up with their tongues.

"See that? Candy calms them down. Gummy bears are the best." And just like that they were all asleep purring like kittens. "They'll nap for hours."

"Wow," Nora said. She looked at them and thought they were cute, snoring like that. Then in one corner, she saw one who didn't eat the candy and recognized it as the one that caused all the chaos. "What are they?"

"Dunno. The University is still busy trying to classify it.

But they're relatively harmless. The guys classified them as Nightmares. Your small garden variety ones. Don't know why. I didn't name them."

"Where did you get them? Is it even legal?"

"Um, that's complicated," was the best explanation he could come up with. He leaned casually over the rim of the pen. "A few years ago I knew a guy who traveled around parallel worlds for exotic animals for sale. He ended up in one of those dark dimensions and picked up a couple of specimens. Ergo these critters. Almost legal. As long as we don't eat them."

That didn't reassure Nora, but she wasn't in a position to judge or go to someone about this. "Aren't you concerned about customs or even contamination? Or the legal cost of processing?"

The blank look he gave revealed how much or how little he thought about it. "Look, lady. I sell these. They don't give off poisonous gases or venoms or pollutants or even toxic waste and they're relatively easy to handle."

"So," Deb said. "What did you call them again?"

"Nightmares."

"Nightmares." Deb tested the words to those hyper hairballs. "What does that mean?"

"You'll find out." He reached down and scooped up a sleeping nightmare and plunked it into Nora's arms against her will before she could back away.

She never realized a nightmare could feel so warm. And so purry. It actually cooed in its sleep. Do nightmares dream? She rocked it back and forth as if were a baby.

"So," Deb said but in a whisper. "What do you think? Cool, right?"

Nora gave the one shoulder shrug. Sure it was cute and seemingly sedate, but she wasn't sure what to expect with a nightmare. Could she trust one of these things to be a guard pet and companion?

"I guess. Seems tame enough, but are they trainable?" The

sleeping creature in her arms twitched slightly.

"Of course, they're very intelligent."

"Okay, I'll take this one."

"Oh no." He gently but firmly pried the nightmare from her arms and put it back in its holding pen. "For your needs, you don't want that one."

"Why not?"

"One. This one is rather calm, too calm for what you need."

"Isn't that the point?" she shot back. She wasn't willing to take on anything that difficult to train. So yes, call her a little lazy, but she didn't want to spend too much time and energy training one. It was one of the reasons why she'd never bothered to get a cat, when she kind of sort of wanted one. "A calmer one would be easier to housebreak and be left on its own when I'm at work."

"Not necessary," he said and deposited the purring one onto the pen and reached down. Nora chanted in her head, please don't get the screaming one and groaned when he did. It squirmed and tried to claw at the floor as it tried to escape Vic.

"No."

"It's not that bad."

"Not that one."

"Why not? Look, see?" He held it up at eye level to her. Its face contorted in pure terror and then rage and barked at her.

Nora backed away and plugged her ears. "Get that out of my face. Why can't I get the quiet one?" She pointed to the one she had held minutes ago.

"No, no, that's not the one for you. And to be honest most of them, on average, are kind of slow to train. They're pleasant but rather dumb. From what I can tell you need something with a bit more personality and intelligence, and best of all it only poops once a week. So you only have to change the litter box once a week."

Once a week. That was a plus, Nora thought. But she dreaded how much after one week of holding it all in. But despite that, it didn't change the fact it was a nightmare screaming in her face.

"That's tempting, but I can only imagine the size of the poop it produces and what kind of stuff it excretes. Nothing weird or anything?"

"Well," he dragged that word nice and long. Yeah she thought so. "Creatures like that from another dimension have their own physical reality, so they usually poop edible glass marbles that make you see through space or mini black holes condensed in a cube. But fortunately for you, as part of our service plan, we send in a guy to pick it up. Here." He literally dumped it into her arms.

She tried to push it back, but he stepped away and she was forced to hold a nightmare in her arms. Nora looked down at the nightmare, and the nightmare looked back up at her. She held her breath and tried to remain still. The nightmare wiggled about and shifted its entire head to place its mouth on her arm, which it gummed rather sloppily.

Ugh, gross, Nora thought.

"See," Vic said. "It likes you."

More like it liked to taste her. It gummed a couple more times, then gave up and curled itself into a ball. Well, she thought, at least it didn't pee on her.

"So. Cash or card?"

By some miracle it remained quiet during the whole trip home. It was luck that she avoided everyone, including Mrs. Katts, who might have had the misfortune of being curious and peering through the bars.

She gently lowered the cage onto the coffee table. She peeked inside. It was rolled up into a ball. Thank God, it was still asleep.

She sat down and opened the manual. She flipped open to the first page.

Owning a Nightmare. Good luck.

Well at least, they were honest.

The first rule to handling a nightmare is let them know who's boss. So be The Boss.

That sounded straight forward enough. Great. Now tell me oh wise and powerful manual, she thought. How? She flipped to the next page.

Rule 2. Nightmares are relatively easy to feed. They'll eat--

Whoa wait a sec. She flipped back to the previous rule. Was there a missing page? She held the pamphlet by the spine and shook it. Nothing fell out. She opened to a random page.

Rule 43. Pick a name, and a pick a good one. That will neutralize any negative auras it builds up, because obviously it's a Nightmare and it's tempted to be an annoying one.

She flipped back to the first two pages. Where was the pertinent information?

...Eats meat, grains, plants, eggs. . . Basically anything. They're not picky.

That's it? She flipped thru the pages, front to back, and still nothing.

"Are you kidding me?" She checked the index page. It had no index page or table of contents. She slowly squeezed the pamphlet into a tube and flung it against the wall with a thump. The noise must have awoken the nightmare, because the plastic box shifted and jumped, moving closer to the edge of the coffee table until it fell off. Nora jumped back in shock, afraid if the bars popped open. A low muttering growl emanated from inside.

Nora went over to the small cage and peered in to see how awake the nightmare was. The mutterings started to get quieter and quieter, until it became one continuous chant of muh muh muhs. Was that normal? Nora couldn't tell what it was doing.

Her head was half a foot away from the case when the nightmare let out a loud roar. Nora recoiled three steps back so sharply from the sound, she tripped on her feet and fell backwards and bumped her head against the wall. Inside the box, the nightmare made a cooing noise. Nora could have sworn it was enjoying itself at her expense.

"You did that on purpose, didn't you?"

Since the nightmare couldn't or wouldn't answer back, she just assumed it did. She wanted to kick the carrying case to teach it a lesson, but with her luck it might set it free.

The manual was by her leg, and she checked to see if that was a normal behavior for a nightmare.

She flipped through a random page.

Rule 3. Nightmares can be jerks if not under control. Refer back to Rule One.

"Now it tells me that," Nora said miserably. And it still didn't specify how to keep it in line.

Rule 14. Do not damage the containment box. It is laced with barrier spells and prevents it from breaking free.

A prison. That's one good thing--

But keep in mind. It still won't stop it from being annoying. It is still an intelligent and sentient creature so Rule 1, 3, 5, 6, 7, 13 and 17 still apply.

Terrific. Basically, she still had to let it out and "deal" with it. But right now, it was acting like it was the boss in this relationship.

"Okay." She stood up and walked over to the carrying case, and realized she didn't have a name for it yet. "You..." She held back the urge to strangle it by wherever its neck was. "Are you going to behave? Because I'm the boss, got it?"

"Bleah," it said.

"Are you going to behave?"

Silence. It stopped muttering.

"Is that a yes? Well?"

It stuck its tongue out at her.

"I'll take that as a yes."

She slowly unlatched the door and took a step back.

Fifteen seconds of silence, then the nightmare rolled out

with a thump into the wall.

Nora took another step back from her nightmare as it slowly uncurled feet and antennae. It twitched and turned its head left and right sniffing around the floor. The nightmare stopped itself and stared at Nora.

"Hey," Nora said lamely and waved at it.

The nightmare curled into a ball and rolled itself towards her.

"Ah! Keep away!"

The nightmare stopped a foot away from her and looked up. Then it sniffed the ground at her feet and grimaced.

"Well I'm sorry my floor is not pristine enough for you."

It continued sniffing along the floor and paused for a couple of seconds, then resumed its scent trail. Nora followed after it as it scurried along the floor until it reached the couch. The nightmare took two sniffs along the fabric, then proceeded to gnaw on the corner.

"Stop that!" She ran to the couch with a rolled up newspaper and smacked it several times against her hand. It looked at her and then the newspaper, and ran.

"Wait!" She cornered it against the wall and couch, and as soon as she reached for it, the nightmare slipped under the couch.

Nora lowered her head to peer through the space under the couch. Two red eyes stared back at her. How was it possible for that nightmare to squeeze itself under there? She grabbed the manual and flipped through the pages.

Rule 22. Nightmares are agile and have collapsible bones.

"Collapsible bones? That's weird, and ew." She jammed her hand underneath, and the nightmare scurried further away.

"Aw come on..." she stopped herself, realizing she hadn't named it yet.

"Okay, fine. Suit yourself." She was too tired to try to reason with a nightmare.

Against her better judgement, Nora left her nightmare alone while she went to work. And when she returned, she was surprised the place was still in one piece, which probably meant her monster was still hiding under her couch. She knelt down and then spread flat on the floor to stare at her nightmare. "All right, you." She still didn't have a name for it yet. "You are really trying my patience." Nora stopped herself. Patience. It wasn't the coolest sounding name, but it was apt, since it was driving her patience up the wall and it was the perfect adjective to negate the negative mojo the manual had warned against.

"Patience," Nora tested the name out loud. Eh, good enough. "Your name is now Patience."

Patience stared and then narrowed its eyes at her. "Bleah!" Patience said.

"Well, tough. The manual said I name you and that's your name for now on. I name thee Patience. So deal with it."

Patience's response was to shift and move its body until it actually turned its back to her. Nora dropped her head to the floor in resignation. This was going to take a while.

For the rest of the day, Nora decided that she would ignore Patience until it decided to behave like a proper pet. She wasn't going to move the couch and drag it out. If it wanted to eat, it would come out on its own. She had enough experience with cats to assume that. She ignored the stubborn furry lump and stirred the macaroni on the stove and heated the pan of beef stew on another burner. Briefly, she glanced to the side to see if there was any movement from under there.

Nothing. Not a peep.

"I hope you like beef stew," she said to the couch. "I forgot to pick up dog or cat food or whatever monsters eat at the pet store. So..."

She spooned the stew onto a plate and walked to the couch. The thing underneath didn't say anything.

She tapped her foot against the couch leg. "Patience, are

you still under there?" Nora took the silence as sullenness and kept on talking. "I have lunch."

Still no response.

Nora sighed heavily. "Aw, come on." She sank down onto floor next to the couch. "You are not being fair. What do you want from me? Do you want to go home? Honestly, I don't know where or how." She shoved the plate to the edge of the couch. "Eat. I may not be what you want, but we might as well make the best of it, so eat or don't. That's up to you."

She sat down on the couch and dug into her macaroni and cheese and turned on the TV. "I hope you like The Simpsons." Patience didn't respond, and Nora took that as a yes.

Going to bed was an ordeal. As soon as she walked into the bedroom she forgot for a second that there was someone else in the apartment because she left the door open. She climbed into the bed and closed her eyes. She opened them and thought she had forgotten something. Then she heard it.

"Muh muh muh…"

She sat up and stared at the open door. She scrambled out of the bed and slammed the door shut and locked it. Still unsatisfied, she jammed a chair under the doorknob and shoved some socks and a scarf under the space under the door.

She spent the rest of the night hidden under the covers with her cellphone next to her hand to call 911 the moment the nightmare broke the door down.

By Day Seven, she reached her breaking point.

"Okay!" she yelled at the couch. "I've had it up it up to here," she held her hand up to her neck. "With this. Look, I know this isn't ideal, but we're stuck with each other. Are you even listening to me?" She kicked a couple times on the cushions. "I don't like the ideal of explaining to the super the smell of dead nightmare because you starved yourself to death. So come out, right now. Well?"

Nothing. Nora thought or at least assumed it was doing it

to be defiant. Even though she knew it wasn't a dog, she thought it was worth a shot. And since it wasn't going to do what she ordered, she was going to have to be less subtle.

She grabbed onto the armrest and pulled and pulled at it until the couch was two feet away from the wall. She climbed over the back and looked down. It was curled up into a ball.

"Ah hah!" she said, and leaned down to grab it. Patience bugged its eyes out and proceeded to roll and run at the same time, barely dodging her hand by inches. "Crap!" She nearly toppled over. It kept on rolling across the floor. "Get back here!" She chased after it.

Nora moved to the right, Patience rolled to the left. And when she moved to the left, it leaped onto the coffee table. It scurried across the surface with its feet until it reached the edge and then slipped off and fell with a thud. For several seconds there was complete silence.

Oh shit, Nora thought. She ran to the other side. Was it injured? Dead? It couldn't die, could it? She didn't bother to go back to the manual to see if it could be easily injured, she just ran to her nightmare.

The nightmare was lying at the foot of the coffee table on its side. Its eyes were closed, and its tongue was hanging from the side of its mouth.

"Oh crap, I killed it." She didn't mean to. It just happened. How was she going to explain this to the pet store when they came to pick up its poop? They were going to think she was a monster killer. Sure, it was annoying, but it didn't deserve to die.

She bent down and gently touched the side of its head. Immediately its eyes popped open, and Nora fell backwards onto her butt. Starring at the now awake nightmare, she wasn't sure if this was a good thing or a bad thing.

Patience scrunched its eyes and mouth up tight and then it began to whimper and moan.

"Oh no, please don't cry, Patience." She scooped it up into

her arms. She didn't think it might try to escape or bite her. She held it and examined the head/body for injuries. She carefully turned its head/body around, and gently parted through the fur and found a small red bump.

She rocked and cooed, trying to soothe it. She grabbed a first aid kit on her bookshelf and sat down on the couch, carrying the nightmare in one arm. "Okay, okay, Patience, don't panic. It's just an itty bitty bump." She opened the first aid kit and cradled Patience with one arm. She smoothed out the fur to expose Patience's bump, and dabbed it slightly with a cotton ball soaked with alcohol to clean the area.

"Okay," she said and uncapped a tube of Polysporin. "It's going to sting a bit, so don't bite me." She dabbed the ointment on the small abrasion. Nora expected any second for it to squirm, writhe about, or bark at her. Eerily, Patience was quiet and behaved.

Once she was finished, Patience moved its body so that it was face to face to her. It was actually disconcerting for those red eyes to stare back at her.

"Uh hi," she said. "Remember me? I tended to your wounds."

The nightmare blinked and stared for thirty seconds. Nora hoped it understood a truce or, at the very least, gratitude. Patience's toes curled and uncurled themselves five times, then it pushed its body up, rolled off her lap, and pushed its body next to her.

It purred, and Nora hoped this meant it liked her and wouldn't give her any more trouble.

Famous last words.

After she had healed it, it began to follow her around. It trailed at her heels as she walked to the bathroom.

"No!" she said. "Wait. Hold. Heel." She firmly pushed it out of the room with her foot and closed the door. Geez, it was just as bad as a cat.

When she went to the kitchen to make dinner, Nora could hear the tiny click of nails on the hardwood floor as Patience pattered after. When she stood by the counter, opening a jar, it weaved around her ankles, then jumped up and down and made yipping noises.

"Hold on, hold on," Nora said to the jumping nightmare. 'I'm fixing dinner." She decided to make spaghetti for both of them.

The moment she said dinner, the nightmare bounced even faster.

As soon as she placed her plate on the table and its plate on the floor next to the bowl of water, it barely waited ten seconds. It tore into its meal and slurped its water messily.

"Wow, Patience, you were hungry." As soon as it finished, its mouth was completely clean. No stray sauce, or even wet fur.

"At least you're clean."

Nora drew the line when she climbed into bed. Patience hopped up and walked around in small circles, then burrowed its body down on the blanket. She was not going to sleep with a dimensional monster. That would be too weird.

"No, not on the bed." She pointed on the floor. Nora didn't know how, but Patience somehow widened its eyes and trembled its mouth while making small whimpering noises.

She sighed in resignation. "Okay, fine. But just for tonight. Tomorrow, I'm getting one of those pet beds." She pulled at the blanket over her shoulder and sighed dramatically.

"Don't you dare eat me."

Patience didn't respond; it was already asleep.

Nora stared up at the ceiling. Was it possible for nightmares to have separation anxiety? So much for home security. She was expecting something a little tougher.

Around two in the morning, Nora woke to the sound of a thump. She thought she'd accidentally kicked Patience out of bed with her foot. She lifted her head and saw it was still in a ball asleep, but it woke seconds after Nora sat up.

Nora froze when she heard a glass break outside her room. Oh shit, another break-in and worst of all, she was here to witness it in her bedroom and her bat was outside her room. Even worse, the footsteps were getting closer to her room.

"Patience," she whispered. Panic was replaced with the realization that this was what she bought the nightmare for, but now that she looked at the little fuzz ball she wasn't so confident with its ability to deal with full-sized intruders. God, she thought why did she agree to buy a small one? If Patience confronted the intruder, it might get killed.

The footsteps stopped at her door. Thoughts of getting robbed, raped, and then murdered ran through her mind. She reached for her cellphone. Patience hopped off the bed.

"Patience, no!" she whispered.

Not heeding her warning, it scurried to the door. Then it slowly shimmied its head and most of its body under the space of the door until its feet and butt remained. It wriggled two more times, and Patience's entire body slipped entirely under the door and to the other side.

From behind the door Nora heard this:

"What the--?" A male's voice.

"Rawr!"

"Oh my god! Ahhhh!" There was a thunk, then a wet crunch, and then silence.

"Patience?" Nora climbed out of bed and opened the door. She couldn't block out the image that the intruder had clubbed her poor nightmare to death.

The hall was empty. Nora looked down. Patience was standing next to a bag that had a crowbar and a knife on top.

It looked up and smiled in satisfaction.

"Patience?" Did the burglar run away? There were no blood trails on the floor. She walked to the front door; it was closed. She went back to check on Patience, and had to ask the question out loud.

"Where did he go?"

Patience's response? It burped, and out from its mouth came a baseball cap.

She wasn't sure how was she supposed to explain this to the cops.

Sorry, officer, but my nightmare ate the intruder before I could call you.

She knelt down and patted Patience on the head. "Good nightmare," was all she could say. But at least it solved her home security problems.

Sylvia Son is a writer that lives in Mississauga. She has a degree in English from York University. Her novella, *The Guest of Honour*, made the shortlist in the 2014 Ken Klonsky Novella Contest for Quattro Books. She likes horror movies, improv, and board games, but not at the same time — although she has played *Ultimate Werewolf* and it's sort of the same thing.

MINETTE DANCES WITH THE GOLEM OF ALBANY
BY PAUL WARTENBERG

I'm wasting time shouting at the deejay. He pretends to nod and shake his head in alternate turns, before sliding his headphones over his ears and turning up this lousy German technobeat to full volume.

I don't care if this jerk thinks he's being edgy by ignoring the dance hits of 1985. I just want him to play my favorite song. It's not like I'm asking for Madonna or some disco hit seven years ago. It shouldn't be this hard to get Laura Branigan's "Self Control" purring through the dance club's speakers.

I love that song. I can't help it, it speaks to me. I do live among the creatures of the night. Humans, too.

The dance floor here is swarming with them, all movement and heartbeat and breath and warmth. It's in the middle of a two-story space, balconies with chrome railing circling above. The night club is new; think I read it opened a month ago, definitely owned by someone who's so in love with neon lighting they likely didn't save enough money for the cognac or bourbon. Decent turnout, but I give it about six weeks before it closes due to that rampant drug dealing in the ladies' bathroom. I can smell it from here. Not even good quality powder, either.

I look for my lovers. I see Caden upstairs flirting with a pair of young women in Lycra shorts, lace stockings that go all the way up, and unbuttoned short-sleeved jackets hiding slim attractive bodies. They're college age, roommates because they're so dissimilar physically. He's holding a pool cue; guess there's some billiards set up on that floor. Nice. If there are any healthy males up there I might flirt with myself, I can use a little hustling as part of the fun.

It takes me more time to spot Kimber working an older couple sitting at a table near the bar. From here it looks like she's tagged a married couple, healthy-looking but aging, out for a night's fling to stir some excitement in their mid-life crises. Hmm. Either way, this night's hunt for stimulation can scratch the urges coursing through my blood. Both ways, ahhhh, very tempting but I've seen the confusion from throwing too many players into an orgy before their mindsets are properly set...

Oh no. Gods help me. I see him. He's staring right at me, and I can tell why. Not that he should be attracted to me like that, despite my youthful sexual appearance. He shouldn't be able to smell my scent, not in a crowd already this sweaty and active. If my pheromones are doing anything in this crowd of humans, it'd work them all up into an exuberant unfocused craving. No, that's not him at all by that glare in his perfect glass eyes. It's a look of a predator fixated on prey.

Dammit. I've got a Golem on me tonight. Not at all good.

I can tell he's a Golem. There's always something off about the face between the eyebrow ridge and the nose. None of the crafters can ever get that right. This one's different, though. His red skin stands out underneath that Army surplus clothing like a prolonged reckless all-day visit to a tanning salon. Nobody's bothering him about it though; being that tall and that broad-shouldered, I'm guessing the club crowd is mistaking him for one of the bouncers.

He's just standing there on the edge of the crowd that's circling the dance floor. Nothing is stopping him from marching towards me to start an attack. I take that back; something is stopping him, and I need to figure that out right now.

Fortune favors the bold, my mother told me four lifetimes

ago. If he's not attacking me right now, I can risk this.

I slide between the warm bodies, making my way through the dancing throng toward him. His glare remains intense as I get within an arm's length of him. I'm at his mercy right now. We wait as the song finally ends and there's a minute of buzzing as the deejay annoys tonight's crowd with a lame joke.

I smile with the comfort of knowing that for the moment I'm safe. I'm going to see if this one's smart enough to answer questions. "Are you here to capture me or kill me?"

The Golem does not blink. I've never known one made to do that. Up close, those eyes of his are a marvel of sculpting, glass baubles masquerading as puppy blues. He responds with a noticeable Southern drawl. "My orders are to kill you."

I glance about the club. "I guess you can't do that in front of an audience, can you?"

"I am here to kill only you. My orders do not say to kill others." The accent is clearly Deep South, but the pronunciation and word use are scholarly, proper.

"A Golem with a conscience." I say it but I'm doubting it. It's more likely practical concerns. Golems don't have a conscience, or souls. Some of them, though, they can think and reason. Like this one. I can deal with this one. "Do you have a name?"

"My maker did not require to grant me a name. It is not needed for me to obey."

"Well, what is needed for you to obey?" Standing this close, I can examine his forehead. Okay, he doesn't have the Hebrew script tattooed there, so no Aleph to remove to stop him. "Aha, you're the type with the scroll rolled up under that tongue of yours, yes?"

The Golem tilts his head as though debating if he should be open enough to discuss this matter. He tilts it again as though my questions are really something he isn't expecting. Poor twitchy golems. This is what happens when rabbis fail to build these guys to blink like normal people. "Why are you talking to me?"

"Because I don't want to die and you don't want to kill." The speakers in the club thrum with a hard backbeat, a new song stirring up the crowd into a fresh rhythm. "Here. Dance with me."

I take his hand. It's red clay all right, solid yet soft. One tug on his arm does nothing. He is big and bulky, after all. The second tug convinces him to follow me through the throng onto the wood floor.

I start with a simple shimmy. "Tell me you know some moves."

The Golem just stands there, imposing. He looks at the others around us; I can tell he's thinking this is a trick. "I do not dance."

"Not true. I think everyone can dance." I twirl arms up, circling him, bumping my hip against his.

"I see." He makes an effort to move his legs. I watch him kick one leg out a few inches, then lift the other, back and forth. The Frankenstein. How appropriate.

I feel soft hands on my shoulders. I don't need to turn to know it's Kimber coming in to join me on the floor. "Hey lover," she whispers in my ear, close enough to kiss. "Is this guy part of the plans tonight?"

I turn to face her, placing my hands on her hips, and she does the same as we start to partner. "Change of plans, Kimmy. I may have to let you and Caden roam free for the rest of the evening."

"I don't think Caden's eager to let this guy bother you." Kimber looks upward.

I follow her stare to the upper railing where Caden stands, both hands on the chrome bar. He looks like he's willing to jump right down and make himself useful. I shake my head at him. I know he's trying to be the honorable defensive boyfriend – it's a reason to keep him – but he's hopeless against this threat.

I return my attention to Kimber. "Kiss him for me." I lean in and kiss her as well, long and passionate on her lips. I have no illusions this could be a bad night for me. She's warm and tastes of scotch. I hear some cheering from the nearby perverts but that doesn't bother me for the moment. I part from her, feeling her breath on my face. "Keep him safe. This is something I have to do."

Kimber nods and slips her arms from me, stepping away from the floor and hurrying to the stairs. I return my attention to the Golem. "Okay. This needs to be an early night for me, it seems. Let's find another place to dance."

It takes finding a quiet street about three blocks away from the night club. There are no shops open, no apartments or dwellings, almost no foot traffic involving the locals.

"So how bad does your Maker want me dead?" I ask as I move a little faster in my steps, creating distance between myself and the Golem.

"He is not my Maker, but my Master." The Golem slows his steps. He's going to play to his strengths.

Golems make excellent hunters of my kind. Dhampyrs may have speed and power, but that's nothing against a persistent and unstoppable opponent. There's no real life to take, no blood to drink, no way to wound him and keep him down.

There's nothing to stop him once an order's given. I could get on a plane and fly to anywhere in the world; that Golem will follow me, even if it takes a lifetime. I can try to dance and keep away from him, but all he will need is one second grabbing onto me and every physical advantage I have is gone.

"Very well." I toss my hand purse atop a car's roof and kick off my high-heels. I need to unencumber myself. "Let's dance."

All my awareness becomes fire. Caden likes to call it "dialing it up to eleven" when I described the sensation to him, I don't know from where he got the phrase. My vision, my hearing, my scent, my touch all speed up as I speed up. Taste doesn't help me at the moment.

I leap, jumping to and fro, seeing how the Golem moves. He merely reaches down with his red clay hand and touches the street.

Pavement turns from solid to a wave, rippling outward, rushing towards me. I see it coming and jump higher than the rocks and bits splitting from the surface at the speed of a bullet.

"Clever," I shout down from the narrow banister of a darkened building. "But you really shouldn't leave the streets in a bad shape. The city's budget is just not up for fixing a lot of potholes nowadays."

"Thank you." I am after all dealing with a conscientious Golem here. His touch makes the street surface respond to him, and the ripples and cracks formed by his attack smooth down. I think he actually improved on it. If I survive this I have to ask the local high temple priests about making a few of these guys and lending them out for repair work. Oh, I forgot. The unions would object.

I watch the Golem approach the building where I'm perched. I know he's going to make the building answer to his command to strike me, so I jump across the space of the city canyon. The opposite building has fire escapes crossing the facade, and I grab onto the railing and swing my body higher.

I look down at that Golem, considering my options. Can't bury him; he'll merge with the dirt and use it to attack. Can't drown him, water will only soften his clay and he'll squeeze the excess like a pressed sponge when he gets out. Arrows, back in the day, were laughable. Bullets today, just as much. With a sword, I could cut him into pieces, and he would pull himself together.

My father – monster hunter that he was before he retired to that college – showed me twice how to deal with a Golem.

One of the ways back then was heat and lots of it. It would be nice to find a kiln to drop him into; pity there's not one handy. Despite it being hot and sweaty on that dance floor back at the night club, that's not hot enough.

That means I need to use the second way.

"You know these attacks can hurt other people if you're not careful," I shout down at the Golem as I climb towards the rooftop.

He's crossing the street, having looked both ways for traffic. Once he reaches the sidewalk he looks up at me. "That is why I am being careful."

I dangle from the ledge when I reach the top, staring down at him. "Did your Master order you to bring back proof you got me?"

The Golem does his head tilt thinking gesture again. I swear I see a slight upward curl of his lips. "Yes. The Master ordered me to bring your head and your heart."

"Gruesome, but unsurprising." Usually, Golems are reliable enough to follow an order to the letter and comma placement. But always look for their doubting soul-driven owners to question that dedication to duty.

I push my legs against the brick and mortar of the building to fly outward, tumbling into space. It's not like I can fly: as the young ones say "Get real." Dhampyrs just jump well and land on our feet. Good thing I kicked off my high heels during this dance; landing on those things now would be a pain.

My agility and senses accelerate to match my heartbeat, and then faster as I approach the sidewalk. My body twists feet first to the ground, and I bend at the knees, then the hips, angling one arm down to perfect a three-point landing. I sense the cracks in the concrete where I land, but nothing in the way of debris exploding outward, there's not enough impact force for that.

My senses return to normal speed as I stand. The Golem shifts his body to face me, and leans one hand against the building. I stay alert; he may use that structure as an attack.

I raise both arms to him as a gesture of goodwill. "Your Master didn't specify I had to be completely absolutely dead when you bring him my head and heart, I take it?"

The Golem does not respond right away. He pulls his clay fingers into a clawing scrape against the brick. "I am thinking about your question," he states with caution in his tone. "You are planning to talk me into taking you alive to the Master. That is out of the question. You will try to kill him if I do that."

Interesting that he keeps referring to a Master and not Maker. "I can promise you I won't kill him." I keep my hands up. "You are familiar with the oaths?"

"There are several I know."

"What is your name?"

The Golem shakes his head. "I told you. I never had a name. I have no need."

"Then where were you forged, where is the clay from which you rose?"

He pauses before answering. "The City of Albany, Georgia." It explains that accent, if not the crisp enunciation.

I speak as calm and direct as I was taught. "This I vow to the fire, this I vow to the wind, this I vow to the river, this I vow to the stone. This I vow to the Golem of Albany, I will not kill your Master, not this day or any other."

He drops his arm from the wall. "I know that vow."

"Thank you then, Mr. Albany." I lower my arms as well. "Now you can take my head and my heart and all the other intact body parts to your Master now."

"That is not my name." It's not that he's offended by it, just annoyed.

"I need to call you something."

"No, you do not."

"I will refrain from that, then." I smile, trying to keep him in a good mood as well as soulless automatons can be. "Please lead on."

The taxi I waved down in Manhattan drops the two of us in front of an unpleasant-looking office building in Queens. The driver's an aging ugly Irishman, so I don't kiss him as part of the tip. I do let him inhale enough of my body scent to stay aroused for the rest of the night, well into whenever he gets home to pleasure his unsuspecting wife.

"I had tokens," The Golem repeats what he's been saying the whole ride to here, holding out the oddly shaped coinage of the realm. Sad truth about them, these clay boys can get single-minded about things.

"I had money," I answer with a friendly gleam of my sharp canines, tapping him on his broad shoulder with my hand purse. "I'm a vampire in New York; I'm rich and can flaunt it. Besides, if we get on the subways, we're dealing with others who might jump in, ruin the evening."

"You are not referring to the citizenry," he says, "you are referring to others of your kind."

"Our kind," I emphasize, "and I take it you've met some of them already. Depending on how long you've been in town."

The Golem pauses like he's been whenever he gets a probing statement from me. "We have been here in the city for some time. I should not say for how long."

"Fair enough." I gesture to the darkened nine-story office edifice the Golem gave the taxi driver as our destination. "If you have the key to let us in, please guide the way."

I'm able to see the directory of floors and listed businesses near the elevator once we get inside. It's dimly lit, due to half the light fixtures being empty. A quick inhale of the air as the car arrives and the door slides open lets me know how many people are still inside this structure. Just three humans, although I'm not sure which floor yet.

The inhuman scent mixed in with the human, I pick that up strong and certain. Certain of who it is. The bastard.

It's one of those old slow elevators, so I take the moment

143

to keep probing with questions. Any driblet of information will help. "I got to ask you: why did the rabbi who made you, well, make you?"

The Golem did not look at me, even though I was standing right there next to his elbow. "The Maker summoned me, made me to protect the assembly foremost. The Synagogue first, but then the city itself."

"Protect it from what?"

"The war."

My eyes go wide. "The Civil War?"

"What?" The Golem finally turns his head toward me, those glass eyes rolling in their sockets just a bit before he realigns his vision. "Not that far back. Perhaps I misused a word. There was a fight between the Black humans and the Beige humans. The threat of violence was everywhere. The rabbi called upon the rituals and made me, providing the scroll of life and service. I stood at the door, among the chosen as they walked and chanted. And time passed, the fight moved elsewhere and the city calmed."

"Oh, that," I reply. "You mean the civil right marches and riots." I take a moment to remember. It wasn't that long ago by my own measurement of time, but it is such a blur to me. "What year was that?"

The Golem opens his mouth just so, then closes it. His need to blink has to be frustrating sometimes. Finally he whispers, "I did not recall the year. I never do, I just realized that."

I place a hand on his arm. "I didn't mean to upset you."

"I am not upset." His tone goes back to grim and serious. "It is just not my job to remember such things."

The elevator slowed to stop at the eighth floor, sliding open for us to exit into a darkened hall. I don't smell any humans here, which is good for what I plan to do. No interference or hostages; like the Golem, I'm not keen on bystanders getting caught in a fight.

Neither of us needs light to see where to go. Golems have

their own way of seeing, and a Dhampyr like me has all twelve senses heightened to incredible degrees. The hallway only leads in two directions, and I can tell by scent which end of the hall that bastard is waiting in.

The Golem opens the door to a dimly lit room. It's office space, but without the walls or partitions most workplaces have. I get the feeling it's something for lease that hasn't been fully furnished yet.

The only furnishing in here is a massive and ornate altar. A set of candle stands circle it as though a ritual is underway. Wax drips down half of the stands where wicks had burnt out; most of the remaining lit tapers are nearing extinguishment. I hope the place is insured, as I think the safety sprinklers are off.

The bastard I've been smelling since entering the building is lying on the altar, eyes closed, arms crossed, what I recognize as smug satisfaction radiating from his still form. The idiot doesn't even realize the Golem he sent out has returned with someone still alive. For a Dhampyr himself, he's always been this clumsy and dimwitted, and so easily caught off-guard.

"Pathetic," I announce. Lawrence has to hear me even if he hasn't heard my breathing or my heartbeat by now. The ones born this century, so lazy. Barely ever needed to hunt back when it was a necessity, never trained in the arts to survive.

Lawrence's eyes open in shock, and his reflexes make him tumble off the altar knocking one of the stands over. Lucky it's one where all the candles burnt out.

He takes a second to realize I'm standing here very much alive and pissed. Lawrence glares at the Golem. "Dammit, Bo, did you have to screw up the instructions like this?"

"That is not my name." The Golem takes that serious.

"Don't blame him," I interrupt. "Someone here forgot how mystic commands depend entirely on the exact wording of those orders."

Lawrence glowers at me, which is a good sign because it means he's gotten over his infatuation and has moved on to hate.

I leap onto the altar, showing off my legs as I twirl to a provocative sitting pose. "What are you doing back in town, Laurie? There's a protective order still in force, last I checked."

"The laws of mortals do not apply to us," he sneers, exposing a curled fang.

"You're still in that world-view, child?"

Lawrence takes a step towards me, but glares at the Golem and doesn't move any further. He's trying to figure out if he's lost control of his clay puppet. "Do not presume that I am some immature whelp, if only because my vampire father sired me two hundred years after your own birth. I should call you crone by that regard. We are immortals, Isa; to us, time is without meaning, with our passion the only redeeming flame in our eternal night."

I shake my head. He is stuck in that world-view of arrogant superiority. He never had to deal with the life experience I earned with more than a century of hiding among normals and avoiding teams of hunters. Born in a high-rise penthouse, thinking he earned the key to it. And he's stuck speaking some rehearsed speech of bad poetry at me. How many years did he have to write that dreck?

On the bright side, he's calling me by the name I used back in the Second World War. I already know how to get the Golem to stop his pursuit.

I wait on making the move. I need to give Lawrence one more lecture before I whip his backside. "You're an immature whelp, Laurie, because you've convinced yourself you own everything in your sight. You thought you owned me when we met, and you didn't learn your lesson then when I brought your petty little blood empire down and left you scrambling two steps ahead of a police manhunt."

Lawrence tries to open his mouth, but I snarl at him

before he can even think of a reply. "Shut up. The only reason I had that fling with you was because you have the stamina of all Dhampyr males, which pleased me for that weekend. Then you turned into this egomaniac who..."

"I was going to marry you!" Lawrence screams, eyes flaring red, taking three steps closer. Good.

I scream back. "You put a *collar* on me! Tried to get me to join you in killing some poor girl just hitting puberty like it was some pagan ritual of yours! And like all jerkass men, you couldn't handle the rejection!"

My senses dilate as my perception speeds up. I don't leap off the altar as much as I step off, but at the rate I'm moving I am crossing the floor towards that bastard. Fast as a heartbeat, if there was anyone in that room with a normal heartbeat to measure by.

It's rare to see a fellow vampire not react by adjusting to the same body speed, but Lawrence hasn't learned, has he? A bullish mind with a stubborn refusal to stay at peak perfection. As I'm dancing right past his arm I see in the corner of my eye his slow response, his head turning just a little bit faster as I get behind him.

By the time he's even thinking about moving as fast as I am, it's too late. I've got him, arm pressing against his neck and my other arm wrapping under his armpit and hand clasping his jaw. He's strong as I am, but I've got him pinned, bending his back ever so much to my shorter frame.

The Golem steps forward. "You promised you would not kill him."

"I did indeed promise." I press my hand hard against Lawrence's pale neck. "I didn't say anything about hurting him." I lean in to whisper loud in his ear. "And I can hurt you, despite what you've said about my frail girly body."

My ex-boyfriend doesn't need to gasp, but he does so anyway. "Bo... I command you... now. Kill... her... Kill..."

"No, now here's the thing, like I told our friend from Albany here, I'm not interested in dying anytime soon." I pull downward just enough, make Lawrence feel his spine twitching a little more. "Speaking of, I doubt any school let you study to be a rabbi, did they? So you had to get a Golem from someone else. You're not his Maker, are you?"

The Golem answers but keeps walking towards us. He's not using any tricks at the moment to attack, because he might hit my hostage. "He is not my Maker, but my Master."

"Right. So that means you picked our clay friend here off of someone else." I look at the Golem. "How did he do it? Buy you? Steal you? Did he kill your rabbi?"

The Golem stops in his tracks. "He killed him."

"And then stole you." I keep my hand on Lawrence's throat, but free my arm to work on something else. I press my body against his back, probably giving him one more thrill having me rub against him like this. Doesn't matter. This is almost finished.

"He was wasting away, in some two-bit hick town," Lawrence hisses at me over his shoulder. He doesn't seem to feel where my hand is, checking his pockets. "His Maker was using him as a study tool for other rabbis, lining him up for Halloween festivals as a freak show attraction for the local children. He has so much more potential under the will of someone stronger, smarter, more intent upon controlling the chaos of the night."

"I would like to point out, Laurie, how you're not stronger, and you're certainly not smarter." I let go of his neck and push him away. Hard, forcing him to stumble against that joke prop of his. "If you were smart you'd have learned to make your own. If you were really smart, you'd have done a better job of finding a better hiding spot."

He rubs his neck, and tries snarling again, this time showing his ill-shaped canines. "What hiding spot?"

"The one you used to keep the Golem's key on you," I answer, holding it up.

It's a pretty little thing. A dangling iron chain looping into a ring encircling an orb. A glass orb similar in size to the

Golem's artificial eyes, but uncolored. I see it's covered in minute etchings: Hebrew text intermixed with a small symbol. I am impressed by the rabbi's work; he somehow transcribed the Seal of Solomon onto it as part of the ritual.

Lawrence shows a hint of fear for a second, then bursts out laughing. "You fool! The Golem is still compelled to obey all commands given him. My order still stands, no matter what you think you can tell him!" He realizes he's giving me a little too much time to give an order than can hurt him, so he raises his hand to point at me. "Bo, kill this stupid bitch before she utters another word."

"I cannot follow that order, so she can keep speaking if she likes," the Golem answers. He returns his attention to me and resumes walking. "I do, of course, need to fulfill the original order while doing so."

I take a few steps back, panicking a little bit. Okay, so this was a risky move. But I can still win this. I start circling the room, swirling with purpose trying to get back to the hand purse I've left on the altar. "Golem of Albany, I hereby command you to repeat the exact order Lawrence gave you regarding me."

The Golem keeps walking, but he responds. He repeats the order as exactly as he can, which means he talks in Lawrence's speech pattern. "Golem Bo, I am ordering you to begin your search in this city of New York, across all five boroughs and beyond if need be, to hunt down this woman Isabella DeJouie, with this specific appearance from this picture I need you to memorize. I am ordering you to find Isabella DeJouie, for she is no woman but a vampire, a night creature, to kill her, to bring to me her head and her heart. Now go."

"Good impression," I tell the Golem.

"Thank you," he answers with a nod as he keeps marching in my direction, which keeps changing as I've gone back to doing our dance. "I have excellent hearing and vocal control."

I reach the altar, with Lawrence on the other side offering me a twisted grin. I grab the hand purse before he realizes why I'm there. "How's your catching skills?" I toss the hand purse at the Golem.

He can move as fast as regular people when he needs to, and the Golem does a good job catching with both hands. "Is this a weapon?" he asks.

"Yes." I answer. "Open it."

The Golem peers inside. "What am I looking for?"

"There's a locket in there. And my wallet. You can look at both."

The Golem's clay face shuffles into a glower, but he reaches inside and pulls out the necklace. He flips it open. "Who is this?"

"You're looking at a painting of an old boyfriend of mine," I reply. "A dashing figure from the wars of independence across Nineteenth Century Europe, a Bohemian gentleman name of Ernest." I sigh. "A long time ago. Long time. That there is my heart."

The Golem's expression changes when he looks at me. Somewhere along the way, he learned some touch of pity. "I understand. And for the wallet?"

"Look for my driver's license." I turn to grin at Lawrence. "He asked for my heart and my head. My photo's a head shot, you can use that to present to him."

My mistake of a romantic partner slams both hands to the altar's surface, cracking the cheap concrete. "You'd do well to remember that the order I gave Bo is to kill you. Bring you dead to my feet, you whore."

"Technicalities," I smirk back. "Check the name on that ID."

The Golem looks at it, then looks at Lawrence. "The name on the license says Minette Van Austen."

Lawrence's body language wavers. "That changes nothing, she's..."

"That's my real name," I interrupt him again. "Isabella

DeJouie was an identity crafted to fake a death back when I needed to, standard practice for immortals." I grin. "It's not *my* fault you didn't do any research before giving the order."

The Golem's voice boomed throughout the near-empty room. "Agreed."

His feet stomp against the floor, shaking the altar and driving Lawrence back in fear. "The order is impossible to resolve, as the name no longer exists. All other aspects of the order are invalid. I now answer to the person in possession of my Maker's key."

Lawrence steps back more hurried than before. "Impossible, no. Isa... I mean Minette. Give me my key back."

"It's not yours, it belongs to that rabbi you killed to get it." I walk the other way, towards the Golem. "And how do you think this poor thing feels about it?"

"I feel nothing." As he says this, I can hear the dark tone in his voice. "But I remember his compassion to his people and his city of Albany."

I turn and glare at Lawrence. "So what do you think is going to happen next?"

I swear this has to be the moment a real thought finally works its way through that thick skull of his. Lawrence turns and runs. He really runs, I see him blur against the shadows cast across the room by candlelight. He smashes into the window overlooking the street eight stories below and falls. If he's done any learning about it, he may actually survive the jump. Not that I care if he does.

I smile at the Golem. "That scared him."

The Golem does not smile back. "Were you prepared to give me the order to kill him?"

I reach out my hand, gesturing for him to hand me back my purse. "Actually, I wasn't. I gave my vow, after all." I wink though. "Didn't say anything about scaring him."

The Golem nods, and I see a glimmer of a smile. "Typical air-breather mendacity, of course."

151

"Of course." I do sigh inwardly. I have to make some calls when I can to the right people. Government agents, and the Vienna Council has to know. Lawrence is too dangerous to be given leniency this time. "Before we leave, let's put these candles out before the place burns down."

There is just one last unavoidable thought this night that needs an answer.

"Bo?" I have to ask the Golem as we're waiting at the subway station – he insists, and this time of night a taxi is hard to find – for the Ghost Train to carry us back to my not-so-secret lair. As he stares at me with those unblinking glass blues I add, "I know, no names. But why did he, you know, call you that?"

The Golem sighs. Giving how he doesn't need to breathe, his attempt to fake having lungs is something else he needs to work on. "The Not-Master was watching *The Dukes of Hazzard* too often, labeled me with an unwanted nickname."

I glance the poor clay boy over. "You don't look at all like John Schneider. You've got a fake buzzcut hairstyle, for starters, and..."

The Golem glares at me with the horrified expression of judgment that only a serious non-human can offer. "You watched that show, too?"

Wow. I know *Dukes* is an acquired taste, and the episodes got dumber when half the cast went on strike, and didn't the network just kill it this year? But this poor Golem is really upset about meeting any fans. "Well, I, you know. I get bored sometimes. There's only forty-two channels on my cable connection. Hey, here's the deal, I will not call you what Lawrence did, okay? I'm not like him, so I won't do that to you."

The Golem keeps glaring, giving it more thought, has that wary stance I've seen in many a lover when I've talked them into something kinky. "Okay. I accept your vow on this."

The Ghost Train arrives at the station, its destination

reading "Out Of Service" but already carrying a handful of *Lilin* and secret agents for the evening. As the doors open for the two of us to board, I can't help but grin, "Besides you look more like James Brolin to me."

Getting a Golem to groan is one of those moments in life you have to treasure.

Paul Wartenberg may be a long-time Florida resident, but he's made two visits to New York City so he thinks he knows where all the fun landmarks are. In spite of being born in Albany, Georgia, he's ninety percent certain he is not made out of the red clay common in that part of the map.

Paul has been published in anthologies *Strangely Funny*, *Mardi Gras Murder*, and *History and Mystery, Oh My!* He published his own anthology *Last of the Grapefruit Wars*, has self-published shorts and novellas such as *The Hero Cleanup Protocol* and *Body Armor Blues* as ebooks. He was last seen feeding his cats and giving them ear rubs.

JINNI
BY FRANK SAWIELIJEW

What would soon turn out to be the best day in Anne's life was Jann al-Sahar al-Raghba's first day of work after a long vacation. He poured out of the bronze lamp as a blue mist and took on a more substantial form to greet his new mistress.

"Hahaha, I shouldn't have drunk that last shot of vodka. I'm seeing ghosts now," Anne said, with the slurred voice of a woman who's had one drink too many.

"Not a ghost. A jinni," he replied with a respectful nod. "You have found my lamp and rubbed it. Therefore, you are granted three wishes."

Anne scratched her head. She wasn't sure whether the creature in front of her was real or just a figment of her imagination. It was blue, floated in the air, wore a turban and had a ridiculous moustache.

It was close to midnight, she was tired, she had drunk more shots of vodka than she could count, and she had even lost a shoe on the way home. Considering her current state, she concluded that the creature must have been a hallucination.

"I didn't know alcohol could cause hallucinations like that," she said, scratching her head. "This is just a lamp I found in the trash. Jinn aren't real."

"Jinn exist," said Jann al-Sahar al-Raghba. Being one himself, he was pretty sure about that. "You found this lamp. You brought it home. You decided to polish it. And polishing a lamp containing a jinni…"

"... summons it," Anne finished the sentence. She poked Jann. His skin had the consistency of a soggy marshmallow. "I can touch you. I can talk to you. That probably means you're real, right?"

"Yes."

"And I can really make three wishes."

"Yes." Jann cleared his throat and recited the common terms of service of a jinni's wish-granting contract. "You are granted three wishes of your choosing. Once you have made your wishes and confirmed that you want them, the jinni is obligated to fulfill them. You can wish for anything except more jinn and/or more wishes. In the case of more complex wishes that might be divided into several sub-wishes, it is in the jinni's judgment whether to allow it as a single wish or split it into two or three, depending on how many elements the wish contains. Other than that, there are no restrictions as to the content of the wishes."

"Uh." Anne thought about it for a moment. "So I can wish for anything?"

"As long as that wish doesn't ask for more wishes or more jinn, yes."

"Hum."

She thought about it for a much longer moment.

Three wishes. She could wish for anything she wanted. Simple and obvious choices like a billion dollars would be a waste of a good wish, of course. Why ask for a limited amount of money if she could have an unlimited amount? Why even ask for such mundane things as money when she could have anything she could think of?

"All right. I think I know what I want."

Jann nodded. "Your wishes are my command. What is it?"

"I want the most awesome hair in the world," she said, running her fingers through her decidedly average hair. "I want to be able to control its growth, so I can grow it out to waist-length in a day, then buzz it down and keep the buzzcut for a month without having to trim it. I want to be able to change its texture from straight to wavy at will, and its color, too. Just a single thought and poof – completely different hair."

Jann nodded again. "It shall be done."

"For my second wish, I want the best husband in the world." She grinned. That was something the jinni probably heard often. "I want him to be as strong as Rambo, as eloquent as Shakespeare, as smart as Einstein. He should be funny and witty and handsome, and be able to give good foot massages, and cook, and be skilled at constructing stuff so he can repair things around the house when necessary."

"This, too, shall be done."

"And for the third, I wanna be queen. A real queen, not just a figurehead. I want to rule a country, make the laws, lead the armies, get all the tax income." She paused for a moment, looking for the proper word to describe what she wanted. "I want to be an absolute ruler."

"Are these three wishes your final decision?"

Anne thought about it. She thought about it for a long while.

Then, she said, "Yes."

"Then so be it."

Jann touched her and vanished in a puff of blue smoke.

"Huh." Anne scratched her head. "And now?"

This might have been the hardest job Jann had ever received. Most people tended to wish for simple stuff – money, houses, fame and fortune. Those were comparatively easy to achieve. Her wishes, however, were difficult. He had to improve a part of her body. He had to find the perfect man – not just any man, but one who fulfilled all her requirements. He had to make her the absolute ruler of a country.

At least he had some magical skills to help him with his tasks. He just hoped he wouldn't make any mistakes, especially during the fulfillment of the first wish.

He swam through her bloodstream, trying to catch something that contained her DNA. Any cell would do – he would change it and then use a simple spell to apply the changes to her entire body.

Changing someone's appearance was always a challenging task. To fulfill that kind of wish, Jann had to modify the person's genetics. Anne's wish was particularly difficult. She wanted an ability humans didn't ordinarily have. He'd have to get creative.

He grabbed a couple of cells and took a closer look at the genetic information contained within. Then, he put on his magic glasses. They allowed him to look at her genetic code like a programmer would look at that of a computer program. After fulfilling many "I want to be beautiful" wishes, he knew exactly what to look for. It didn't take him long to find the relevant code for the appearance of her hair.

But this time, it wouldn't be as simple as changing a couple of basic properties. He had to come up with something that allowed her to change the appearance of her hair at will – and even accelerate or slow down its growth. The programming language of the human body was a delicate thing. A bad line of code could have horrible consequences. He had to be very, very careful.

"Let's see… this is the part that determines color, this one determines texture… I'll have to make them into variables… and write a function that allows them to be changed by thoughts…"

He spent over an hour writing and re-writing the hair control plug-in until he was satisfied with it. He didn't want to brag, but he was really proud of his work. It looked better than anything millennia of evolution could ever come up with.

He checked and double-checked the code to make sure there were no issues with it before applying the changes to her body.

With a spell, he went out of her body and increased his size to normal human proportions again. His first task was done. Her wish was fulfilled.

"I have done as you asked, young lady," he said. "Your first wish was to have perfect hair, the appearance of which you could control with your thoughts. You can do so now."

Anne closed her eyes and concentrated. Within seconds, her shoulder-length hair grew out until it reached way below her waistline. Then, she opened her eyes again and went into her bathroom. When she returned, she held a mirror in her hands.

"Let's see, then." With a thought, she changed her hair from straight to curly, from curly to wavy, and back to straight again. With another thought, it became red. Then blonde. Black. Blue as the sky. Green as grass. And back to her natural brunette again.

She grinned. "It works. This is amazing. Your wish-magic really works!"

Jann nodded. "Of course it does. I'm glad my work is to your satisfaction. I hope you will be as pleased with your other wishes."

Again, he vanished with a puff of smoke.

Anne let herself sink into her couch and played with her awesome new hair. She couldn't wait for the jinni to return with her perfect husband – and a fancy crown to put on her head.

A perfect husband or a perfect wife were wishes Jann encountered very, very often. Usually, he'd just go and fetch whatever conformed to the current standards of "perfect", but this time, he actually had to find someone who was – more or less – perfect. Strong, intelligent, handsome, skilled... that girl was clever. She had actually specified what she wanted, rather than trusting a jinni's interpretation of "perfect."

Of course, for him that meant more work. Men like that

didn't grow on trees. Especially in this day and age, being good at everything was a rare trait. But, luckily, he could travel through time and look for the perfect man in a more likely place.

The Viking Age.

He teleported himself into the 9th century A.D. and hovered over Scandinavia, searching for settlements that might house one or more Viking aristocrats. Contrary to popular belief, they weren't sword-wielding savages but well-spoken, intelligent and highly competitive men of high achievement. And what would be better husband material for Anne than a man who tried to beat even his own king at both riddling and fighting?

Jann found a mead hall that looked like it currently had a feast going on and floated down to pay the celebrating Vikings a visit. They were so focused on the duel of wits taking place within, they didn't even notice him.

"What's going on?" he asked one of the spectators.

"A duel, of course," the spectator answered. "Hakon had come up with a riddle that was so difficult, it kept everyone guessing for months, but nobody managed to get it right. Well, until Egill came along and solved it, and now it's on. They're throwing riddles at each other until one of them gives up. And then they'll probably continue with swords instead of words."

That was just how Vikings rolled. For them, everything was a competition. And that's why Jann had decided to travel back to the Viking Age – Anne had wished for a man who was great at everything, and here, people always held competitions to prove they were.

He'd just wait for the duel to conclude, then try to win the winner for Anne.

"There is a road," Egill said to Hakon, "which leads over another road. They cross, but do not touch, as one's below, the other above – and on the top, there is another crossing both. What is the name of that topmost road?"

Hakon scratched his head. "A road above two others? Could it be... no, that's probably not it..."

Egill grinned. "I've answered four of your riddles. You've only answered three of mine. Do you really want to give up already?"

Hakon mumbled something that was probably an insult. Then, he thoughtfully stroked his beard as he searched for an answer. "Three roads... one on top... what could it be?"

The spectators were whispering amongst themselves, sharing the answers they had come up with, but none spoke aloud. The riddle was for Hakon to solve on his own.

Finally, he let out a sigh. "I have no idea. I give up."

"Oh, you do? But the answer is so simple!" Egill said with a huge grin on his face. "It's the sky!"

"The sky?"

The people in the crowd where whispering again. It seemed like none of them had guessed correctly.

He nodded. "The sky. The road at the bottom is a river – you can sail it with a boat, so it is a road of water. The road that crosses but doesn't touch it is a bridge. And above them all is the sky, the road used by the birds in their flight."

The crowd cheered. Egill had beaten Hakon in the battle of wits. But when Hakon drew his sword, it was clear that the duel was far from over.

"You might have bested me in riddling, Egill, but will you be able to match my skill in combat?"

Egill drew his sword and grinned. "You wish to embarrass yourself even more? Oh well, it's your choice, Hakon."

"I'm going to shut your damn mouth!" Hakon shouted and charged at Egill.

Egill kept his wits about him and dodged Hakon's wild slash. His opponent was enraged, and he planned to use that to his advantage. He parried and evaded Hakon's blade, managed to flank him with quick sidesteps and kept him on his toes with savage counterattacks. One of these grazed

Hakon's forearm, drawing blood.

Hakon dropped his sword. First blood had been drawn, and that concluded the fight. He had not only lost the duel of wits, but also the duel of might.

The people cheered for Egill, chanting his name. Jann was impressed by the Viking's skill. If he was as good at cooking and construction work as he was at riddling and fighting, he'd be the perfect husband for Anne.

"Excuse me!" Jann shouted, waving at the victorious fighter. "I'd like to have a word with you."

Egill looked at the jinni with surprise, but he came over without hesitation. He hadn't seen a jinni before, but he correctly concluded that this strange blue-skinned guy probably had a good offer to make.

"What do you want?" he asked. "And what are you, anyway?"

"I'm a jinni, a magical being who serves a wonderful mistress," he said, introducing himself with a polite bow. "And that wonderful mistress is looking for a husband. And a man like you is exactly what she wants... well, as long as you fulfill some requirements, that is."

"Oh?" Egill raised an eyebrow. "And why would I be interested in her?"

"She's the queen of a small kingdom. If you marry her, you would be a king."

That got his attention. With a broad grin on his face, he asked, "What are those requirements?"

"She wants a man who can cook, is good at building and repairing things, and can give good foot massages."

"Well, I can turn even smelly old fish into something halfway palatable, and I once helped a friend build his longship." With a chuckle, he added, "And I can massage more than just her feet, if that's what she wants."

"Great. You're the perfect husband for her, then. Congratulations, you're going to marry a queen."

"That's the most unexpected thing that ever happened to

me, and believe me, I've been in some very unexpected situations." He shrugged. "But it's definitely the most pleasant surprise I ever had."

"I bet it is. Now, come with me. It's time to meet your new wife." Jann took Egill by the hand and both vanished in a puff of smoke.

The Vikings who witnessed it were shocked. Their hero, taken away by an evil spirit! That was worthy of a story. And more than a thousand years into the future, linguists and historians would crack their heads wondering about that unusual tale so different from all the other stories from the Viking Age...

"That's a queen?" Egill asked, not really convinced that the drunk woman lounging on her couch was the ruler of a kingdom.

"Well, not yet. But she's going to be one very soon. It'll take less than a day, I'd say," replied Jann.

"Are you my husband? You're pretty cute," Anne said, throwing a flirty smile at Egill. "Come, join me on the couch. I'd really like a foot rub now. Oh, and you could tell me a story. Something exciting. I hope you're good at telling stories, I asked the jinni to bring me a man who's good at that."

"Uh... yeah. I'm a Viking, after all, and you know Vikings are good storytellers..."

"A Viking?" A visible wave of excitement washed over her face. "That's *super hot*! Oh yeah, I'm totally into you. Just come here and take me, right here, right now."

"Uhm... I'll just go and fulfill your third wish while you enjoy the company of your new husband," Jann said.

"Yeah, you go do that. I'm gonna have some fun with my *Viking!*"

Again, Jann disappeared in a puff of smoke. This time, he went to a small nation somewhere in Eastern Europe. He didn't even know its name – he had set the destination of his traveling spell to random small Eastern European country not in the EU. Hopefully, it was a place where overthrowing the government wouldn't lead to an international intervention. That is why he had specified the country to not be a member of the European Union. The less resistance there was to a sudden change of government, the better.

He really hoped the people – and especially the military – wouldn't mind suddenly having a drunk foreign woman as their queen. But he was a jinni, and he knew magic, so somehow, he'd manage.

As in most countries, the government was busy governing while the people were busy minding their own business. Nobody expected a coup to happen today, or any day in the near future at all. Life wasn't great, but it wasn't bad either, and things were pretty fine overall. Nobody wanted to overthrow the government.

Yet.

Jann approached a few pedestrians and questioned them about politics. He told those who seemed like they might join a revolution to meet him in front of the parliament building and join his protest against some made-up governmental shenanigans. Of course, they weren't real, but people these days didn't waste too much time fact-checking when they could waste it on blind activism instead.

Once he had assembled a crowd of twenty people, he addressed them with a speech.

"People! Citizens! Are you tired of your government doing whatever it wants without asking for your opinion? Do you want something better than what you have right now? Better policies, lower taxes, more freedom?"

The small crowd cheered. Of course they did. Who wouldn't cheer for the vague promise of things generally improving?

"Then follow me! We shall overthrow the government and give this country a new ruler, a better ruler! Revolution!"

"Wait, what? I thought this was just a protest," one of the people said.

"Yeah. Yeah, I thought we'd just stand around and hold up some signs or something," said another. "This is a bit much, isn't it?"

"A bit much? Listen to yourselves! Are you cowards? Are you sheep? Look how the oppressive hand of the government is keeping you down! You don't even dare to strike back against it!"

"Uh... I'm not really kept down by the government. They're not doing anything too bad," someone said.

The others nodded. None of them remembered the last time they had been kept down by the government. The government was corrupt, sure, but it wasn't particularly oppressive.

"If you help me overthrow the government, you get a million of whatever your country's currency is called."

"A million isn't that much–"

"Two million."

"Long live the revolution!"

The others in the crowd joined in, cheering and yelling.

"Keep it down, people! We don't want anyone to stop us before we even enter the parliament, okay?"

The crowd fell silent. If someone stopped them, they wouldn't get money. They didn't want to risk that.

Jann entered the building and the spontaneous revolutionaries followed him.

"Oh, wait. I forgot something. I'll be right back," Jann said, disappearing in a puff of smoke. He teleported himself to his own personal weapon chamber – every jinni had one, as they often needed weapons for their work – and fetched a couple of guns and swords. With enough weapons to arm his little army, he teleported back.

"Here. Take these. We need to intimidate people. Maybe even kill some," he said as he handed the weapons to the revolutionaries.

"Why do I only get a sword?" one of them asked. "I want a rifle, too!"

"I don't have enough rifles for everyone. You want the two million monies? Then stop complaining."

Nobody else had any complaints to bring forth. Jann was quite happy with these people - they didn't even ask how he managed to teleport away, even though most people tended to be shocked when they saw him use magic. Apparently, the lust for monetary reward was stronger than the fear of the unknown.

They burst into the parliament, interrupting a speech by the president himself. A few shots fired into the air silenced not only him, but all the politicians in the room. Jann approached the president and handed him a stack of paper.

"This is a revolution. Just sign this new constitution, and you'll be allowed to leave with your life," Jann said.

The president skimmed through the handwritten constitution and frowned. "Absolute monarchy? Complete abolition of the parliament and democratic votes? I can't sign that!"

"Just a little reminder here: we've got guns. And swords. You have neither. Are you sure you don't want to sign it?" Jann asked, threatening the president with his rifle. "Oh, and of course, we can also offer you significant monetary compensation and a large mansion to retire in if you hand over your country peacefully."

"A tempting offer, but I'm still not sure whether I should--"

"A tempting offer? Don't you dare surrender our country to this mob, you bastard!" a politician yelled.

"What did you expect? I always said he's not to be trusted. Haven't I always, from the day he became president, told you what an untrustworthy person he is?" said another.

"Hah! Good thing we always managed to block his reforms, isn't it? Ah, it's good to be in the opposition..."

"Yeah! Boo! Bad president! Bad!"

"Then again," said the president as he took a pen from his pocket, "abolishing the parliament doesn't sound like such a bad idea after all."

The president put his signature under the document Jann had given him and handed it back. It was done. Anne was now the sole ruler of this country.

"You can't do that, we have a vote on this!" one of the politicians said.

Jann fired his gun into the air. Plaster rained from the ceiling where the bullet struck.

"Guess we'll have to get a new job now," said another politician. He got up from his seat and left the building.

Bit by bit, the house of parliament emptied, until even the most stubborn of the politicians realized they had lost.

"So, about the money and the mansion..."

"You shall receive it once the new queen arrives to take over the country, Mr. Ex-President. You won't be disappointed."

The president sighed. "I'm still not sure if this was the right decision for my country. I could've waited until the police arrived – your little mob wouldn't have stood a chance. But it definitely was the right decision for myself. I'll never have to deal with this thrice-damned parliament ever again."

"It was a good decision," Jann replied with a nod. Of course it was. Had the president not given up so easily, Jann's job would've been a lot more difficult. "Now, just wait here while I go fetch the queen."

The coronation ceremony had been pompous and joyful. The people of the country that was, from that day onward, known as the Kingdom of Annesland hadn't been bothered too much by the sudden change of government. Instead, they appreciated the addition of a new national holiday on which they could celebrate instead of having to work. Right after her coronation, Anne had wedded Egill the Viking in a marriage ceremony just as pompous. The people had been slightly disappointed by that – had the wedding happened on a different day, it would have resulted in two new holidays rather than just one.

Anne quickly adjusted to her new position and, with the help of her Viking husband, actually became a competent ruler.

"This is amazing," she said to Jann while she tried to braid her hair into the shape of a crown. When it didn't really work, she cut it off and grew it back out again. It would be back to waist-length in less than a minute. "I got my magic hair, my perfect husband, and my kingdom. Just like that. I rubbed a lamp, you came out, I made three wishes, and now here I am."

Jann nodded. "Yes, that's how it works. Whoever finds and rubs the lamp of a jinni gets three wishes. And then, those wishes are fulfilled."

Anne shook her head. "It's crazy. You just went *poof*, and when you came back my wishes were fulfilled. It all seemed so effortless. Like you just snap your finger and make stuff happen. How do you do it?"

"Magic," answered Jann, grinning broadly. A jinni never revealed how much work it was to fulfill those wishes. "But now it's time for me to go. You were happy with my performance, yes?"

"Are you kidding? Yes, of course I was!" Anne let her hair cycle through all the colors of the rainbow and demonstratively stared at all the banners on the walls, bearing her own coat of arms. "I got everything I asked for. Everything I ever wished for, even. I couldn't be happier!"

Jann smiled and nodded. He could be proud of his achievements. A glowing customer review like that was a jinni's most treasured reward. He couldn't wait to brag about it to his peers. They'd be so jealous.

When Anne's hair had reached her desired length, she turned to the mirror to attempt the crown of braids again.

This time, she was more successful.

"So, Jann..." she began, but when she turned around he wasn't there anymore. "Uh, Jann? Where are you?"

When she looked more closely, she noticed that not only was her jinni gone, but also the lamp he had come with. It didn't surprise her. There was nothing more to do for him here. She had gotten her three wishes, and now he was free to be found by someone else.

She shook her head and grinned. How easy a jinni's life must be, she thought – with a snap of their finger, they could do everything. Anne wished everything were as effortless for her as it was for them.

And then, she cursed herself for not making a wish that granted her a jinni's abilities herself.

Again, she shook her head. Maybe it was better if she didn't know how their magic worked. Things that looked effortless, she thought, often took more effort than people thought.

As an eccentric Russian noble who should rightfully be Tsar of Bulgaria but studies history in Frankfurt (Germany) instead, Frank Sawielijew loves to forge wild tales set in the weirdest of worlds. Historian by day, writer by night, he likes to explore a myriad of genres but feels at home in the very broad over-genre of speculative fiction. He writes in both English and German, self-published his first book in 2013, and has had a handful of short stories appear in various anthologies. When he's not working on something, he wastes his time watching campy 1980s B-movies and playing *Thief*, the best game ever made.

WEREMAN OF A SOUTH PACIFIC ISLAND
BY ROSALIND BARDEN

Donald is quite the talker. Occasionally he has something interesting to say, but I must wade through an ocean of his dilettante ramblings to get there.

Such was the case with his trip to an obscure South Seas island for screenings of antique silent movies on their original silver nitrate film.

"Of course it was expensive," Donald explained during a "little" cocktail party that jammed his hillside home, a party he threw for an acquaintance of an acquaintance's birthday, but really to talk about himself. "That's why it was exclusive, don't you see?"

Donald got on the topic of his recent trip after a party-goer noticed a curious souvenir in the powder room: a badly taxidermied parrot, cigarette in beak, perched on a beer can of foreign make.

Beemie, a close friend he claims is not really his friend, told Donald about the jaunt. "Beemie travels compulsively. Or, he used to. I'm sure you know he's a confidant of all major fashion designers of any note whatsoever. If Beemie doesn't know you, I'm sorry, but you are no one. Sorry!" Though "sorry" is hardly an emotion that applies to Donald.

To his rapt cluster of listeners at the party, Donald off-handedly listed his other fellow-travelers: an unsmiling artist, a divorcée he referred to as "Madam X" who was formerly wed to a bon vivant known for a misunderstanding involving Dubai and jars of jam, a "boring" businessman sans wife--"Madame X was hitting on him, embarrassing really," then some software emperors from "around San Francisco-ish--I'm sure you've met the type."

All in his listening huddle nodded. Of course, I knew they'd likely never met such people, nor fashion confidant Beemie, but polite and sensitive as always, I said nothing. I also knew Donald would cattily gossip about them later ("Did you see how they nodded as if they had?").

Rounding out the travel group was a trust fund baby who opted for the trip to avoid rehab, a fading celebrity, and a smattering of other idly moneyed types Donald referenced only vaguely. Probably the ultra-wealthy who don't speak to the likes of Donald, thus breaking his heart every time. Poor thing. I do feel sorry for him sometimes. He tries too hard.

"But why did you have to go so far in the middle of the ocean to see movies?" asked one of the eagerly nodding types, an aspiring model/starlet barely out of her teens and barely squeezed into a wisp of clothing.

"Darling," his condescending voice now, "Silver nitrate prints are explosive. It is illegal to show them anywhere in civilized countries, except for a handful of approved venues with projection booths built literally like bomb shelters--I know you think I'm being colorful, but it's true. Look it up on the Internet if you don't believe me. Plus, they need a police permit, local council approval, ambulances standing nearby, military on alert. Ridiculous. And these approved venues are so stingy with their screenings. Always claiming they lack funding or some such story." A dramatic roll of the eye and more nods from his eager audience who really had no idea what he was talking about, only that he was talking to them.

Not me. He talks to me all the time. Being his therapist and all.

Thus the obscure chain of South Seas islands, an independent kingdom that did what it felt like. For the right price, it was fine with this group watching as many explosive films as they wanted.

Through the glass walls, I saw the birthday boy sitting alone outside by the pool in the chilly night air, staring forlornly at the Hollywood lights spread below like a carpet of Christmas glitter. Donald didn't notice him; hadn't noticed him since he absently air kissed the boy when he arrived at the party he foolishly thought was for him.

After a chartered jet flight to the kingdom's main island, the group got their fill of silent film screenings. Nothing exploded, and, "I was getting bored. I mean, how many movies with no sound can you take already?"

The tour arranger had thought of everything except musical accompaniment, a requirement for the silents which were never designed to be completely silent. The wealthy stared at the glittering silver images with their nearly magical shimmering quality that so few living have seen, while listening to the coughs, labored breathing, crunching, and other annoying body noises of their fellow moneyed humans. Finally, a local official rounded up a group of choral singers from a church. "Amazing singers, but didn't really go with the movies."

Fortunately, the screenings only lasted two days before protests of boredom shut them down. Only Beemie objected. "Such a baby. He thinks he was a silent film star in a past life."

Suddenly, Donald's manicured fingers flew to his mouth. "Whoops! Beemie had me swear never to tell another living soul." His audience tittered as Donald wickedly smiled.

Cruel, he is. I've met Beemie a few times at Donald's parties. It's sad how obviously Beemie cares for him. Or, cared.

Then, on to the "nature tours" and where Donald's story finally became interesting, to me.

"They put us on a boat. They called it a yacht, but I think all of us have been on better, so there was much complaining all around. Took us to one of their islands. All green and lush, and no one lives there. Nature preserve. They had these cabins which were not first class. No one was happy. Took us walking through the jungle pointing out some rare parrot found nowhere else on the world. It squawks at us, and the trust fund baby shouts back to this parrot, 'I don't care!' Frankly, we were all feeling that way. Bugs bit me. My feet hurt. I ruined a nice pair of shoes in the mud. Please!"

After the tour operators liberally doused the guests with rum, "from the Canary Islands, of all places," the muttering settled down to some jolly partying.

"But the odd thing was, they forbade us to venture outside come nightfall. Upsets the rare parrot's sleep, they tell us. They herded us into our cabins and locked the doors!"

The aspiring model/starlet gasped, the reaction Donald was hoping for, so he pressed onward.

"They put me in a cabin with Beemie, which is fine, as long as he's drunk. When sober, he's so depressing. Always going on and on about his pets. Why he keeps them, I can't tell you. They're supposed to 'support his emotions,' or some such nonsense."

This is a dig at me. I've recommended he get a pet as an emotional support animal, but really to train him to care about something other than himself. I've yet to be successful.

I don't like it when he makes these passive-aggressive remarks aimed at me. I saw an imperious flash of his eye in my direction before he continued.

"We were both far gone drunk, and would not tolerate anyone commanding what we should or should not do. Beemie declares, 'Parrot be damned! We shall sally forth!' Did I say one of his pets is a parrot? The thing's squawking gives him migraines."

One of Donald's eager listeners started talking about a parrot he owned and liberated in a park for the very same squawking reason, but Donald cut the man off without looking at him.

"There were bars on the windows too." Several more

listeners gasped. "But the cabin was so old, so rotted with the tropical damp, Beemie was able to smash through the wall. Turned himself into a human battering ram. Didn't know he had it in him. Of course, he took off his jacket first. After he smashed that wall, he brushed the splinters from his sleeves, and carefully--even drunk as he was--donned that jacket again. A designer gave it to him--very famous--of course, I won't say which one, because everyone who knows, knows, and those who don't, well, do we really talk to them?" Frozen smiles from all the listeners, not willing to admit they hadn't the foggiest idea who this designer is or was. Poor things. The knots they twist themselves into so he'll notice them. Become a friend. Introduce them to his world of glitter.

Won't ever happen.

"The designer made the jacket expressly for him. None exists anywhere else in the world. Beautiful, beautiful jacket. I confess, I'm often so jealous. Are you surprised?" he asked no one in particular. "I know my books teach a positive way free from negative paths such as jealousy. But if you actually read them, you know I say everyone is human and we should never beat up on ourselves for our feelings."

His listeners smiled and murmured agreement. Several named a favorite book.

That's where Donald's wealth comes from: his books, his shows about his books, his t-shirts with his favorite positive sayings. He produces films now, too. I'm sure the aspiring model/starlet is hoping he'll cast her in one.

Won't ever happen. He has casting people to do that.

"So, we're arm-in-arm, marching through the jungle, singing a song we're making up as we go along, something like, 'Parrot be damned!' We're loud, and I'm thinking this trip is finally getting fun!"

Donald stopped and frowned. Abruptly, he added, "By arm-and-arm, I'm not saying what some would say I'm saying. Beemie is well known to like the men, though he

175

denies it. As I've told the press many a time, 'Donald is not like that!' You know I'm against judging, but he really needs to face his life reality. As I do. Daily."

Many eager nods from the eager listeners, though I could tell from their eyes they didn't believe him. I'm sure they'd all heard last year's scandal, with his former assistant's gossipy tell-all tome and the interview with the prom queen from his long ago high school.

Being bisexual, Donald, technically, is not like Beemie. So, he's actually not lying. Clever that way, he can be.

"It was all fun. Until that wereman thing came. That's how Beemie lost his jacket. Everyone asks, but he won't speak of it. Awful loss."

Wereman?

My drifting mind was brought back to sharp attention. But, Donald, as he usually does, wandered off to the trivial, about some fashion "revulsion" the divorcée (Madame X) dared wear, "embarrassing herself completely. I mean you could see her huge butt right through it. But the boring businessman liked it. Did I tell you he's divorcing his sad faithful wife now for this horror woman?"

Then other islands, a nude incident that caused a local tribal chief to start shouting, and they had to pack up and flee to the boat in a hurry. The drugs came out, which technically is a public whipping, or maybe even a public execution crime in this particular kingdom. A huge fine/bribe had to be paid all around, but it, "made things less boring-like, thinking we could be dragged to the airport--that's their capital's center I think--and whipped to death. Kind of sexy, really."

I stuck around, just in case he might return to the wereman thread, but he didn't. The party wound down. The birthday boy had left early on. The others drifted away, hope in their hearts that they might be invited to another party, or cast, or become his girlfriend/boyfriend. The aspiring model/starlet lingered to the last. As I left, she was still fawning over him.

Maybe she made it to his bed. Hard to tell. But she'd not make it further than that. She was no more valuable to him than a parrot, but she'd find out soon enough.

Me? I had time. An hour weekly, sometimes more if he felt "needy" or "emotional." I'd draw the details from him carefully. If he sensed I was interested in the odd turn his trip had taken, he'd clam up on purpose. He'd toy with me, pretending to be about to tell, then not. He did that once about a two-headed monkey he saw tied to a post outside a producer's house in Santa Fe. That's the most detail he was willing to let me have.

He's wicked that way. I don't like him. A therapist doesn't have to like her patients.

For the next several weeks during his sessions, he moaned about the guilt he felt for being bored watching rare silent films. Then another several weeks venting his anger at silent films of the exploding variety for causing him to feel guilty and bad about himself. "Those are negative emotions. It's unfair that a bunch of old movies should strive to hurt me so much."

Gradually, stealthily over the weeks, I danced around the edges of his sexuality, steering him toward Beemie. It was a dance on the point of a knife. Either I'd lure him to worries of his Beemie-feelings and entice him to speak of the wereman, or he'd suspect what I was about, and go mute with a chuckle and evil glint in his eye.

He's an intelligent man. Very sharp. We've been together so long, he knows my wants. It's difficult to trick him.

I pretended I was far more interested in Beemie's jacket, and all the lustful subtext it could represent.

"So, did you take Beemie's jacket?" Finally, finally, I'd brought him to that fateful night.

"No!"

"Where are you keeping it? Do you put it on sometimes?"

"Oh, my God! No! I don't even see Beemie. Not really. I

told you. He's depressing. I gave him some of my books once, you know. Audio versions. I question if he reads anything. I'm sure he listened to none of them. When I asked him if he had, he had such a cagey tone to his voice, and... "

"Donald"--I have to be sparing in cutting him off. His ego gets challenged easily. I must save my moments. "Why are you avoiding telling the truth about the jacket?"

"Oh, my God! I don't have it. The wereman took it."

"Are you the wereman?"

"What is this? No! We were singing in the jungle. This song we were making up about the rare parrot--'Parrot be damned!'--something like that. I was drunk. Why are you looking at me like that? I didn't have sex with Beemie. Stop looking at me like that!"

Ah, yes, I had him in just the state of anxiety about his sexual feelings toward Beemie where I could push further.

"What does this wereman represent to you?"

"He doesn't represent anything. He just burst out of the jungle at us, rushing. We could barely see anything. It was so dark under all the palm fronds and vines and things. But he was so white, he stood out. He grabbed Beemie's jacket. Ordinarily, Beemie would have fought an army to keep his jacket. You can check with anyone."

Then he stopped to give me his deprecating look of pity. "Though you don't move in those circles, so I suppose it would be hard for someone like you to 'check with anyone.'"

He was trying to dance away by using his snob tactics. I could care less about him and his glittering society acquaintances. But I dislike how he enjoys trying to hurt me.

"Do you often stroke Beemie's jacket?"

"Why is it always sex with you? No! I don't have it."

I gave him my cool, skeptical look. "What does Beemie have to say about the jacket?"

"He doesn't talk about it. He was terrified. The wereman grabbed Beemie. I ran." Realizing this might sound cowardly, he quickly added, "But I did turn around to see if

Beemie was okay. I saw him slip out of his jacket to escape. That man kept holding onto the jacket. His hands, his whole body, were white-white. Like chalk. It was horrible. He had this long ratty blond hair that looked like he'd never ever washed it. Long, long curvy nails. Clearly, he never gets them properly trimmed. I don't think Beemie would take that jacket back if the wereman said, 'Oh, sorry. Here, it is. I took it to the cleaners and everything.'"

Donald was breathing more heavily. Sweating even. This memory was bothering him.

"Why?"

"There was something just wrong about that man. Just wrong. We kept running and screaming back to the cabins. Everyone woke up. The others were locked in their cabins and couldn't get out and started panicking and screaming. It was so chaotic. Finally, the tour guides came out and hustled us to another cabin, because Beemie had knocked the hole in ours. It was stacked full of those old exploding movies. I guess they'd been thinking of screening more--probably because Beemie complained he hadn't seen enough.

"They were planning on leaving us in that cabin alone with those old movies. I think I fainted. Beemie grabbed at the people and started crying. So one of the tour guides, a local kid from another island, said he'd stay."

Donald was exactly where I wanted him. Talking jag. His hands nervous, trembling. I said nothing, kept a blank face, let him keep talking.

"The kid didn't want to tell us anything, but Beemie started shaking him. I'd never seen Beemie so aggressive. But, of course, he'd just lost that jacket--Oh, my God! please don't say a word about that jacket!"

Donald began gasping like he was about to sob. I remained silent. Reassured, he wiped back his nearly-tears and continued.

"Finally, the tour guide starts explaining. His English wasn't great, but we could understand. He said it was a wereman. Beemie thought he said 'weird-man.' No, he said--clearly--Beemie doesn't know what he's talking about--'wereman.' The wereman, not weird-man, only comes out and hunts after sunset. That's why tourists can't go out at night. Long ago, there used to be people living on the island and ground-type animals as rare as the parrot, he said. But the wereman ate all of them. Now, only birds, like that damn parrot, survive because they can hide up in the trees. So, to get dinner, the wereman goes fishing. We didn't believe him. We're thinking a chartered fishing boat, a proper captain. How could this wereman, completely naked--he had no shoes, nothing--how can he afford go fishing? So this tour guide tells us to look out the window. He does a lot of pointing too. Like I said, didn't have the best English."

Donald had to pause and wipe his sweating brow. I gave him a tissue. He actually mumbled "Thanks," to me. Unusual.

"We're at one of the barred windows that looks out over a steep drop to a little bay with a nice beach, where we lounged around during the day to recover from that ridiculous nature hike. Wonderful fine sand. Sugar-like. Unbelievably clear water that you do not see in the Mediterranean anymore. Beaches too crowded there, even ones that are supposed to be 'secret.' Always swarming with yachts. Awful. So, we're watching this beach. The moon is up high now so we can see clearly. Out of the palms and whatnot comes him. Beemie says, 'Where's my jacket?' The man took his jacket and isn't even wearing it. Did he just drop it in the mud? I know Beemie's thinking this because he starts to cry. I tell him to shut up, because I'm afraid the wereman will hear and charge up the cliff. I was very afraid."

Donald stopped and was silent so long I worried that I'd learned as much as I could, when he said quietly, "It's hard for me to say how afraid I was because I know my books tell people to release their fear, that fear doesn't really exist except in their minds. But I was afraid."

He looked up at me in a troubled way, seeking my understanding, as he so rarely does. I let a look of sympathy drift upon my blank countenance and gave him a nod.

Feeling supported, he continued with a deep breath. "The wereman wades into the waves, which are strong now. Earlier, they were gentle and even I took a dip. The wereman is a good swimmer, because the crashing waves don't faze him at all. He's diving in and out. He's easy for us to spot because he's so white. After diving for a while like this, he comes up with this huge shark. Absolutely huge and it's fighting for its life, thrashing around. But the wereman has the shark tight in his arms, and he starts eating the shark alive, tearing out hunks of the shark with his teeth. The shark is panicking, fighting, but it doesn't do any good. The wereman drags the shark back to the beach, through the crashing waves like it's nothing, then continues ripping it apart with his teeth. The poor shark is still struggling, but it's half-eaten. The sand turns black with blood. It was so horrible. I think we both threw up. Then the wereman drags it into the jungle and we can't see anything more.

"We were so afraid, yelling to leave that instant. Of course, we couldn't. No one could go out with that wereman hanging around.

"I demanded we use the silent films to blow that wereman up, since they're supposed to be so explosive, like dynamite or something. The tour guide gets confused and says, 'Aren't the old silver movies valuable?' That stops me, because I suddenly felt like my life had no value. Maybe that's why I'm so angry at those films."

He looked up at me. "Am I worth less than them?" His face was so worried.

"No."

I kept it simple, said nothing more. No need to divert him now and have him wander back to his meanderings about guilt and silent movies.

It worked. Donald nervously nodded and plowed on, sweat dripping from the end of his nose.

"The tour guide kept talking, I think to distract us. We got in our heads that we'd turn into weremen too, because we'd stepped in the island's mud and drank the rum--never mind the rum was from Gran Canaria--we were so confused at that point we couldn't get our islands straight. So, he tells us there's nothing wrong with the island. The wereman came from one of those old wooden sailing ships hundreds of years ago. This ship comes to the main island and the sailors want to come on shore. But, the shaman or whatever senses something wrong, so they won't let any of the smaller dinghies get close. At night, some sailors try swimming to shore, but the locals spot them and kill them because they're afraid. They don't know what's wrong with this ship, just that something is. Late at night, by the moonlight, everyone on shore sees a man attacking the others on the ship. But there was something strange about the man, not normal. The chief orders the warriors to throw burning spears at the boat. This finally motivates the sailors to take off.

"They later learned the ship stopped at this little island. The only man who came off was the wereman. He swam to shore and attacked everyone he saw. Some of the islanders were able to escape in their canoes. He ate the rest of them. Beyond that, the locals have no idea where the wereman came from or how he got that way.

"Beemie starts demanding, really angrily demanding, if the ship was French or English. Of course the kid has no idea. Beemie gets this tour guide, who is just a skinny kid, around the neck. The tour guide starts crying, then gasping like he can't breathe. It took me forever to pull Beemie off. I had no idea how strong he is. He never goes to the gym. If you ever saw him, you'd think, 'fat boy!' Where does this strength comes from? It was strange. He's upset and looks me in the eye and says, 'I will never speak to you again.' I was so hurt. I told him it wouldn't help to kill the tour guide on top of everything. I'm sure that kingdom has penalties for that sort of thing.

"I don't know if he was serious, but he's barely spoken to me since the trip."

Donald suddenly made a strong point of adding, "Not that we're close. I only bump into him at openings and things like that." Then he switched as quickly to a safer line of talk. "Heard he's reconciled with his pets. Spends all his time huddled with them in his flat. Never goes out. Heard the pets are getting sick of him."

Donald was quiet for as long as it was possible for Donald to be quiet. He gripped the sides of the chaise with his trembling hands. He was pale. After another moment, his eyes, big and childlike, looked up at me. "Was I wrong to feel afraid?"

"No, Donald, of course you weren't."

He nodded and looked at me in the needy way I so rarely see.

His eyes turned suddenly away. In a whisper I had to lean close to hear, he said, "Since the tour boy was just lying on the floor not moving, I decided to take action. I found the cabin key in the boy's pocket. I unlocked the door, grabbed one of the film canisters, and ran with it outside. Beemie was screaming, 'What are you doing?' I was going to blow up the wereman. I knew he must still be around the beach somewhere, so I threw the film down the cliff. It bounced and bounced. The case broke open, and it spilled out over the beach.

"I'm not a strong man. I can't defend myself. I always meant to take that Boxing Smack Down class in Venice Beach, but keep putting it off. What do I wear to Boxing Smack Down? I have no idea. I don't know martial arts. Beemie wasn't helping at all, so it was up to me." A pleading look at me again. I gave him an understanding nod.

"The movie didn't blow up. It just sat there on the beach, the silver glittering in the moonlight. It was so beautiful, like a looping silver ribbon. Beemie came out by now. He's so angry. He loves those old movies. Can't imagine why, apart from his silly fantasy about being a reincarnated silent screen heart throb. Obviously, good looks did not translate to this life. He starts shouting that he's going to push me over the cliff. After what he'd done to the boy, I was terrified. I can't defend myself! I told you that," as if I was disagreeing with him.

I gave him another reassuring nod.

He settled down. "Okay. When Beemie grabs me, he sees the film too. He starts to cry and go on about how beautiful it is. He's so loud. I know the wereman can hear and I keep telling him to shut up. Sure enough, the wereman comes out of the jungle. He sees the film and runs his hands over the loops. He holds it up to the moonlight and moves it around, so it glitters more. He's hypnotized by it. Beemie is so stupid. He yells down, 'Don't touch it! Keep your hands off!' The wereman looks up. Beemie dives flat to the ground. Coward. So, I'm the only one standing there for the wereman to see."

He started to fully cry now. I handed another tissue.

"I think Beemie hates me. The wereman looks directly at me. I know he's going to charge up the cliff and kill me. I know it. But then, he looks at the film, looks at me, looks at the film. He decides to drag the film into the jungle and he disappears. He didn't want me. He wanted that old, stupid movie more than me."

Ah, Beemie's ego, bruised.

"Do those movies make you feel jealous? That wealthy people, and Beemie, would travel half way around the world to see them, not you?"

Donald is jealous of everything. I had him now.

Donald shot me a look like a pouting baby. He sobbed, "Beemie said the same. He said I'd just destroyed history and art and everything. He said he would tell on me. I told him if he did, I'd tell about the tour boy. That shut him up. We didn't sleep all night. We just sat as far away from that boy as we could. I knew the wereman wouldn't come back. Because he liked the movie better."

A sob choked out. "We told the tour people it was the wereman who stole the film and did that to the boy. I'm sure they didn't believe us, but only told us not to say anything to the others. They gave everybody more rum and took us to the next island."

Our time was up, but it took a moment before he could stand and make it to the door.

I'd gotten him into quite a state. I called in a delivery prescription and gave the heads up to his new personal assistant to make sure Donald took a pill the moment he got home. I expect to hear about his fear and guilt for months to come. I'll suggest he cancel his upcoming book tour. He's really is in no condition to be out in public with too much noise, commotion, cameras.

But it's been all worth it.

Home now, I settle into my favorite chair, with a tiny cup of the dense chocolate drink I learned to make on one of my travels. Comfortable by the fire on this rainy Los Angeles night, I write his odd story in my journal I keep for this purpose.

My profession does have its rewards. Sometimes.

Over thirty of Rosalind Barden's short stories have appeared in print anthologies and webzines, including the U.K.'s acclaimed *Whispers of Wickedness*. Mystery and Horror LLC has included her stories in their anthologies *Mardi Gras Murder, Strangely Funny, Strangely Funny 2 1/2*, and *History and Mystery, Oh My!*, winner of the Florida Authors and Publishers Association President's Book Award Silver Medal. Ellen Datlow selected her short story "Lion Friend" as a Best Horror of the Year Honorable Mention after it appeared in *Cern Zoo*, a British Fantasy Society nominee for best anthology, part of DF Lewis' award winning *Nemonymous* anthology series. *TV Monster* is her print children's book that she wrote and illustrated. Her satirical literary novel *American Witch* is available as an e-book. In addition, her scripts, novel manuscripts and short fiction have placed in numerous competitions, including the *Writer's Digest* Screenplay Competition and the Shriekfest Film Festival. She lives in Los Angeles, California. Discover more at: RosalindBarden.com

AND EVERYTHING NICE
BY B. DAVID SPICER

I'd known when she'd get there for several days, so I made it a point to have important business elsewhere at just that precise moment. Richard and Claire would be disappointed, of course, but not pissed off. They never got pissed off, which sometimes pissed *me* off because I lived for that sort of trouble, which is how I ended up in so many foster homes anyway. Richard would look sad and shake his head. He'd say, 'Andrew, we're very disappointed in your behavior. What more can we do to help you adjust?'

Poor Richard didn't get it. I didn't want to adjust or be adjusted. I *enjoyed* being maladjusted, I reveled in being a social outcast, a freak dressed in black, who wore eye makeup and listened to Bauhaus, The Cure and Siouxsie and the Banshees. They called me a Goth, and I supposed I lived up to that description, but in the 90s, everyone was *something*, a goth, a punk, or whatever. It all made sense back then.

The new kid, a six year old girl named Sandy, showed up right on schedule. Claire told me that Sandy was an orphan, like me. I watched from my usual perch on the roof, a cigarette between my teeth. I saw the social worker's car pull up to the curb and stop. Miz Jacobs, who insisted she not be addressed as either miss or missus, heaved her linebacker-built body out of the car and opened the back door for a tiny little blonde girl, all bouncy curls and pink lace.

I rolled my eyes, just knowing that Claire would expect me to play dolls with this little ray of sunshine. Would she *finally* get pissed off when I refused to have anything to do with the brat? That idea had possibilities. Spite was my forte, my artistic specialty.

Sandy clutched a pink teddy bear, which made me wince. Having a teddy bear was bad enough, but did it have to be pink? Insult on top of injury. She stood on the sidewalk as Miz Jacobs introduced her to Richard and Claire. Claire knelt to shake her hand, but Sandy dropped her bear and wrapped her arms around Claire's neck in an enthusiastic hug. Some cigarette smoke stung my eyes just then. The girl hugged Richard with the same fervent energy.

I met Sandy just before dinner that night. Richard did the honors. "Sandy, this young man is Andrew. He lives here too. I know he might look scary..." He never got to finish, because Sandy did a repeat performance of her hugging act and wrapped her arms around my head. I didn't remember kneeling down for her to do that, but I must have. She smelled like cotton candy, but in a good way. She kissed my cheek and beamed her 10,000 watt smile at me. "Hello Andrew!"

"Uh, hi, Sandy."

"Can we be friends?"

I blinked and shot a sideways glance at Claire, who had a hand over her mouth. "Sure."

"Oh, goody! I've never had a friend before!" She hugged me again, and I think that's when her victory over me was complete. I'd known this child for less than five minutes, and she'd already swept away fifteen years' worth of carefully cultivated cynicism and emotional indifference. I didn't realize it then, of course, because I'd never loved anybody before, and had no idea what had just happened, but I'd just fallen in love with her, the pure kind of love a brother feels for his younger sister.

So Sandy settled into our little world, and right away I noticed she didn't act like other children, that is, like *normal* children. I've seen lots of kids, of course, whiny, demanding, temperamental little monsters for the most part, but not Sandy. She never complained, never got upset, never made demands and never whined. Her mood varied from cheerful exuberance to bubbly ebullience, with both ends of her emotional spectrum improving throughout the day. Which meant that she woke up happy and went to bed happier. I've never seen anybody else as happy as Sandy, neither before nor in the decades since.

That isn't to say that her life wasn't without complications. For instance, she sleepwalked. Some mornings when she woke up, she'd find herself in the kitchen, or the living room, or once, the treehouse in the backyard. So, we all fell into the habit of checking in on her throughout the night, even me, because we couldn't bear the thought of her hurting herself. Which leads me to the strangest event of my life.

One Saturday night I'd burned through two or three smokes while sitting in my usual spot on the roof, when I heard the back door open below me. Sure enough, Sandy came into view, fully dressed and wearing her pink jacket. She crossed the yard quickly and deliberately, exiting the gate on the far end without slowing down. I considered calling out to her, but instead I jumped off of the roof and landed with a huge bounce on the trampoline in the back yard, and dashed through the gate after her.

I managed to catch up enough to keep her in sight, mostly because my legs were so much longer, but something furtive in her movements made me decide to follow her instead of just picking her up and taking her home. She moved with a purpose and had a definite destination in mind, and I suddenly realized she couldn't be sleepwalking. Was Sandy running away?

I kept her in view, but stuck to the shadows. I could have saved myself the effort because she didn't look behind her, not even once. A stray dog out for a stroll gave her a sniff and growled. I almost couldn't believe it, because animals reacted the same way to Sandy that people did: they adored her, even Richard's evil cat, Galahad, purred and rubbed his head against Sandy's face. But the dog lingered, snarling and barking at her.

"Get the bell out of here, you son of a birch!" She hurled the words at the stray, which tucked its tail and slinked away. Something bothered me about her words, not just the obviously edited curse words, but the cadence of her speech, which sounded different, wrong in a way I couldn't define. She scowled at the dog for a minute, an expression I'd never seen on her face before, and resumed her trek. Her little fingers curled into fists, clenching and unclenching as she steamed through the night.

She left the neighborhood where Richard and Claire lived, crossed through the old commercial district and entered into the area Claire called 'the blight' because of all the rundown houses and criminal activity. Sandy ignored the scenery and continued her determined march. An old man on a ramshackle porch whistled at her and suggested she come inside for a Popsicle.

"Go fork yourself!"

"That's no way for a little lady to talk!" He cracked open another Natty Light and poured it down his neck. "Come over here and be a good girl."

"I'm not a lady, and I'm sure as spit not gonna be a good girl. So stick your head up your bass!" She moved on while the old man laughed so hard he spilled his beer. At the end of the block, she made an abrupt turn and climbed the porch steps of a cinder-block house. She pounded on the door with both of her tiny fists.

"Johnny! Open the door, you faking bathrobe! Wake up you drunk son of a pitch!" She pounded on the door, screaming in Sandy's voice, but not with her little-girl inflection. Her words had taken on a different sound, the way she said them had changed. She almost sounded like a New Yorker now. "Open this door, Johnny, before I kick the shirt outta you!"

I ducked behind the decaying heap of a car where I could see what was going on. Finally, the door opened and a bookish man in his late thirties opened the door, still tying the belt of his ratty bathrobe. He spoke to her through a screen-door covered in dead bugs.

"Little girl, why are you outside at this hour? I'm not buying any Girl Scout cookies..."

"Do I look like I'm selling funking cookies?" She stabbed a finger at him. "You put me in this body, you sasshole, now you're dumbed well gonna get me out of it!"

"What?"

"It's me, you moron! Tony Casino!"

The man blinked for a minute. "Tony?" He opened the screen-door, knelt down and stared into Sandy's face. "Tony Casino? My God, is that really you?"

Sandy crunched one of her fists into his nose, and he toppled backward onto his butt. "Of course it's me, you idiot! Now get me out of this kid's body and back into my own."

He slowly stood up. "I think you'd better come inside."

Sandy heaved a huge sigh. "You'd better not jerk me around, Johnny." She strode past him and into the house. He followed her, but left the front door open. I dashed onto the porch and pressed my ear close to the screen-door.

"So, Tony, what happened?"

"You tell me! One minute you're talking that witchcraft mumbo-jumbo, the next thing I know, I wake up as a girl!"

"That wasn't supposed to happen. The incantation was supposed to protect your life and make you immortal."

"Well, Joey Martoleone put two in my chest, so your spell isn't worth skip!"

He chuckled. "Skip. That's funny."

"No it's mucking not! I can't even cuss! I have to kiss sitting down, and I can't even cuss!"

"Kiss sitting down?"

"Kiss! Hiss! Pass! Oh, Christ, you see what I mean? What's going on, Johnny?"

"Something went wrong."

"No shut?" She hissed out a lungful of air. "This is getting so old."

"Look, Tony. I think the spell worked, just not like we expected it to. You are alive, after all. And you're still you. Sort of."

"I'm only *me* when *she's* asleep!"

"She?"

"Yeah, the girl who this body belongs to. A glitch named Sandy. Itch. Ditch." Another sigh. "Get me a beer, Johnny."

"Uh, I don't think..."

"Get me a beer, Johnny. I'm not really a little girl, get over it." I heard a can crack open and the sound of someone swallowing noisily. "Oh, that's good."

"Tony, tell me how this works again. There's another personality in that body too?"

"Yeah, a little girl. She's all cuteness and rainbows, enough to make me puke. Everything she owns is pink! Pink, pink, pink!"

"You're only in control of the body when the girl-personality is asleep."

"You got it. But I'm always aware of what's going on, even when she's awake. I see everything she sees, I hear everything she hears. I can't shut her out." I heard her take a noisy sip of beer. "This is the first beer I've had in months!" She slurped at the can again.

"The people you live with don't drink beer?"

She laughed. "No, they're Mormons, they don't drink or smoke. Or cuss."

"Sounds awful." Johnny laughed.

"Shut the truck up, Johnny. Why can't I cuss?"

"My guess is, that the girl, this Sandy persona, is stopping you. She must have a very strong personal prohibition against cussing, which somehow prevents you from doing it either."

"That little stitch!"

"Hey, at least she let you have the beer." He chuckled.

I heard her slam her fists onto the tabletop. "All right, Johnny! Enough screwing around! How do I get out of this body and back into my own?"

"You don't."

"Wrong answer, Johnny..."

"At least for now. I'll need to research what's happened to you. It could take some time. Your body, your original body, was cremated, so that's gone for good. We might be able to transfer your spirit into a different host though, one more acceptable to you."

She sighed. "Fine, how can I at least get control of this body all the time? I'm sick of watching Sandy play with her dolls all rucking day."

"That, I think I can help you with."

"Really?"

"Yeah. Since there are two personalities trapped in the same body, one of them must be removed so you can be in control. The girl is the dominant personality, which we know because she is in control by default, and you are only in control while she's asleep."

"Great, so what do we have to do?"

"Kill the other personality."

I gasped, but quickly covered my mouth. I peeked around the corner of the door frame and could see Johnny sitting at the table in the kitchen.

Tony frowned through Sandy's face. "Kill her? Why would we have to kill her?"

"To allow you to have complete control of that body until we can figure out a way to move you into another one. It's the only way." He frowned a little. "Is there a problem, Tony?"

"Well, yeah, I mean, she's just a little girl. I don't think I want to kill a little girl, Johnny." She shifted uncomfortably in her chair, looking like both a child, and a grown up.

"Wait a second." Johnny stood up and left the room for a minute, when he came back he had a silver ball on a chain necklace. "All you need to do is put this around your neck just before she takes control. After a minute or two, her essence will be dissipated and you'll be in sole possession of the body."

"That'll kill her?"

"Think of it more as an exorcism. Her spirit will be set free. Or, you can keep playing dolls and sitting down to kiss." Johnny grinned. He didn't have many teeth left.

"Fine, give me the necklace. I'll do it. Tonight. I just put it on?"

"She'll just have to wear it for a few minutes, and then she'll be gone. She has to be in control while she has the necklace on in order for it to work."

She dangled it in front of her face. "It doesn't look like much, does it?"

"It's a potent talisman, designed to expel demons during a possession. It might not look like much, but I promise you it'll work."

"All right. I'll give it a try."

Johnny shifted in his chair. "You, uh, aren't gonna do it here, are you?"

"Well, why the bell wouldn't I?"

"It has a better chance of working in the girl's usual environment. If she's scared, she might put up a fight."

"So what if she does?"

"If she passes out, it'll be *you* who gets exorcised."

She sighed. "I think you just want me to go away. That's fine, I'll be back tomorrow night, Johnny, and when I get here you'd better know how to get me out of this body. I think I want Joey Martoleone's body. He's a young, good looking guy, popular with the ladies. I hear he's got a big cork, so I'll just move in and kick his bass to the curb, and put that nightstick to some good use."

Hearing this foulness spoken with Sandy's voice made me queasy, but I'd already resolved to prevent Tony Casino from doing anything to Sandy. I heard her push her chair away from the table and I leapt over the side of the porch and ducked behind the car again. Sandy came out of Johnny's house and stopped on the sidewalk.

"I'll be back tomorrow, Johnny. You'd better be home, and you'd better know what to do to get me out of here."

"I'll try, Tony. Good luck."

She flipped him the bird. "Prism off." She started down the sidewalk toward home. I waited until Johnny had closed the door before I started following her. I paced her until we'd gotten to within a few blocks of home when I sped up to walk beside her.

"Hello, Tony."

She scowled up at me. "Andrew? What are you doing out here?"

"Following you. I know what you're planning, Tony, and I won't let you kill Sandy."

She stopped walking and shook her head. "Hey, I don't like it either, she's a cute kid, reminds me of my own daughters at that age, but I can't stay in here forever."

"So you're gonna murder a child to get what you want? Does that make you feel like a tough guy, Tony?"

"Go truck yourself, or better yet, go listen to more of that dopey music and let your Dark Lord truck your mass-hole." She clenched her fists and hissed through her teeth. "See? I can't live like this anymore!"

"I won't let you kill, Sandy!"

I expected another acid retort, instead, she took off running, heading toward the park. For a six year old, Sandy, and by extension, Tony, could run extremely fast. I had to give it everything I had just to catch up to her. I snatched her off the ground and held her up in front of me. Which proved to be a painful mistake. She aimed a punch at my prominent nose, and I dropped her. She popped up, kicked me in the

195

shin, and ran through the darkness.

I cursed, noting that the words came out unmodified, and set off after her. She ran toward the playground equipment and started climbing up the tube-slide, but I grabbed her feet and dragged her out of the tube. She kicked like a jackrabbit, and I struggled to hold on to her. I saw the end of the necklace dangling from her pocket, and gave her legs a yank. She twisted and kicked some more, and the necklace fell out of her pocket. I let her go and she started up the slide again. I picked up the necklace and went for her feet again.

"Let go of me, motherbucker!"

"Watch your mouth, little girl."

"Go to well!"

"I'll see what I can do!" I pulled her out of the slide and maneuvered her around. I spun her around so she faced away from me, the necklace falling over her head and onto her chest. She kicked her leg backward into my crotch. I went down like I'd been shot. She rolled away from me and jumped up to hammer away at my nose again. I pulled her toward me and wrapped her in my arms, and held her immobile. She didn't smell like cotton candy, which is what Sandy always smelled like, but rather like old cigarettes and beer-sweat. In fact, she smelled like the old man who worked at the video store downtown. It almost made me gag.

"What are you doing? Let go of me!"

"No, Tony. It'll all be over in a few minutes."

"What the cell are you talking about?"

I held her with one arm and gave the necklace a tug with my other hand. "You won't be sharing this body with Sandy much longer."

Her eyes widened and she struggled like her life depended on it, which in a way, it did. "No! I'll give you anything you want! I have money! In a hiding place in Jersey! I'll give it to you!"

"No thanks."

"Look, I know women! You like women, right, Andrew?"

"Goodbye, Tony."

"No! Let..me...go!" She writhed in my arms until she realized its futility. "Well, ain't this about a tucking hitch." Those were the last words Tony Casino ever spoke through Sandy's lips. A moment later, I smelled cotton candy, and heard Sandy speak in her childlike cadence again.

"Andrew?"

"Hello, Sandy."

"Why are we outside at night?"

"You were sleepwalking again, so I came to get you." I released my grip on her and gave her a smile. "You walked really far this time." I took the necklace off of her neck and put it in my pocket. She didn't seem to notice.

She looked around and shot me one of her brilliant smiles. "We're in the park! I love the park! Can we play, Andrew?"

"We can play in the morning, sweetness. Right now it's time for sleep. We should go home and go to bed."

"Okay." She took my hand and we walked home together. She changed into her pajamas and got into her bed. I tucked her in and kissed her cheek.

"Goodnight, Andrew!"

"Goodnight, Sandy." I waited for to her close her eyes and fall asleep, and I watched over her all that night, and many more thereafter, the talisman clutched in my hand, but Tony Casino never made another appearance.

B. David Spicer lives in Ohio, where he earned a BA in English from Ohio University. His first name is Brian, but thinks B. David Spicer sounds more artsy and pretentious. He's a member of the Horror Writers Association who writes crime fiction, science fiction, horror stories and scripts for independent comic book publishers. His short fiction has appeared in several short story anthologies including *Out of Phase* from Sirens Call Publications, *From the Corner of Your Eye: A Cryptids Anthology*, and *Pernicious Invaders* (both from

Great Old Ones Publishing), *Dark Light Book Four*, and *Hope & Love Anthology* (both from Crushing Hearts & Black Butterfly Publishing), *Torched* (Nocturnal Press), *Strangely Funny II* (Mystery and Horror LLC), *Tales With a Twist*, and *The Rudderhaven Science Fiction and Fantasy Anthologies II* and *III*, (all three from Rudderhaven Publications) as well as several upcoming short story anthologies. He's written comic book scripts for PLB Comics' *The Fall: Vengeance and Justice*, *The PLB Comics Halloween Special*, and contributed stories to Acid I Comics' *A Taste For Killing*. You can contact him at: bdspicer@horizonview.net

A FAMILIAR PROBLEM
BY DANIEL HALE

Dultarius Broadkent, Under-Cunning class sorcerer, member of the Northern Ohio Arcane Arts Society, was hunting for a familiar.

He shouldn't have had to, which was the galling thing. He lived on his late grandmother's estate, precariously perched on a lumpy hill that overlooked a narrow, unpaved road. The backyard was an overgrown wilderness of uncut grass and, somewhere in the tangled depths, her garden. Forest surrounded it on all sides and, usually, the requisite number of chirping, chittering wild life was favorable.

Traditionally, familiars would appear before their masters when they were needed.

That was why practitioners tended to live in wild, or at least comparatively remote, places. Sooner or later, a local spirit would coagulate in the mind of a squirrel or a chipmunk, or a stray cat, or even the air itself if no other form was available. It would then act as a repository of magical knowledge, aiding the practitioner in his art dutifully, and loyally.

That was tradition. But tradition was having a hard time of it, these days.

Dultarius trudged through the forest, conscious of his brown terrycloth robe and his staff (he'd bought it at a hobby shop. It had a tiny pair of antlers carved on the upper end, and a black rubber guard on the bottom). It was the latter part of autumn, nearing sunset, which was just as well. Technically, the forest was a municipal park, and it was always embarrassing to conduct magical business in the way of people trying to use the disc-golf course.

The forest should have been waking up at this time of the evening, alive with things that squawked and scurried when the sun went down. There should have been bats fluttering from branch to branch, and raccoons bounding away at the sorcerer's approach. Instead, the only sounds were the snapping of weeds against his legs, the sucking of mud on his soles, and the muttering of pseudo-Latin profanities under his breath.

The sun had set completely by the time the sorcerer returned to his property. He was shaking with the rising chill and pent-up exhaustion; like most practitioners, Dultarius was a dedicated insomniac, his nerves strung together with cheap coffee and over-the-counter uppers. Magic, even the simplest, required sacrifice of some kind, and peace of mind was considered the minimum. The very best sorcerers could go weeks without sleep, and not so much treaded the line between genius and madness, as collapsed across it in debilitating giggle-fits.

Dultarius was on his third night of wakefulness, and at his sharpest, mentally speaking. He decided he would rather risk doing research on his own for a change than try winding down, and letting the tension go to waste.

He practiced out of his grandmother's old gardening shed, a husk of peeling blue paint and rusted nails. The hinges hung loosely from the rotted wood, the doors bowed out against the padlock.

As he approached, Dultarius felt the hairs on the back of his neck stand on end. He could feel static electricity throbbing against the doors. Aether mail.

He gritted his teeth; he hated getting ae-mail. Bad enough it cluttered your head with spiritual flotsam, but it also felt like running into a wall of charged carpet. There was no way out of it, either. Not if he wanted to use his laboratory.

So, gripping his staff and closing his eyes, Dultarius

reached out and touched the doors.

Dultarius Broadkent. The Northern Ohio Arcane Arts Society bids you greetings. Your most wise and valued counsel is requested next Saturday hence at three, A.M., for our monthly Sabbath and bonfire. Marshmallows and S'mores shall be available, and —

Dultarius muttered the delete cantrip. He'd been reluctant to attend the meets ever since they introduced therapeutic skyclad demonstrations. It wasn't that he was insecure. It was just that most practitioners were not pleasing to look at, even with their clothes on. Ritual nudity brought to mind a whole slew of forgotten modern conveniences, such as hot baths and electric razors and skin creams.

Great magus, help me! My fortunes have been ransacked by a horde of half-orcs. Aid me, and I will ensure a quarter share —

Astral spam. Delete cantrip.

Don't trust your magic to an animal. Improve your spells in ways you never thought possible. Receive guidance and advice at the equivalent of a Great Fiend level practitioner. Automatically updated on all the latest approved rituals and workings, with such helpful features as Component Calibration and Spell Correction, and full customization options for physical form and personality. Esotere presents The Very Familiar. Will one sacrifice of newborn baby-value to summon yours today.

The haze of static dissipated, the last words of the ethereal advertisement echoing in Dultarius' head. Another aspect of ae-mail that disturbed him was its uncanny knack of coincidence. It made him feel like his actions weren't due entirely to his own initiative.

Still, the study and practice of magic would never have

gotten off the ground if its disciples let philosophy worry them. Dultarius had commissions waiting. He needed a familiar.

So he entered the shed, and set about preparing a summoning ritual. He fished a nub of chalk out of the rusted watering can, and drew a circle on the wooden floor. He drew Transaction runes around the edges, adding Esotere's corporate sigil to receive the deposit.

Newborn baby...it was unquestionably steep, but the fortunate thing about the magic economy was that it left you a certain degree of freedom through interpretation.

Dultarius had no children. He could think of nothing he physically owned that had the same value, and he couldn't just steal a baby, or it would mean the Amber Elementals coming down on his head. What worth was a baby?

Sleep. That was it. His own mother had given birth to eight children, over an eight year period. She was a stout lady with a kick that could fell a ghetto troll, and she'd trained herself to run on half an hour's sleep each night. Of course, she fainted constantly and was known to speak in tongues, but she managed well enough, all things considered.

Dultarius only slept two or three times a week anyway. Just imagine how much sharper his skills could become by sacrificing a few hours?

He had to write small to fit the runes into the circle. It got somewhat cramped near the end, but Dultarius lit seven candles around the edges, raised his staff, and spoke the contract.

"Esotere," he invoked. "By air and wave I call you! By contract and compact and consent I grant you! By market and barter I meet you!"

The circle set off a faint hum, like a baseball card of infinite size brushed by the spokes of the wheel of the cosmos. The hum rose in pitch, higher and higher, before attaining a height beyond octave and going completely silent.

Dultarius waited as his request was processed. Then, a voice like the shaping of wind in a throat of wood spoke from the nowhere inside the circle. *"Do you grant Esotere leave from the consequences of your actions?"*

"I do."

"And do you swear, by the Fourteen Contravenes and the Abra Accords, that you will not knowingly tamper, alter or in any way change the nature of the Very Familiar in such a way as to invalidate its enchantment?"

"Yes."

"Do you desire to be made wise of further of Esotere's Great Workings by invoking our newsletter?"

"No."

"Do you understand the terms and conditions of this compact?"

Terms settled in Dultarius' mind like a brick in a pond. He did not have to consciously examine them to agree. "I understand," he said.

"It is done," said the voice. And a creature appeared in the circle.

Dultarius stared at it. It was definitely animal, if only in broad terms. It was about two feet tall, and blue in color. It was covered in something more down than fur, more fluff than feather. Its mouth was somewhat elongated, and had something of both beak and muzzle about it. Its eyes were oval-shaped, and filled brim-to-brim with blackness. Its ears were wide and triangular.

"Hello!" Its voice was light and whimsical, with an inoffensively English lilt. It was as charming and dapper as an insurance mascot. "I am your *Very Familiar!*" The copyright charm beneath the creature's word flashed a brief and unmistakable charge into the air. "What would you like to call me?"

Dultarius stared at the unlikely creature. He felt at once disappointed and amazed. The thing was clearly an artificial construct, a spirit creation of pure magic. It was vaguely translucent; he could see the clutter of rusted tools he never got around to throwing out in the back of the shed. And it was friendly, or at least polite. Most familiars were intransigent, and easily distracted. This one seemed on the ball, eager to serve —

"You have not responded," said the Very Familiar, in a tone of mild concern. "Would you like to name me later?"

Very eager. "I'll call you, um, Jeeves." Not especially imaginative but it was the only thing he could think of. He recovered himself. "And I," he said grandly. "I am your master, Dultarius. I charge you to honor my command and give me counsel as —"

"Hello, Dultarius!" the Very Familiar said brightly. "I am Jee-vess!" It pronounced the esses separately. "You will notice that, with my Intentions Intensive Perception, I can perceive your every command on a mental as well as verbal level, allowing me to understand what you want better than even you do!" Jee-vess smiled brightly, perhaps. It was difficult to tell through the beak-snout. "Now, how would you like me to look? My Perception tells me that you enjoy raccoons. Would you like me to look like a raccoon? Oh, and incidentally, my Arcane Encyclopedia Capacity means that I can fill you in on even the most esoteric of esoteric knowledge! For example, did you know that the Tanuki, a forest spirit native to Japan, takes on the form of a raccoon with enormous —"

"Stop! I command you!" Dultarius thought quickly. "Look like a bat. And no interesting bat spirit facts, please," he added.

Jee-vess blinked, and began to fade into invisibility. "Very well. I will be a bat. Please remember that my Chameleonic Personalization Capacity is still in the beta stage of testing."

Jee-vess shimmered, fading away to nearly nothing, coiling mistily at the edges. After a moment substance returned, showing Dultarius Jee-vess' new shape.

The ears were pointier, and erect, more like a Doberman's than a bat's. The wings were flat, triangular shapes sticking out of Jee-vess' back. Otherwise, the Very Familiar was unchanged.

Dultarius decided that it didn't really matter what the thing looked like, so long as it was useful. "Right, well. Let's get started. There's an old lady who needs a plumbing charm to reconnect the drains."

"A plum charm," Jee-vess said. "My Celestial Positioning Perception indicates that this is early autumn. Plums are more preferably planted in late winter or early spring. I might recommend a temporal divergent enchantment to accelerate harvest. Three broken pocket watches of at least Edwardian make or earlier are required, and must be submerged in a solution of—"

"No, no! I said plumbing, not plums!" Dultarius rapped his staff on the floor. *Act like its master*, he told himself. Be imperious. "Clean thy ears, creature, lest I cast you into back unto the deepest pit—"

"Casting the pit from the plum will require a measure of apple cider vinegar shot through with ground calcium carbonate, injected into the plum with a brass syringe—"

"Desist! Cancel! *Shut up!*"

Jee-vess waited politely. Suddenly Dultarius was regretting very much giving up on full nights of sleep. Obviously talking a few centuries out of date would not be helpful. Perhaps he should try this a step at a time. "I need a household spell."

"You require a domestic spell," intoned the Very Familiar. "Maintenance or enhancement?"

"Maintenance, please, Jee-vess."

"Maintenance. Utilities, or upkeep?"

"Utilities," Dultarius said, desperately.

"Heating, cooling, electricity, broadband-cable-and Internet connection, water—"

"Water!"

"You require a water utilities spell." The Very Familiar was becoming more monotoned by the second. "Do you wish to resume discontinued water access? If so, please be advised that circumnavigating the local Utilities Board would be a contravention of article thirteen of the Sorcerous Malfeasance Act—"

"I just want the drains reconnected!"

"You require reconnection of drains to the main systems. You will require: one schematic of the house's floorplans, one fresh piece of yellow chalk, and a rusted copper pipe."

Dultarius gathered the ingredients quickly. He cleared a space on the worktable and laid out the schematic. At Jee-vess' instructions, he sketched the pipes beneath the house, and connected them to drains in the kitchen sink, the bathroom sink, the toilet and the tub. He wiped rust from the pipe, dabbed it as best he could over the lines, muttering incantations.

"The spell will require thirteen hours to take effect," finished Jee-vess. "Would you like to upgrade to high-speed Evocation for an additional Cherished Treasure Sacrifice?"

"No." Mrs. Gardner had paid an advance, with the remainder on completion of the job. Dultarius had been cheated out of such commissions before, when just the evidence of the furnace working or the peeling repaired in the paint was put down to coincidence. He added a thematic flourish to the working, so that a light yellow glow would emanate from the drains. They said they wanted the job done quickly and without fuss, but in truth they wanted the magic to be a little showy.

"Did you find this spell helpful?"

Dultarius looked up from the schematics. "What? Oh, yes. You did well, servant."

"On a scale of one to five, one being unhelpful, five being—"

"Four and a half," Dultarius said, absently. "That's enough."

"Would you now like to submit your Esotere registration?"

"Not now! We've got another job."

The next was slightly easier; an adjunct professor at the local community college wanted a tincture of charm. The dirty old letch had insisted it was just to make his students pay more attention to his lectures, but the way he licked his lips and kept his hands in his pockets revolted Dultarius.

But work was work, so he asked the Very Familiar which potion would be best. The creature began rattling off the ingredients.

"About what I expected," Dultarius said. Still, it was useful that the creature was so knowledgeable. "I need a variation for a man in his mid-fifties."

Jee-vess was silent for a moment. "You will need two tablespoons of name-brand wart cream, six ounces of shavings from a wooden plank no less than ten years old…"

The useful thing about living in his late grandmother's home was that it was so packed with junk and rubbish. The old bat had been too lazy to do much cleaning, and Dultarius could usually find most of what he needed somewhere.

"I'll rate that a three, by the way. Right, I think that's enough for the night. How do I turn you off?"

"Never fear! Your Very Familiar will automatically disperse of its own volition. To re-summon, simply speak my name—"

"Right, yes." Dultarius shut the shed door and replaced the padlock. "Good night."

It took the sorcerer most of the evening to fall asleep, and the relief came and went so quickly he hardly noticed. *Ah well*, he thought. *You get what you deal for.*

After a breakfast of burnt bacon and coffee, Dultarius delivered the charm tincture to the professor, positively throwing it at him to avoid touching his shaking hands. At least the old fool was happy enough to pay him without questioning too deeply about the tincture's contents.

Dultarius was worried. This was nothing new; no magician could learn the craft without turning just a little twitchy. Paranoia was healthy, and even comforting. Surliness was a given.

But Dultarius was starting to feel positive. That was definitely unheard of. After the initial teething troubles, Jeevess had proven as efficient as Esotere had advertised, with nary a flaw to be seen. Traditional familiars could not even be relied upon to give exact measurements to ingredients, making for some alarming variations in potency and toxicity.

And yet the Very Familiar had provided the knowledge with ease. That seemed wrong.

Subsequently, when Dultarius felt moved to check in on Mrs. Gardner, he was practically relieved to have the old woman harangue him about the state of the drains. "All I've gotten out of you is a pretty light coming out of the drains! I'm still having to use the neighbor's toilet."

Dultarius adopted his best expression of learned serenity. "Mrs. Gardner, I did tell you when you came to me the enchantment was fraught with subtle intricacies. Magic is not entirely subject to our own design—"

"Neither is my stomach!" snapped Mrs. Gardner. "I've called a plumber. You'll give me back that advance, young man."

"Like hell I will!"

"Then I'll tell the police about your scamming old ladies!"

Dultarius would have dearly liked to hex the horrid woman into a puddle of flesh and cartilage. Unfortunately, the only curse he could perform on the fly undid the stitches in the recipient's clothes. He would rather not have to punish himself with that in addition to being sued for molestation.

When Dultarius returned to his shed he was two-hundred dollars poorer, and very desirous for a good, flesh-melting curse. "Jee-vess, I conjure thee!"

The smiling pseudo-bat faded back into the summoning circle. "Hello, Dultarius! I'm pleased to say that an update is available for my Astral Communications Capacity. Never again will you clutter your threshold—"

"I command you to tell me why your plumbing spell didn't go through!"

"All spell and enchantment effects are held in suspension pending registration."

"Registration?"

"Full access to all features of your Very Familiar requires registration of your true name with Esotere, in addition to the subscription fee for the Arcane Encyclopedia. You may pay by monthly installment of your happiest memory per month, or one year's worth of memory, per year."

"You didn't tell me that before!"

"I'm sorry, but you indicated you understood the terms and conditions of Esotere's compact. Esotere is not responsible for false understanding once consent is given."

The details of the compact were already an incomprehensible slurry of jargon in the back of Dultarius' mind. "Then why did you tell me the spell at all?"

"Non-registered users are granted a free trial of their Very Familiar up to their first enchantment. The enchantment will not go into effect until registration is complete."

"But you gave me knowledge without asking me for my memory!"

"Agreement to the terms and conditions of the compact automatically signifies subscription to the Arcane Encyclopedia. Unless otherwise specified, Esotere grants the user basic subscriber privileges."

"You mean you've already taken one of my memories this month? But I don't remember…um. Forgetting anything…"

"In accordance with the compact, Esotere examined your most recent memories and selected the most treasured. Greta

Smallbrooke met you for coffee."

"She did? Wait. Who's Greta?"

"I'm afraid I cannot tell you without violating the terms and conditions of the compact."

"But...hang on! What about the charm tincture?"

Jee-vess blinked, and looked apologetic. "I have no recollection of a charm tincture, I am afraid."

"I asked you for it just after the plumbing spell!"

"Potions, tinctures and elixirs are a stationary form of magic, and lack the full benefits of a genuine spell. Esotere does not charge for instructions on their preparation. However, I assure you that the only tincture you've asked me for was a muscle liniment."

"What! But I specifically asked for a charm tincture for a fifty-year-old man!"

"Ah," said Jee-vess, regretfully. "It would appear my Spell Correction Directive was a tad overzealous. It seemed to me unlikely that a man over the age of fifty would need to enhance his sex appeal. Please bear in mind that much of my functions are still in the beta stage. However, if you would like to send an error report to Esotere, I am sure—"

"Right, that does it," thundered Dultarius. "Creature, I expel you from my sight! You can tell Esotere I am deeply unsatisfied with their product!"

An expression of deepest horror spilled onto Jee-vess' face. Its snout-beak gaped, its useless wings trembled.

The lines of the summoning circle slowly acquired a white luminescence, like sunlight shot through ice crystals. A chemical smell, septic and metallic, seeped into the shed.

Jee-vess suddenly looked very animal; it paced the circle uncertainly, watching the glowing lines and whimpering.

The circle was shrinking. Before it, it looked to Dultarius like a tiny dust storm was pouring out of the white. Black, minute particles spat and shook, crashing together in rabid crests before racing towards the trapped Very Familiar.

Dultarius watched Jee-vess dissolve from the legs up, torn

apart into to strands of spell-life, themselves torn away into vaguest components of wizardry, into light and time and intent.

He stared into the creature's eyes as it was ripped apart, did not look away even as its yowling rose to wall-shaking decibels.

At last, the circle was emptied. The light died, the shadow specks dissipated.

Dultarius looked around. The shed seemed even emptier than it should have been. As if a vacuum had been planted into the walls that fed on some vague yet all-encompassing vitality.

He cleared his throat. He smiled absently at the nothingness. "I suppose I shouldn't expect a refund?"

Daniel Hale is an amateur storyteller living in Canton, Ohio. He has had stories published in Mystery and Horror LLC's *All Hallows' Evil*, as well as *What Has Two Heads, Ten Eyes and Terrifying Table Manners?* by Mega Thump Publishing, *The Last Diner*, by KnightWatch Press, *Creature Stew* by Papa Bear Press, and *The Myriad Carnival* by Glitter Wolf Publications. Find him at: danielhale42.wordpress.com

ATTACK OF THE RAD-ZOMBIES
BY D.J. TYRER

Damp Valley was very much the essence of small town America, being a town of relatively small size. It was nothing special. It was poor. It was located in a valley that was, as the name suggested, rather damp.

Things changed when Shady Acres Funeral Home opened with a wide new and surprisingly shade-less cemetery on the edge of town. Around the same time, people began to see mysterious tanker trucks bearing hazardous waste symbols driving down the back roads. Where they came from, where they were going and just what they were carrying were all questions that nobody knew the answer to; very few were actually interested. Even the *Damp Valley Concoctor* carried just a couple of brief lines on the tankers, whilst running multiple two-page spreads on Shady Acres and all the benefits that having a cut-price burial ground would bring to the area. Only a couple of local environuts cared about the trucks and nobody much cared what they thought.

John Schwartz had hoped that the opening of Shady Acres would get him into a job and out of his parents' basement, but despite applying to be a gravedigger, a grass-cutter and even a headstone polisher, he had had no success. The closest he had come to a job at Shady Acres was as a mourner at the burial of his grandma on a rather bare hillside. The ceremony was quite moving given that they were allowed just a fifteen-minute slot to lay her to rest. Had he not been attempting to mourn at high speed, John might have noticed the tire tracks that indicated several heavy-laden trucks had passed through that section of the cemetery.

"Lovely," sniffed his mother as his father drove them and his sister, Kelly, home.

There was a simple buffet for friends and family upon their return, a quiet and somber affair; then the day was over. John was put out by the fact that his great-uncle wasn't leaving till the morning, meaning he had to give up his bed for the third night running. The basement was okay, but sleeping out in the gazebo wasn't.

"I can't wait till everything's back to normal," he told Kelly as he headed out into the garden. Unfortunately, his words would come back to him as if he'd tempted fate.

The next day passed uneventfully, mostly in front of the TV playing *Call of Duty*. His great-uncle was gone and John was back in the basement, and glad to be there. He felt just a little guilty to be glad the entire funeral business was out of the way. John had loved his grandma, but the hassles of playing host to relatives who'd gone unseen for years had made it more unpleasant than necessary.

Supper was some cold pizza left over from the buffet.

Not entirely full, he headed upstairs to the kitchen to see what else was left. John was hoping for meatballs, but had to make do with a little Canadian bacon.

"It's a hard life," he muttered as he devoured some.

John was just swigging from a can of cola when he heard a sound from the backyard; it sounded as if someone had stumbled over the ride-on mower.

Wondering if it was a burglar, he went over to the window and twitched aside the curtain. There was definitely someone outside; he could see a shadowy figure, but from the way they shambled about, he was sure it was an old person. Oddly, they seemed to be illuminated by a soft green glow.

"Probably Mrs. McKay," he muttered, thinking of their neighbor from down the road who had dementia and really needed to go into a home. She sometimes wandered into her neighbors' homes and gardens in a confused state.

John walked to the door, opened it and stepped out.

"Hey, Mrs. McKay, that you? You okay?"

There was a sort of gurgling rattle in response. Sometimes, the old woman would make inarticulate sounds like that.

"Mrs. McKay?"

The figure shambled nearer, into the area lit by the lights of the house.

John gasped in shock. "Grandma?"

It was definitely her. She looked as she had as she lay in her coffin, only disheveled and dirty with soil, clearly having clawed her way out of the earth.

"Grandma, you're alive!" John felt a wave of guilt. She must've been in a coma and nobody realized. "Oh, man, let's get you inside where it's warm."

He stepped towards her and reached out to support and guide her. As he did so, she lunged for him and snapped at his fingers with her dentures. He recoiled in shocked surprise.

"Grandma!" he exclaimed, reproachfully.

"Problem?" called a voice. It was their neighbor, Mr. Swanson, peeking over the fence. Then, he obviously saw who it was. "That your grandma, kid?"

"Yeah," John called back, retreating as she shambled towards him, arms outstretched, fingers twitching, jaws snapping. Her eyes were oddly blank and the whites a yellowish-green.

"Jeepers! She was buried alive – terrible!" Swanson came through the gate that connected their drives. "Can I be of help?"

His approach caught the old lady's attention and she turned and shuffled towards him, instead.

"Hello, there..." he began to say, only for her to leap at him, grab him. Her touch seemed to sear his skin. He struggled for a moment, then she tore out his throat in a bloody spray. John was most surprised that her dentures had stayed in.

"Grandma!" John exclaimed, affronted. "You can't bite Mr. Swanson!" It was a terrible way to behave.

Then, as she crouched over his twitching body and began to devour his flesh, something clicked in John's brain and he realized that the strange, dead eyes and the lust for human flesh could mean only one thing: Zombie!

John didn't have to pause to consider what to do: he'd seen every zombie film going. There was a baseball bat just inside the house; John's father had one ready just in case a burglar broke in. John dashed back inside and grabbed it, then ran back outside it.

A good swing smashed his grandma's jaw so that it dangled grotesquely from one side as she lunged towards him.

A second good swing smashed in her skull and a third pulped her brain so that she fell still in a disgusting, pulpy mess at his feet.

John stared down at her, uncertain whether to be horrified or elated at what he'd just done.

"What's all the noise?" It was his sister, Kelly, in a dressing gown, obviously roused from bed.

"Um, nothing..."

"Yeah, right. What've you done, John?" She walked towards him.

"I've killed Grandma. Again."

John had felt terrible that a joke with a rubber spider had caused his grandma's fatal heart attack. To literally pulp her head was even worse, even if there was mitigation in the fact she was a flesh-craving zombie.

Kelly thought he was joking till she saw the bodies; there

had been no denying it, then.

Eventually, she'd helped him move Mr. Swanson's body over into his yard, hoping the police would assume he'd been attacked by a rabid raccoon or a Mexican or something. Now, they were wrapping Grandma in a blanket and loading her into the trunk of their dad's car. Luckily, John could drive, even if he couldn't afford a car. He just hoped Dad wouldn't notice the car was gone.

"You know," Kelly said, as they drove through Shady Acres, "there's something weird about this place."

"What, other than the fact Grandma came back?"

"Yes, doofus! Aren't you paying attention?"

"Of course, I am! I'm keeping a close eye on the road; and, don't call me doofus!"

"Sorry, doofus! But, look around: the grave plots are all glowing..."

"Glowing?" He glanced quickly around, wary of taking his gaze from the road for too long. John was not a very confident driver.

"Yeah, glowing green."

He thought for a moment. "I remember... Grandma's eyes were sort of glowing... and her touch seemed to burn Mr. Swanson..."

"What can it mean?"

"Radiation!"

"Radiation?"

"Yes. Remember those tanker trucks people said they saw?"

"Yeah."

"Well, I think they've probably been dumping toxic waste in the graves; *radioactive* waste. That must be what brought Grandma back from the dead."

"That's not good," Kelly murmured, "we could all get cancer!"

"Worse than that!"

"Worse?"

"If the radiation brought Grandma back as a zombie and there is radioactive waste in all these graves..."

"Well? Oh..." Her face fell.

"Exactly. There could be a heck load more zombies about to push their daisies right out the ground..."

"What do we do?"

"Dump Grandma, for a start."

They reached her grave and tossed her back in. They'd leave the soil and smashed casket for Shady Acres to explain. As they did so, they could hear scrabbling and scratching coming from nearby plots; it seemed it mightn't be the only open grave they'd have to explain.

"Now what?" Kelly asked.

"I think we should take a look around the funeral home itself. See if we can find any clues as to what's going on, who's behind it. Then, call a town meeting."

"Yeah," we could do with some evidence in that case."

They drove down to the funeral home and climbed out. They headed round to the back and sneaked in,

"Quiet," whispered Kelly, "I can hear someone."

There was music and someone singing along, rather off-key, and some squishy, sawing sound they couldn't quite place.

They crept over to the door of what proved to be the embalming room, where a man whom they recognized as the chief undertaker was elbow-deep in a twitching, glowing corpse, singing along to *Jeepers Creepers*, a smile on his face.

"Fascinating, fascinating, fascinating," he said, softly, as he grubbed about in guts and organs. "To imagine radiation could do this."

Kelly took out her phone and filmed him for a minute, before following her brother, who was headed for an office.

A quick search found some vaguely-worded contracts from a company called Nukem Disposal. They took them and headed back outside.

"Not a moment too soon," muttered John as they saw zombies pulling themselves from their graves.

They jumped back in the car and John put his foot down.

A zombie stumbled into the road and Kelly shrieked, but John just kept going. The car slammed into it and sent it flying.

"Boo-yeah!" he exclaimed and kept racing along.

"Dad! Dad! You've gotta wake up!"

"Wha'? Wha'?" Their parents looked at them in confusion as they shook their father awake and shouted at him.

"Dad! We need you to call a town meeting so that we can warn everyone about the radioactive zombies!"

Conveniently, their father was the town mayor, so he could call the town together on a whim.

"What are you talking about?" their mother asked as she rubbed bleary eyes.

"I killed Grandma!"

"No, John, we told you, it was a tragic accident; she could've gone at any time," his mother told him.

"No, not then; now! She came back from the dead and I smashed her head in!"

"Son, that's a terrible thing to say," his father said.

"No, Dad, it's the truth!" Kelly exclaimed. "Listen!"

"Dad – they're dumping radioactive waste in the graves at Shady Acres and the bodies are climbing out as zombies. Grandma was only the first! We saw others climbing out at Shady Acres!"

"You went to Shady Acres?" Mum asked.

"Yes, to return Grandma's body. We found more zombies. Oh, and I nearly forgot: Grandma killed Mr. Swanson..."

"What?"

"Dad, it's true!" Kelly exclaimed. "Go look at his body."

They showed him their dead neighbor – John was glad to see he showed no signs of coming back as a zombie, unlike in so many movies – then Kelly showed him the documents and the film she took.

"Okay, this could be true..." their father admitted.

The town meeting was called for eight o'clock that morning. As well as phone calls and the use of local radio and TV, a sheriff's car travelled the streets of Damp Valley announcing it over a bullhorn. In addition, occasional gunshots and screams and shouts of surprise helped to alert the townspeople that something was going on.

"From my men's reports," the sheriff told their father, "these zombies have infiltrated the west side of town." He sounded rather gleeful at the fact. "See, Mr. Schwartz, buying those chainsaws *wasn't* a waste of money, eh?"

Their father sniffed. "The main thing is to get everybody here, so we can warn them."

Just then, a deputy entered the office and informed them that the townspeople were ready in the school gym, waiting to be addressed.

Their father led them and the sheriff onto the stage.

"People! People, quiet, please!"

"What's happening?" someone called.

"I'm about to tell you," their father retorted. He took a deep breath. "People of Damp Valley, our town is being invaded by radioactive zombies."

The news didn't go down too well.

"I was woken early for this garbage?" someone shouted. "I'm on night shifts, man!"

Their father struggled to explain, but too many of the townspeople either weren't listening or weren't convinced. The sheriff gamely lent his support, but his overenthusiastic reaction to the dire news was of little good.

However, their skepticism was turned around when the far doors of the school gym burst open and a number of zombies shambled in, seizing terrified townspeople. Their touch seemed to burn clothes and char skin. Those they caught had chunks of flesh bitten from their bodies.

Suddenly, there were cries of "Aunt Edna!" and "Grandpa Joe!" and "Mom – you're dead!" and people began to believe. And, unfortunately, die.

"I've got an idea!" Kelly hissed in John's ear.

He grabbed her and pulled her out the door. Behind them, the crowd was surging onto the stage and out through emergency doors. The sheriff and his deputies were attempting to lug forward their chainsaws through the crowd to reach the zombies, but making little headway through the seething crowd. Suddenly, chainsaws weren't looking like great ideas.

"Don't let them touch you," he told her. "They're so radioactive they can burn you!"

"This way," she replied.

They burst out of the gym and ran across to the school building.

"What's your idea?" John asked her as they ran.

"Iodine!"

They reached the school building, but it was still locked up. John found a rock and broke a window so they could climb inside.

"Iodine?" he asked.

"That's what I said, brother mine."

"I don't get it."

"Let's get to the science lab and I'll explain!"

The lab was locked, but John grabbed a fire extinguisher off the wall and used it to smash the door open. Conveniently, someone had forgotten to lock the store cupboard. Quickly, Kelly found the iodine and decanted it into a number of test tubes, handing some to him.

"Okay, we've got it; but why do we want it?"

"Think about it," Kelly told him. "If you're exposed to radiation, you can drink iodine in order to absorb it."

"So?"

"So, these are rad-zombies, John! They need radiation to

live, um, unlive, whatever it is they do – if we can soak the radiation up, we can stop them!"

"I'm not sure that makes a lick of sense..."

"Trust me, it'll work. Better than a chainsaw, anyway. Come on!"

Clutching test tubes, they ran outside.

"Throw it at them!" Kelly said, throwing iodine into the face of a zombie that shambled before her.

"Watch out!" John barged his sister aside as a zombie reached out for her; its hand brushed his jacket and burnt a gash across it. He tossed a test tube at it and the zombie staggered back, then collapsed.

"It seems to work," he told her.

"Yeah – but, we need more!"

"Dad!"

Kelly wasn't sure if his exclamation was intended to mean they should ask their father or because they'd just spotted their parents being menaced by a trio of zombies. They ran over to them and threw test tubes; the zombies collapsed.

"Dad," gasped Kelly, "we need iodine!"

"Iodine?" he asked, forcing her to explain again.

Luckily, it turned out that the town had a plentiful supply of iodine in store, in case of terrorist attack or nuclear war.

Within ten minutes, bottles of iodine had been handed out to everyone who was still alive: between the zombies' vicious bites and the radioactive burns inflicted by their touch, many of the hapless inhabitants of Damp Valley had been killed or severely wounded in the attack. But, now, the zombies were dropping like lifeless corpses (their former state) and the tide had turned.

When the town was secure, their father took them and a surviving deputy out to the funeral home to detain the undertaker, who was deemed utterly insane.

Homeland Security was called to come deal with the aftermath, destroy the remaining zombies and soak the ground with iodine to prevent a further rising.

Nukem Disposal claimed it had delivered the radioactive waste in good faith and that the undertaker was entirely to blame for the attack of the rad-zombies and a judge agreed, exonerating them completely. Their shareholders were extremely pleased with the result.

Surveying the garbage trucks collecting the bodies of the zombies and their victims, John turned to Kelly and said, "I can't wait till everything's back to normal."

His sister rolled her eyes and told him, "Don't tempt fate, brother mine!"

D.J. Tyrer, who is the person behind Atlantean Publishing, was short-listed for the 2015 Carillon 'Let's Be Absurd' Fiction Competition, and has been widely published in anthologies and magazines in the UK, USA and elsewhere, such as *Warlords of the Asteroid Belt* (Rogue Planet Press), *Strangely Funny II* (Mystery & Horror LLC), *Destroy All Robots* (Dynatox Ministries), *Steam Chronicles* (Zimbell House) and *Chilling Horror Short Stories* (Flame Tree), *State of Horror: Illinois* (Charon Coin Press), and *Irrational Fears* (FTB Press), as well as issues of *Sirens Call* and *Tigershark* ezines. He also has a novella available on Kindle, *The Yellow House* (Dunhams Manor).

GOBLIN GOURMET
BY ROBERT W. EASTON

He stepped back, crouching behind the artificial banana tree, and waited for a sign of the warlock. He knew it was an artificial banana tree because he had climbed it three nights ago and ate four of the fruits. They were hard and flat and he highly suspected that they were really painted wood. Tricksy.

He eyed the booth with the orange sun on it, hoping to lick the rollers. They would taste of rot and grease, his favorites, next to warm, rich blood, of course. It was across the clearing, past the slow river and the upside down waterfall. His brown, scaly lips rose in a snarl, exposing his one hundred pointy teeth. Well, ninety-eight after the berry-stick incident; also cunning fakery.

The hard, shiny floor was extra slippery tonight. His clawed feet were good at finding purchases on wood and ground, even rough stone, but the warlock had coated the area with an invisible shell that made footing treacherous. The shell was lemon-scented, but after licking a patch of the shell down to bare stone, he didn't feel like he'd eaten a meal of lemons.

To cross the clearing and get to the tasty rollers, he would have to walk on his dry heels and shift his weight back and forth, which would leave him vulnerable to attack. To compensate he would have to swing his arms around, and that much movement could draw attention. Best if he could slide, and knew it was clear of watchers. He waited.

Down the big glass passageway, the sounds of the

warlock's weapons started. He smiled a toothy grin and began flailing his way across the clearing. He wobbled to the first table, leaned forward and grabbed one of the blue metal sticks on the underside (it wasn't made of berries, he had checked). He swung his legs under him and slid on his back, racing underneath two more tables. Alarmed, he realized that his speed wasn't slowing. The warlock and his magic!

As he slid under another table, his claws scrambled for purchase. They only tore large gouges from the underside as he passed, bits of a soft rubbery substance sticking to his fingers. He splayed out all four claws on the ground, his nails digging into the hard shell as he desperately tried to slow his slide. He came to a stop with his feet dangling above the river.

He let out a low, spittle flaked, lip-rumbling sigh of relief. Back the way he came, he could see dozens of grooves from his claws in the warlock's lemony shell. He lifted his head evilly and cackled toward the glass passageway that led to his nemesis. The warlock had spent a lot of time fixing the spot that he had licked bare, and it might take him longer to fix these scratches.

He raised himself onto his haunches and looked across the slow river. There was a magical mushroom in the middle of the river that shone its elven light onto the water. He normally avoided light but the mushroom provided a way to cross. His toes curled cruelly around the rounded edge of the river, his thighs coiled, and he leaped. He landed on the mushroom on one foot, and then rebounded, leaping across the remaining distance to land safely, and dryly, on the other side.

A small splash behind him drew his suspicious gaze and he saw the thin metal of the mushroom cap sinking slowly into the slow river, dark veins trailing from it. It might have floated, but it was savaged and twisted from his claw. The mushroom stalk flickered briefly, sparking with dying elven light from the severed veins, and then going dark. He looked down the river and saw he had now destroyed three of the terrible things. Only four more and he would have to start taking the bridge.

He waddle-ran (arms flailing for balance) the rest of the way to the orange sun booth and scrambled onto the ledge. He moved to the side of the magic cooking machine.

The metal rollers, still warm from the day's feasts, smelled fiendishly delicious. He began at the top, and ran his tongue along the entire length, the tip of it reaching down between the rollers and scraping the pan beneath. He could taste the meat, offal and salt, tiny bits clinging to the catch pan. The edges were the best; they didn't get scrubbed as much as the middle.

He made several more passes and then hopped to the side, and carefully licked the spaces between the ends of the rollers and then the part where the rollers attached to the sides. Machine grease mingled with animal fat in a delicate blend of goblin delight.

He gave his attention to the other side and its suite of roller ends before turning to the main course. Perhaps it was unnatural for a goblin to delay pleasure, to save the best for last, but only after he had scoured the back and sides did he turn to the front of the meat cooker. The front was lower and the droppings gathered there in greater quantities. His long pointed tongue daintily savored the slit, finding the juiciest spots. He then plunged in, his clawed hands gripping the fake wooden counter passionately as he plunged deeply into the groove, pushing the droppings to one end before curling his tongue and scooping his treasure out for a single mouthful of bliss. He groaned in ecstasy.

In the distance, he could hear the warlock slowly work his dark magic over the floor of the glass passageway, no doubt doubling the thickness of his lemon-scented barrier. He knew from the last few nights that he had some time. Sated, he lay on the warm cooker and dozed.

When his awareness returned, he realized that the

warlock had silenced his device. His intuition warned him that this was not the regular pattern. Something had changed. He lifted his head off the cooker and looked over the lip of the ledge. The warlock was just there, and appeared to be examining the gouge marks from his claws.

The goblin's eyes darted feverishly from side to side. His belly seemed to be sticking up too high, so he took a deep breath and sucked it in. It lowered a bit, but he quickly ran out of breath and exhaled in a whoosh. He peeked and saw the warlock looking his way, eyes widening in alarm.

He pushed and slid noisily down the cooker to the ground, the wheels spinning madly and loudly. He looked from side to side, and spotted a cupboard. He opened it and flung the glass jars about, shattering them on the stone floor. He shrunk inside and closed the cupboard. There was nowhere to go if the warlock looked in.

His head twitched side to side, mind reaching. The side door. The warlock liked doors. He would enter that way.

He snapped his fingers, and his tome *Malicious Rigormortis* appeared in his hands. In time, he remembered it was trapped (smirking fiercely to himself) and mumbled his opening spell. The book flapped open and he began to thumb through the spells.

Incantation to Implode Thy Own Keep? No, that might damage his favorite cooker. *Lucifer's Fell Pact of Unavoidable Doom*? He didn't have the right tribute. *The Seven Whispers of the Witches to Summon a Kraken*? Hmm, maybe. He kept flipping.

He flipped past *The Terrible Curse of Raining Eyeballs*, the *Spell to Bring About the End of All Men*, *Word of Unendurable Agony*, and *The Whirlwind of the Flaying Whips*.

Outside the side door, the warlock's keys crunched into the lock. Leaning forward, he listened while he read. Lock rattling. Key crunching out and another crunching in. Lock clicking unlocked. Door creaking open.

This one, *The Death Mask of Punctured Pupils!* The goblin

started mumbling. The air inside the cupboard shook, his lips trembling with exertion in the dim light. The warlock stepped inside the booth, boots crunching on the broken glass. Suddenly, a great boom sounded back in the mall clearing.

The warlock exploded into action, running back out the side door. The goblin snapped his fingers again, returning his tome of sorcery to its magical home, kicked the door open and stepped out. Claws scrambling on the broken glass, he leaped, reaching for the counter, catching the edge and dangling by one claw. He pulled himself up onto the ledge, his foot kicking over a broken jar. He looked about frantically, and saw the warlock running for the burning artificial banana tree. The goblin leaped straight up, his claws reaching, grabbing and ripping the malleable fabric at the top of the booth. With a grunt, he pulled himself over and up onto the roof of the booth. The goblin froze in place.

The warlock stopped at a strange, glass cupboard on a column near the artificial banana tree. He opened it and pulled out a long, flat rope. His hands moved in intricate precision as he cast some dark spell and suddenly the entire building shook as if a thousand screaming demons were freed. Employing his fell magic, the warlock summoned rain (indoors!) and then conjured a torrent of water from the magic rope that quickly put out the banana tree fire. Not that it was a real fire, just an illusion, but illusions worked that way, too.

As the warlock's magic countered the goblin's own sorcery, the goblin slowly reached up and pushed a ceiling tile out of the way and drew himself into the small space above. He moved the tile back into place and sighed.

That was close; he'd have to avoid the orange sun booth's delicious aroma of sour milk and meat for a while. Oh well, it would be a few days before the greases got deliciously thick again.

What should I eat tomorrow? he pondered. He hadn't

scoured the raw fish place yet. He cackled evilly in anticipation.

Rob Easton is long time writer of short stories, poetry and roleplaying adventures for his friends and family. Caught between the twin passions of reading and writing, Rob focusses his energies on writing short pieces that he can then mine for adventure with his companions. Rob earns his living as a mathematician and pension consultant, and prior to that he worked as a software developer at a military pilot training facility. While earning a bachelor degree in applied mathematics, he was compelled to sneak in a minor degree in English literature. Rob also ran a college level writers' guild, helping fellow writers polish their skills and perform their works in public and on television. He always thought that he would begin publishing fiction after retirement, but having recently begun friendships with several professional writers, Rob has decided to take his craft to the inevitable level sooner rather than later. Rob is currently living in the environ of Calgary, Alberta, Canada, with his wife and daughter and an increasing number of black cats.

THE DIGIT THAT WAS DEATH
BY DAVID COURT

I've been thinking about it a lot recently, and I'd happily bet you a week's wages that I could tell you the most common last words spoken by people just before they die. All you romantics out there would love it to be something like a muttered heartfelt "I love you" followed by a death rattle and the smile that provokes an "Aww. He's at peace now" but I'm sure it's not that.

Do you know what I bet the most common last words are?

"Watch this."

Alternatively, "Look at what I can do" or "Check this out" or some variant or other. Said with some bravado by some drunk and/or enthusiastic boy or girl just before they fail miserably at whatever they were trying to do and go on to meet their maker. Who – if you believe in that sort of thing – should by all rights be waiting at the pearly gates tutting and shaking his/her/its head. Or whatever deities do to register disapproval these days, I'm not all that au-fait with theology and stuff.

I'll admit that I'm over-dramatizing what happened to me, but it's not that dissimilar - only my words in front of a whole bunch of trainees on their first tour around the factory were as follows;

"Make sure the machine is disengaged before you place any of your limbs anywhere near…"

I never managed to finish that sentence - well, not *properly* at any rate. There was a whole bunch of screaming and swearing from me as my hand was sucked into the machine, but a bunch of panicked gasps and shrieks drowned that out. I'm sure I saw one of the trainees faint. I couldn't blame them.

A quick thinking colleague of mine thumped the emergency stop button and the gears halted. There were a few moments of silence and I glanced nervously around, trying not to think of the blinding white pain that had replaced my hand. I blinked several times behind my blood-spattered safety goggles, opened my mouth to say something hugely witty that frankly evades me now, and passed out.

I awoke, not to the engine oil and pork fat scented interior of the factory, but to the sterile antiseptic scrubbed surroundings of a ward of my local hospital. My eyes gradually began to focus, the amorphous and blurry pink blob on the edge of my bed sharpening slowly into the image of an amorphous pink blob with features. It was my work colleague Tony, shoveling handfuls of grapes into that gaping obsidian abyss of a mouth.

There were a few moments of uncomfortable silence. He looked at me, and then to the empty bag of grapes. Back to me again and then to the bag. It was a cycle that could have gone on all week for the slow-witted fool had I not interrupted it by speaking.

"Thanks for the grapes, Tony."

He coughed, spluttering fragments of grapeseed and slivers of wet green skin onto the clean starched white linen of my hospital bed. You could see the confusion on his face, his flabby brow furrowing into fleshy trenches. Jokes didn't just go over Tony's head; they tended to find themselves in geo-stationary orbit. My sarcasm was clearly wasted on this fruit-pilfering buffoon.

"Don't... Don't say a word, Tony," I said as I held my hands out to silence whatever profound inanity he was about to deliver. "It was a lovely gesture."

It was as I lifted them up that I could see that my right hand – the one that ended up in the grinder – was tightly bandaged. I tried hard not to think about the probable mess of flesh and bone that the bandages were hiding.

A few words about Tony; we all know somebody like him. That acquaintance with so little common sense that the fact that they've managed to survive past their teenage years was almost rock-solid evidence of the existence of God. There are some people who make their way through life, and then there are the Tonys in our lives who ricochet through it like a pinball bouncing from bumper to bumper. That empty vessel that makes the most noise, that person who could even fail a personality test.

They say you can't choose your family, but, sadly, unless you've worked your way to a comfortable height up the corporate ladder you can't choose your workmates either.

Tony and I were both line managers at Boarwell's Snacks, proud suppliers of Boarwell's Pork Scratchings. You may have seen our adverts on the television – The one with the CGI dancing pigs singing, "We use everything except the Oink!"

You'd remember it if you saw it – it's a horrible thing from the murky depths of a marketing persons psyche. Quite why you'd trust a chorus-line of pigs betraying their own species and condoning cannibalism, I'll never know. You should be grateful that you only have to catch it on television once every month and don't have to put up with that jingle piped round the factory for thirty-seven and a half hours of your life every week. More often than not, I ended up dreaming about those fucking pigs.

Anyway, I digress. Both Tony and I began employment at Boarwell's at about the same time. I'd worked my way up through the company through intelligence and bloody hard work, and Tony had followed suit through sheer bloody luck and coincidence.

Tony's only really competence is a gift for being incompetent. I know I'm not really one to speak with the accident that led me here, but I'd lost track of the number of times I've had to stop Tony absent-mindedly placing his hand into a mincer or getting himself locked into one of the huge ovens we have dotted around the factory.

I was relieved when a doctor walked over, sparing me from having to engage in small talk with the oaf.

"Ah, Mr. Barclay," he muttered as he read over my notes from the clipboard at the edge of my bed, his tiny green eyes darting left to right. "You're a very lucky man, Mr. Barclay. Mmmm. Good. Other than some superficial scarring, most of your hand escaped relatively unscathed."

My brow furrowed. *Most* of my hand? What classes as most of a hand? That could be just three fingers, right?

The Doctor stared down at Tony who, typically, took excessively long to realize that he wanted him to move. It took a spluttered "If you could just..." from the doctor before the fat lout got to his feet with an uncouth grunt and moved aside.

Doctor Biskind (even without my glasses on, he was close enough now for me to read his name badge) started unwrapping my bandages. I prepared myself for the worst, as the layers were slowly unwound, revealing more and more of my right hand. I was relieved to see that it was mostly unharmed until he finally removed the last of the off-white gauze and I see the true extent of the damage.

My hand was flushed and skinned in parts, but then I saw it. The little finger, attached to the rest of my hand by thick neat black stitching. The skin on it was lighter than the rest of my hand, and it was a good half an inch shorter than I remembered.

"Ah, yes. Your little finger," says Biskind, noticing my reaction. "We couldn't save it. Mmmm. Yes. It had been completely crushed. You were lucky though in that we had one in storage we were able to transplant. It'll be a little tender for a week or so, but there shouldn't be any lasting nerve damage and you should be able to carry on your life as normal."

I held my right hand in front of my face, tensing and relaxing the muscles. There was a twinge of pain even through the painkillers but I realized how lucky I'd been. One careless mistake could have –

No. *Not* a careless mistake. I distinctly remembered engaging the safety mechanism on the machinery. The only way that the accident could have happened if somebody carelessly or absent-mindedly *disengaged* it and didn't remember to –

I was just about to glare accusingly at Tony before Doctor Biskind interrupted, gently placing his hands around my wrist and turning my hand over so the palm was failing up towards the ceiling.

He pushed his glasses down the bridge of his nose and peered at my hand over the top of them, his tiny eyes narrowing in intense concentration.

"Mmmm," he mumbled. "Like I said, there was a little. Mmmm. Nerve damage. Probably be a little while until they've all nicely knitted together, yes? Soreness. Mmmm. Probably be a little while until you can use it, so I'd just try to keep it…"

Suddenly the little finger – this foreign digit – spasmed wildly. Without any effort, it jerked up and down, tapping a staccato rhythm on the bedsheets. The other three fingers and thumb remained perfectly still. We both watched for a few moments until it settled down and lay quite still again.

"Mmmm," murmured Biskind, his vocal affectation seeming somewhat – and somehow - more excited than it had previously, "Extraordinary. You heal fast, Mr. Barclay. Mmmmm. Do try not to overexert yourself though, eh?"

He awkwardly patted me on the shoulder, an uncharacteristic show of affection. With another subtle "Mmmmm" he got to his feet and smiled down at me.   As he walked away, Tony smiled gormlessly on.

"Do you want a lift back home?" he asked, rivulets of grape juice dribbling down his chin.

I thought it prudent to take a cab back home, Tony's driving being on a par with both his management prowess and factory safety acumen. For Tony, the Highway Code was just something that happened to other people.

I fixed myself something to eat and tried to watch some television, but my mind kept going back to the accident. I hadn't made one single mistake with the safety gate in my twelve years at Boarwell, and refused to accept responsibility now. It had to be that lumbering idiot. Admittedly, I'd gotten away relatively lightly from the accident, but not through any help from Tony. I could remember it clearly – even as my hand was slowly being pulled into the machine he was looking around blankly, completely at a loss about what to do. Twelve years training, and he couldn't even remember which bloody button to press to switch the machine off in an emergency – it had taken a colleague of mine who'd been with Boarwell for less than a year to do so.

I slept uneasily that night, dreaming about lowering a pig with Tony's face into a grinder. He was staring at me throughout the process, a sad and empty expression fixed on those porcine features. Even as the gears pulped his legs into a scarlet mess, his expression didn't change. Even in my dreams, Tony was too stupid to realize what was going on around him. As the top of his head vanished between the whirring blades, a chunk of him flew towards me and landed neatly in my hysterically laughing mouth. I was suddenly choking, a globule of Tony's gristle blocking my airways. I struggled to breathe, becoming overwhelmed with panic as my vision filled with dull red.

My eyes opened, wide-awake now. After a few moments of bewilderment and the confusion that comes from waking from a nightmare, I realized my predicament hadn't ended. I was still choking, my mouth held open and something firm pressing hard against my uvula.

I realized in horror that the thing that had pushed itself down my throat was my own hand. My little finger – this new unwelcome foreign digit – was trying to choke me, trying to pull itself down, clawing against the red raw surface of my throat. I pulled on my arm and despite my finger trying to hook itself against my teeth on the way out, it was yanked loose and I collapsed back against my pillow and took in deep mouthfuls of air.

I hold my right arm in my left, attempting to steady it. My saliva-covered and blood-flecked little finger twitched angrily, like a reed in a hurricane. It almost looked as though it was struggling to get free itself from my other digits. As my heart rate and breathing returned to normal, the finger's frantic movements slowed little by little until they were all quite still.

A nightmare? Perhaps. It was true that I'd been having more and more sleepless nights (which I'd put down to the pressure of my increased workload at Boarwell's) but I'd never had anything like this happen to me before. I'd fallen out of bed or even painfully whacked my head against the headboard during previous night terrors, but trying to choke myself was an interesting new development.

Come next morning, my memories of the nights events vanished along with the darkness. I'd put the whole event down to nothing more than a nightmare, probably induced by a combination of the adrenaline produced by the previous day's accident and the anesthetic from the hospital.

A few surprised faces greeted me when I turned up for work next morning. My nocturnal activities had left me drained, but nothing that a morning of reducing pig carcasses to lumps of deep-fried, salted, crunchy monosodium-glutamate infused rind wouldn't cure. It was only when I was in the works kitchen brewing up a strong cup of black coffee to begin the day that I discovered the reason for the confused faces on my colleagues. According to Sandra from payroll, Tony had told everybody he'd met that I'd lost my entire arm in the accident. I think they were – understandably - surprised at my apparent lizard-like powers of regeneration.

Tony walked past me in the corridor without a care in the world, smiling at me as he passed by. My little finger twitched.

Amongst a few dozen emails wishing me a rapid recovery, there was one from the boss Mr. Boarwell. He wanted a meeting with all the line managers (just Tony and me then) in his office at 1700 hours that evening.

I knew how important it was as soon as I turned up when I saw that Boarwell had the special biscuits sitting on his desk for the meeting. It was a well-known fact around the factory that Old Boarwell would only get his pink wafers and party rings out for very special occasions. There was a brief delay whilst somebody found and informed Tony that the meeting had started – The simpleton was (predictably) incapable of understanding 24-hour clocks so was surprised that the meeting was being held two hours earlier than he'd expected.

We both sat there as Boarwell paced up and down in front of his window, with me in reverent silence and Tony in a clam our of crunches as he noisily polished off the rest of the party rings.

He turned to face us and I could have sworn that there was a tear in his eye.

"The cut-throat world of congealed hog lumps has been a good one to me over the years" he muttered in that rasping voice of his, the result of years of smoking cigars and working in an atmosphere thick with pig dust.

"But, Lads - it's changed over the past few years into something I don't recognize. The once simple and humble pub snack world has transformed into a realm of artisan bread snacks. We have crisps, peanuts and maize snacks coming in flavors that we hadn't heard of ten years ago, and even broken bits of bloody pretzel are muscling in on our hard-earned territory. And don't even talk to me about bloody Wasabi peas."

He sat down and spun his chair round a few times. There was an expectant silence in the room that was only punctuated by a faint squeaking.

"Upshot is, boys, the dominion of pub comestibles is a young man's game. There comes a time when the old guard has to step aside for new blood."

I nodded in agreement. I'd predicted that this day would arise – this was what I'd been waiting for. All my years of putting up with that idiot Tony would finally be paid off. I looked over at him, oblivious to Old Man Boarwell's words as he picked at the neon colored party-ring crumbs that adorned the front of his ill-fitting shirt.

"At the end of this month, I'll be formally announcing my retirement," continued Boarwell. "And will also be naming my successor. I haven't made my final decision yet, so you have two weeks to impress me. Which one of the two of you is fit to inherit this fine porky legacy?"

I was fuming as I arrived home and slammed my front door shut behind me. How was Tony even in the running for this? This was the idiot who once locked himself in the factory at night after having set the alarm – the cleaners had found him next morning rooted to the spot, too terrified to move. He was a joke to every employee of that factory – to everybody except his only superior, it would appear.

I was still raging as I lay there in bed that night. Was Boarwell being deliberately difficult, or had he finally gone completely senile? I eventually fell asleep, still seething with rage, and the inevitable anger-fueled nightmare began.

I found myself on a desert plain, a grey landscape dotted with crags and rocky outcrops. A bright sun hung in a cloudless blue sky, the heat almost overpowering. I looked down at myself, clad in black trousers and a torn deli-mustard yellow shirt with black piping around the neck, gold embroidery around the wrists.

I could hear a tune, one unfamiliar to me at first but with every note familiarity dawned. When I saw Tony wielding a branch and standing in front of me, his skin a green tinge (instead of the usual impending-heart attack dark pink) it all became clear.

This was classic nineteen-sixties Trek. I was Kirk, and he was a Gorn. The gladiatorial theme increased in volume and urgency as we circled each other. I leapt at him, delivering that two fisted hand-joined punch that only Kirk could do, but to no avail. In a single move from Tony (that was quicker than anything the blundering oaf could ever manage in real life) I was thrown onto my back and he was upon me, rage in his eyes.

His hands reached for my face and pushed me back onto the hard rocky floor. His thumbs began to press down firmly on my closed eyelids, his weight pinning me down, and I could do nothing but scream.

I awoke, drenched in sweat, to my right hand draped over my face, the tip of my little finger pressing down as hard as it could on my closed eyelids. I wrenched my arm away from my face and switched on my bedside light. The little finger was moving of its own volition, slowing dragging the rest of my arm behind it in what resembled a futile attempt to escape. I grabbed it by the wrist and held it in front of my face. The rogue digit jerked angrily, recoiling and stabbing towards me repeatedly.

It probably went without saying, but something was clearly very, very wrong. It certainly was not normal for your little finger to try to kill you two nights in a row. I rang in sick and booked an appointment with the doctor as soon as they opened that morning.

I sat in silence with the light on for the remainder of the

night holding my right arm tightly and watching for any movement from this accursed finger. It did not attempt to move again.

"Mmmmm. I'd expect the odd muscle spasm from it, but nothing like you've described. I hardly think your little finger is trying to kill you." reassured Doctor Biskind in a patronizing tone that barely hid his obvious disdain at my seemingly incredulous claims. All the time he was prodding the offending digit with the tip of his pencil, but it stubbornly refused to react.

"Let's just put it down to stress, shall we? I'll prescribe you a course of sleeping pills and we'll just see if…"

"No!" I shouted, standing up suddenly. It was only my waking that had stopped the finger carrying out its nefarious plan – sleeping pills would leave me vulnerable and unable to defend myself.

"I'm not imagining this! This isn't just stress! I'll get a second opinion, damn it!" I barked, collecting my jacket and heading for the door.

"My second opinion would be that you're clearly insane", he muttered under his breath, just loudly enough for me to hear before I slammed the door shut behind me.

Standing in the carpark, I was shaking so much with rage that it took me several minutes to gather the necessary coordination needed to light my cigarette. I noticed one of the porters staring at me. As our eyes met, he looked around himself and began to walk over. I'd begun to remove a cigarette from the packet in anticipation of him asking for one, but he shook his head.

"You're the fella who had the finger transplant, aintcha?" he asked, an eyebrow cocked.

"I… am", I replied, hesitantly. I'd seen him before, somewhere. Had he been working on my ward the day I'd been a resident here?

"And has it been giving you... any gyp?"

My heart skipped a beat. What did he know?

"It has!" I remarked. "What do you know?"

"It'll cost you," he said under his breath. "Twenty quid".

He stretched out a nicotine-stained hand.

I sighed, and then went for my wallet. A Scottish twenty-pound note I'd struggled to get rid of despite my better efforts was hastily pressed into his greedy paws. He quickly tucked it into his top pocket and leaned in towards me.

"Does the name 'The Suffolkater' mean anything to you?"

He did that annoying thing with his fingers to indicate quotation marks as he said the name - The immediate expression on my face clearly indicated to him that it did. He'd made the press a few weeks back – he was a serial killer operating in the Suffolk region who had leapt to his death after being cornered by the police. His M.O. was to suffocate his victims, hence the natty nickname coined by some wag at the local press.

"Turns out that even after that fall, there were still a fair few useable bits that wound up in the freezers here. Most people – rightfully so – aren't that bothered about where they get their spare bits from. But if you've worked here as long as I have, you sometimes hear... *stories.*"

I didn't know whether to be relieved or insulted. This was the stuff of horror stories, a lazy trope to be wheeled out in movies. Murderer's hands that, even after their original owner's death, seek to kill and kill again.

"You can keep the money just for the entertainment value," I said, smiling nervously as I walked back towards the car.

I wore an old oven glove on my right hand and tied it to the bed frame though that night, just to be on the safe side. It couldn't hurt, right?

My sleep suffered over the few weeks that followed. Even when that little finger wasn't twitching wildly of its own accord, I was nervously waiting for it to do so. My dreams became more and more violent, invariably centered about killing or causing grievous bodily harm to Tony.

Inevitably, my work suffered. I was often late, having overslept. I was short-tempered, quick to pick any fault with my staff and constantly on edge. I had to go before Old Man Boarwell about a complaint that had been registered against me, and even he admitted that he'd noticed my work had been suffering. This from the man who hadn't noticed *any* of Tony's complete incompetence *ever*. I couldn't justify my behavior – how could I? "Oh yeah, I'm struggling at the moment because I've had the little finger of a serial killer grafted onto me. You'll forgive me for not being that interested in lumps of cold pig rind at this particular moment in time."

My evenings were spent formulating ways in which I could painlessly remove myself from this murderous digit (garden shears and office guillotine were the favorites), but I never seemed to be able to summon up the courage to actually do it.

Predictably, Tony was chosen as Old Man Boarwell's successor. I stood at the back of the canteen as Boarwell made his announcement, quietly muttering to myself. My unrestrained little finger dug its nails into my palm, drawing the smallest amount of blood. I didn't even try to stop it, numb to the sensation. I quit that same day, not willing to suffer the ignominy of calling *that man* my boss.

Whereas my thoughts had previously been solely occupied with murderous rage, they were now shared by my gloating over the inevitable destruction of the Boarwell's Pork Scratching Empire with that idiot Tony at the helm. The clumsy oaf couldn't even balance a coin on its side, let alone balance the books of a nationwide snack company.

It was six nights later as I was sitting at my dining room table, the blade of a mail order Bettaware™ Meat Cleaver poised perilously against the stitches of my murderer's finger, when the phone rang.

"Mate," came the sound of Tony's embarrassed voice. "I need your help."

I let a few moments pass before answering him, a smirk on my face. It had all gone tits-up for him, just as I'd imagined.

"What's up, Tony?"

"This is really awkward but... I have to reset the machines in the factory, but I can't remember how."

You have notes, I thought. *I remember standing over you and forcing you to make fucking notes. We've been through exactly the same process at the end of every single fucking month we've worked there.*

"...and I've lost my notes," he continued. "Could you pop along? There's a beer in it for you."

I held the phone at arm's length for a moment and sighed. That'd be one debt he'd never have to pay off – he knew damn well I never had and never would go for a drink with him. My little finger twitched.

"Okay," I replied, not even trying to conceal the resignation in my tone. "I'll be there in as soon as I can."

I even parked in my old reserved parking space for old time's sake, and of *course* my old key still worked. Tony wouldn't have had the sense to follow the standard company policy of changing the main factory locks when a senior member of staff leaves.

I stepped inside the quiet deserted factory and listened for the sound of swearing, that familiar sound that could be heard when Tony tried to do anything more complex than breathing and walking at the same time.

I found him standing on top of the closed safety panel of one of the big industrial grinders, all powered down but still not the safest place to be. He was looking around himself as though he'd lost something important.

"Evening, Tony" I called out, climbing up the metal steps to the upper level to join him.

"Thank God you're here!" he said, genuinely relieved to see me. He had that same expression that tied-up puppies have when their owners reappear from inside a shop. "Can you remember whether these have to be open or closed before you run the diagnosthingy?"

I stepped towards him, and saw the control panel a few feet away. Tony's key was in it, the red light indicating that it was turned as well. It was active and primed.

"The diagnostic cycle, Tony? Is that what you mean?"

A few feet closer.

"That's the one. One second, and I'll come and join you."

I stood beside the control panel and faced him, my hand sneaking towards the single large blue button upon it.

"One second, Tony," I said. "What's the cycle called?"

This would be so easy, I thought. Just a simple button press. One quick jab and that would be it.

"What cycle?" he asked, looking confused. Like that same puppy would have if you gestured to throw a ball, but threw nothing.

"The something cycle," I shouted, angrily. "I only just told you the fucking word."

I wasn't willing to be a murderer. I couldn't handle that level of guilt or responsibility. However, if I just moved my hand closer to the button...

I didn't mind being an accomplice.

My murderous left finger moved of its own accord, pressing firmly down on the button. The grinder noisily spluttered into life, the safety panels sliding back and sending Tony falling onto the bladed wheels, each of them slowly spinning into life.

Even now, at the very end, Tony failed to have the sense he was (probably) born with. His mobile phone fell out of his hand, splintering between the grinding mechanisms beneath him. He reached down to grab it and his hand became trapped. I watched him slowly vanish into the depths of the machine, bones splintering into dust. He screamed in those moments he had before his lungs burst, staring at me the whole time.

That eternal expression he'd had through most of his adult life, just a look of complete bewilderment.

Alarms sounded before the end, safety mechanisms finally – albeit too late – kicking in. His undamaged blood-splattered head sat there atop the bladed wheels, staring at me with dead, unseeing eyes. To be fair though, they were no less vacant.

I'd worked there long enough to hide any evidence that I'd ever been there. I knew the cameras that faced the car park weren't actually connected to anything, and my fingerprints were wiped off the button. It was only when I was in the car on the way back home when I laughed to myself, having realized that the fingerprints on the button wouldn't have been mine at all.

The little finger had stopped twitching, its murderous intentions presumably sated for now. I looked at it and it slowly bent towards me, almost in a half-nod.

It officially went down on record as a horrible accident, and within a week I was back on the payroll and moving into Tony's office. The little finger hadn't given me any trouble for a while now, and it was only when I read the newspaper a few days later that the digit began to twitch again, my nervous sphincter along with it.

Tony's death wasn't entirely in vain. He'll turn out to be of more use in death than he ever was in life, with his still perfect and undamaged eyes being prime for corneal transplantation to restore a local blind woman's sight.

Those same eyes that saw me consign their owner to a grisly death. The only thing that links me to the crime.

My little finger twitched in anticipation.

David Court was born and resides in the Midlands, UK with his patient wife Tara and his three less patient cats. When not reading, drinking real ale, writing software for a living or practicing his poorly developed telekinetic skills, he can be found writing fiction and has had a number of short stories published in anthologies including *Fear's Accomplice*, *Terror at the Beach* and *Caped* along with contributions to the *Twisted Dark* and *Twisted Sci-fi* series of graphic novels. He's written two anthology collections - *The Shadow Cast By The World* and *Forever and Ever, Armageddon* and plans to release a third - *Scenes of Mild Peril* - in 2016. He can often be found haunting his blog at: www.davidjcourt.co.uk

THE GUNDERSON FAMILY AND THE SEWER-DWELLING REPTOIDS OF ANAHEIM, CA
BY KEVIN WETMORE

By mid-afternoon of the third day at the theme park, Bob Gunderson could see the kids were flagging. This was the furthest the family had driven in the R.V. for a summer vacation, but the kids had begged so much that Bob and Bonnie finally gave in. He never fully realized the distance from Minnesota to Southern California until he had to drive every mile of it.

For the record, Bob was also sick and tired of hearing about Reptoids. He loved his son and he loved his son's enthusiasm for all things weird, but enough was enough already.

None of that mattered, though, as they were at the park as a family, having a family vacation, leaving their troubles behind to have fun.

He pulled a handkerchief from the back of his jeans and mopped his brow. "Sure a lot warmer than home, huh, honey?" Jessie just rolled her eyes and went back to looking bored waiting in line for the pirate ride. "Lord, help us get through twelve," he thought. And then, "What's she going to be like as a teenager?" His thoughts then shifted to the setting sun. He was glad they were beating the crowds out of the park, and even gladder they'd get back to the hotel before sunset.

They had spent three days riding the rides, taking photos with the cartoon characters, eating overpriced food, and enjoying themselves. But Bob knew it was a good thing this was the last day. It would take them two days to drive back to Burntside, Minnesota. The park was fun, but Bob already missed the woods, the lakes, and the natural world of northern Minnesota. This was a theme park in a desert. *No one should have to live in a place like this*, he thought, *but it takes all types*.

He knew the kids were weary because they hardly kicked up a fuss when Bob announced they were leaving the park two hours before sunset. He explained that they had to get on the road at first light, since they had two thousand miles to home and he didn't want to be on the road at night. In order to get home by Friday, so he and Bonnie would have the weekend to rest, they had to leave at sunrise tomorrow.

The kids were fine with that, although they did push back a little when he suggested they not leave the room tonight, but just dine in.

"Geez, we got a hotel room because it is too hot to sleep in the RV, but you kids have gotten spoiled, I think," Bonnie said, looking into the back seat where Jessie sat staring out the window at the unfairness of it all. Bobby, Jr. still had his head buried in that book.

"I suppose I should be grateful that he wants to read, but why such horrible stuff?" Bonnie asked Bob as they drove down the highway towards Southern California.

"He's at that age. Ten year old boys like the weird stuff," Bob reassured her.

"But why monsters?"

"He's curious. It's a phase. Don't worry. Someday he'll discover girls and then we'll really have something to worry about."

The whole trip down, Bobby had read aloud from the backseat about the monsters of Southern California. While the family had been treated to some information about UFOs and Bigfoot, he saved his enthusiasm for the Reptoids.

"Mom, did you know there are Reptoids in the sewers of Anaheim?"

"No, Bobby, I guess I didn't," Bonnie replied, giving a worried glance to Bob.

"At least thirteen people have seen them in the last few years. They have glowing red eyes and they look like lizard people!"

He held up an illustration in the book for Bonnie to see. Sure enough, it was a lizard man with greenish scales, clawed hands, a beaked face with sharp teeth and glowing red eyes. It menaced a woman and a dog that were out walking and apparently had come across a sewer from which the Reptoid had emerged.

"Well that sure looks scary," she told him. "I sure hope we don't run into any during this vacation."

"They only come out at night, and they live in the sewers, so they can be avoided," he assured her. "But it says here that they sometimes mate with humans and sometimes with grays to produce hybrids!"

"Oh, I'm not sure that's a good book for a ten year old boy, Bobby..." she began.

He pulled back in the seat and held the book closer, as if afraid she would reach for it. "Oh, ma, it's fine. I'm not afraid. The Reptoids aren't much bigger than me, and I bet I could take one!"

Bob smiled and looked at him in the rear view mirror. "That's my little monster! Tear 'em to pieces if they come at you, right?"

Bobby, Jr. smiled back, Jessie rolled her eyes even more than usual, and Bonnie again thought they named him well - *he is so much like his father.*

As the kids drifted back into their activities, Bonnie looked over at Bob and quietly asked, "What the heck is a 'gray'?" Bob shrugged. He still wasn't a hundred percent certain on what a Reptoid was.

So, the Gunderson family pulled into the hotel parking lot. Bob and Bobby reattached the jeep to the RV in anticipation of the morning, while Bonnie and Jessie took their stuff up to the room. Bobby Jr. joined them while Bob went to get the family dinner.

Once the family had gathered in the hotel room, Bonnie took charge. Clothes and souvenirs were packed up into family bags. "Leave out the clothes you want to wear tomorrow, and Daddy will take the bags down to the RV tonight."

She pulled back the curtain on the window that looked over the hotel parking lot. In the distance, the moon was just beginning to rise over the Anaheim hills and the land was still giving off the heat of the day, nothing like the northern Minnesota woods she grew up in and loved.

"OK, folks," Bonnie said, closing the curtain and turning back into the room. "Let's have dinner in the room and then sleep. No going out tonight."

"Mo-om," began Jessie, turning the word to two syllables. "Why can't we…"

Bonnie didn't even let her finish. "Because I said so."

An argument was stalled by the return of Bob with their dinner. The family ate and the kids settled down, drifting off to a sated sleep with the air conditioning providing both cool air and white noise.

Bob threw the remains of dinner in a garbage bag. "Let me get rid of this, then I'll load up the car," he told his mate, who kissed him on the cheek and set about finishing the packing.

As he approached the dumpster, he saw it was open and tossed the trash bag in. Then he heard the low hissing. He noticed the red first. Two eyes under the grate in the parking lot next to the dumpster. Then he heard more hissing beyond the dumpster. Something jumped up onto the rear wall of the dumpster just as the grate came up and moved over.

A noise behind him made him look back as a third pair of glowing eyes emerged from under a car. The three creatures were each making the hissing noise and closing upon him slowly. Their movements were threatening. All at once, Bob knew what he was seeing.

"Oh my stars and garters," he said aloud, "You're Reptoids. What do you know, Bobby was right! Son of a gun!"

The one from the sewer and the one from under the car raised themselves up to their full height. Bob guessed they were all about a foot shorter than him at six one.

The one perched on the rear of the dumpster stepped down onto the garbage in order to come closer to him. As its clawed foot raked the bag, it tore open and a head rolled out through the hole in the black plastic. Its hair was long and black and smeared with blood. The face had been visibly chewed. Through the tear in the bag a bloody maid's uniform with a nametag that said "Rosita" was visible. The thing's weight on the bag caused the sharp ends of bones to poke through the plastic.

The Reptoid looked down, and then looked up at Bob in confusion.

"I really wish ya hadn't of done that," Bob said. "In hindsight though, we should have double-bagged it."

With that, hair began to sprout all over his body and his nose began to elongate. His fingers dripped with blood as they lengthened into claws. His snout, once fully extended, opened to reveal jaws full of sharp teeth. His last human thought was, "I wonder what they'll taste like?" and "This is why I hate going on vacation - the cleanup is such a b-rhymes with witch!"

On the first floor of the hotel, Nancy turned to Brian as they lay in bed and said, "There, I just heard it again."

He sighed and muted the television, hating to miss even a second of the show even though he had seen this episode at least twice before. He listened.

"All I hear is traffic, people in other rooms, and your breathing," he told her.

"I swear to you, I heard a wolf outside."

"Don't be silly," he said, taking the television off mute, "There's no such thing as wolves in Anaheim."

Kevin Wetmore is an award-winning horror writer, stand-up comedian, and professor. His fiction has appeared in such anthologies as *Midian Unmade, Enter at Your Own Risk: The End Is the Beginning*, and *History and Horror, Oh My!* as well as such magazines as *Devolution Z* and *Mothership Zeta*. He is also the author of *Post-9/11 Horror in American Cinema* and *Back from the Read: Reading Remakes of Romero's Zombie Films as Markers of Their Times*. He lives in Los Angeles, but has never seen Reptoids.

www.ingramcontent.com/pod-product-compliance
Lightning Source LLC
Chambersburg PA
CBHW060540260626
47161CB00003B/991